THE LAST CAMPAIGN

THE LAST CAMPAIGN

Tim Champlin

GUNSMOKE

First published in the U.S. by Five Star

This hardback edition 2011
by AudioGO Ltd
by arrangement with
Golden West Literary Agency

Copyright © 1996 by Tim Champlin.
All rights reserved.

ISBN 978 1 408 46318 5

British Library Cataloguing in Publication Data available.

Printed and bound in Great Britain by
CPI Antony Rowe, Chippenham and Eastbourne

THE LAST CAMPAIGN

Chapter One

Geronimo moved closer.

The approach of the Apache war chief sent a chill up Russell Norwood's back. He couldn't drag his fascinated gaze from that leathery face. It was a face that seemed to create a hypnotic effect, a face that might be staring from a smoky window of hell — the beaked nose, the wide, lipless slash of mouth. It was a face that triggered many a nightmare among whites of the territory, a face that was the last vision this side of eternity for many others. But the wily renegade had not come to kill. He was here, backed by heavily armed warriors, for a "big talk" with General George Crook, the "tan wolf" as many of the Apaches respectfully called him.

In spite of the tension created by the Winchesters and Springfield carbines in the hands of the painted hostiles who were nervously guarding against treachery, Norwood felt that history was about to be made. Someone else apparently thought so too, as he noticed C. S. Fly, Tombstone photographer, setting up his tripod and checking the angle of the sun. Indians, Mexican officials, American Army officers, and white civilians were all standing or sitting around the clearing close enough for several good exposures.

March 25, 1886. Cañon de los Embudos, Mexico. The date and place were about to be frozen in time.

Norwood, former first lieutenant and now a civilian courier for the Army, was strictly a spectator at this conference. Yet he felt the tension in the air as Geronimo stopped a few feet in front of General Crook, folded his arms across his broad chest and paused dramatically before speaking. The dappled spring sunshine that wove a moving pattern across the shallow ravine did nothing to soften those hard, obsidian eyes as he regarded the general who was seated on the grassy slope before him. The gray-bearded general, casually dressed in brown corduroy jacket and white pith helmet, waited for his adversary to speak. The only sounds were the stamping of horses in the background, the soft sighing of wind in the cottonwoods and sycamores overhead, and the rippling of water over stones in the nearby stream.

When Geronimo continued to glare without speaking, Crook opened the meeting abruptly. "What have you got to say? I've come all the way down from Fort Bowie."

Tom Horn, a scout and interpreter, translated the question into Spanish. Without taking his eyes from Crook, Geronimo replied in Spanish.

Horn turned to the general and said, "He says he left the reservation because many were calling him a bad Indian, and there was talk from Mickey Free and others that he would be arrested and hanged."

Crook nodded slightly as Horn paused to shift the remaining translation into English idiom. "He wants good men to be his agents and interpreters . . . he says when you talk with him, and he goes to the reservation, you put bad men over him. In the future he does not want these bad men to be near where he lives."

Russ Norwood, as bone weary as he was, eyed the general while Tom Horn continued in this vein. He was curious to see how Crook would respond. He knew Crook had no say about the Indian agents who were appointed by the Department of the Interior in Washington. And many of these agents were, at best, ineffective — at worst, thieves and cowards.

Crook chose to ignore the plea and remained impassive until

the interpreter had finished relaying the chief's words. Geronimo listed his well-known grievances about reservation confinement, the law against making *tiswin,* the traditional Indian beer, the chronic shortage of beef and blankets, the prohibition against the right of every Apache to beat his wife if she needed it. Strangely enough, he didn't mention the things that came to Norwood's mind — the suffocating summer heat and dust, the swarms of biting flies and mosquitoes, the filthy living conditions at the lowland San Carlos reservation. But, then, maybe all Apaches were inured to such discomforts.

Before Crook could respond to the list of complaints, Geronimo broke in again, speaking slowly and now gesturing expansively with his hands. At length, Horn picked up the translation. "I know I have to die sometime," he said, speaking as Geronimo, "but even if the heavens fall on me, I want to do what is right. I think I am a good man, but your newspapers everywhere say I am a bad man. I only do wrong if I have a cause. Why don't you speak to me? It would make better feeling if you look at me and smile at me. I am the same man you knew before. I have the same feet, legs, and hands, and the sun looks down on me as a complete man.

"How can I make you believe what I say? To prove to you that I am now telling the truth, remember that I sent you word I would come from a place far away to speak to you here. And you see me now. We have come on horseback and on foot. If all these things had been my fault, would I have come so far to talk to you? We are all children of one God, and God is listening to what we say now."

Norwood recognized the standard ploy. Negotiating Indians — especially this one — loved to wander off into flowery, mostly meaningless, blather that allowed them to hold center stage for as long as possible. He suppressed a yawn.

Crook waited calmly for the harangue to end. Then he replied bluntly, "If you left the reservation because you were afraid of bad treatment, why did you kill innocent people? What did those innocent people do to you that you should kill them, steal their horses, and sneak around in the rocks like coyotes? You are not a child to believe foolish stories you hear in your camp. You were in no danger of arrest or being hanged on the reservation. Two years ago you surrendered in the Sierra Madre and promised to live in peace, but you lied. When a man has lied to me once, I want more proof than his word before I can believe him again."

When this was translated, Geronimo appeared to be offended by Crook's words. He turned his back and walked a few steps away, saying something in his own language to the rest of the men scattered about the ravine. Several of the Apaches grunted and nodded affirmatively in response, while most of the whites sat in uncomprehending silence. Apparently protesting his innocence to a sympathetic audience, Norwood thought dreamily. Somehow it seemed appropriate that this conference was being held at Cañon de los Embudos — Cañon of the Tricksters.

In spite of his odd mixture of clothing, Geronimo was an impressive sight as he strode about, muscular thighs showing above knee-high moccasins. A white loin cloth flapped beneath a blue Army uniform coat that was decorated with silver conchos. The straight black hair was held in place by a wide red bandanna around his head. Hanging from a silver-studded belt, his sidearms consisted of an ivory-handled Colt and a Bowie knife.

When Geronimo finally turned his attention back to the general, Crook said, "You must make up your mind whether you will stay on the warpath, or surrender unconditionally. If you stay out, I'll keep after you and kill the last one if it takes fifty years. Mark what I say. I have never lied to you, but you have lied to me."

Even though the Apache must have known Crook was bluffing,

his manner seemed to change. He quickly became very agitated, and he appeared nervous. As he paced up and down, he toyed with a leather thong he extracted from a coat pocket. Through Tom Horn he began a long harangue about being able to see his kinsman, Kaytennay, whom Crook had brought along after securing his release from Alcatraz.

Although the day was only pleasantly warm, beads of sweat began to roll down Geronimo's cheeks and, concentrating in order to keep awake, Norwood noticed even the backs of the Apache's huge hands were sweating.

Norwood shifted his position to avoid the needles of a buckthorn next to where he was sitting. He glanced sleepily around, trying to gauge the other whites' reaction to Geronimo's change in demeanor. All the faces were impassive. Yet they must have known, as he did, that it would probably take the Army every day of the fifty years Crook mentioned to track down and kill the half a hundred or so Apaches that Geronimo led. Personally, he doubted it could ever be done. So why was Geronimo so nervous? Crook did not play the game of oblique and lengthy verbal negotiations. He was honest and straightforward, almost to the point of being blunt. He had issued an ultimatum. But Geronimo was not ready for a "Yes" or "No" answer. He again spoke to his followers in the Apache dialect.

Tom Horn, the raw-boned, six-foot interpreter, stood to one side, squinting at Geronimo. "Trying to make everyone think he understands the Chiricahua lingo," Norwood muttered under his breath. To Horn appearances were everything. He was wearing a buckskin jacket, a broad white Stetson, and had even blacked his boots for the occasion.

Glancing at the two dozen Apache men and boys who loitered about within earshot, Norwood saw that every one of them was burdened with at least two full cartridge belts. Besides their pistols, many of them were armed with new 1873 model

Winchesters. The boys were wearing new shirts of German cotton of the type that could be obtained in Mexico. Even though there were several young boys in the group, this was no ragtag outfit. They all appeared well fed, and very serious. The only thing that would keep them from disappearing into the Sierra Madre mountains, again to live free and raid as they pleased, was the knowledge that Crook, backed by all the forces of the U. S. Army, would give them no peace. They would be hounded and harassed and kept on the move incessantly until they were gradually killed off or died. Both the Mexican *Federales* and *Rurales* would also be tracking them.

Everyone here — whites, Mexicans, and Apaches — knew it was only a matter of time. The one question that remained to be answered was whether or not Geronimo and the other Apache leaders wanted to surrender unconditionally and live peaceably on the reservations, or eventually to go out living free but running and fighting.

Finally, Geronimo stopped pacing and stood before Crook.

"We will talk again tomorrow."

Crook nodded as if it were the answer he had been expecting all along.

During this last interchange, Norwood had drifted off to sleep.

"Up and at 'em, Russ," said Lieutenant Perry Babcock. "Daylight's a-burning."

Russ Norwood rolled away from the toe in his ribs. Groaning, he wanted to cling to blessed oblivion.

"Just because you're not on active duty any longer doesn't mean you can sleep the day away. You're still in the employ of the United States government."

"Okay, okay. Gimme a minute," Norwood said, running a hand through his mop of blond hair. "Damn! That was the best night's sleep I've had in a week, and you had to go and spoil it." As he smiled, he squinted up at the tall, lank form

12

of the lieutenant, his old friend and now aide to General Crook. Babcock had grown up on an Alabama farm and had always been an early riser.

Russ stretched and yawned mightily. "Must be getting toughened up to sleeping on the ground, or else I was awful tired." He rubbed the sleep from his puffy eyes.

"Well, you oughta know Crook by now. He doesn't believe in any amenities on the trail, like wagons, tents, or stoves."

"You're right about that. Always travels light . . . even in Dakota winters." He unrolled the corduroy breeches he had brought with him and slipped them on. Dragging the gun belt from under his saddle, he swung it around his lean hips and buckled it. He glanced at the activity of men moving around cooking fires in the small camp. "One thing about the general, though," he added. "He lives just like his men."

"None of that spit and polish crap," Babcock agreed. "When we're in the field, he doesn't really care if we're in uniform or not."

"I noticed," Norwood said, wryly, eyeing the dusty blue flannel shirt, unbuttoned to reveal the gray knit undershirt beneath. Tan canvas pants were stuffed into a pair of scuffed boots. A week's growth of dark stubble was beginning to hide the lower part of his face.

Russ instinctively ran a hand over his own chin which hadn't seen a razor for several days, either. But he hoped the reddish-blond hair beneath the mustache wasn't as evident. Then he sat down on his blanket to pull on the knee-high desert moccasins he chose to wear in place of the stiffer, heavier boots.

"You reckon this is the day Geronimo will finally give it up?"

Babcock shrugged. "Who knows? It's their decision now. I think they know they can trust the general to keep his word. A lot of people think primitive Indians are as simple as a bunch

13

of children. They haven't got Crook buffaloed. I heard him remark last night that they were as fierce as so many tigers. He said, 'Knowing what pitiless brutes they are themselves, they mistrust everyone else.' Those were his very words."

"Huh! Crook's no fool. He's got the upper hand, and he'll keep pressing."

Babcock walked over to a still-smoldering cooking fire and snatched a fried corn cake from a skillet setting on a flat rock. "Here yuh go. Last one up gets what's left."

Norwood folded it, stuck it between his teeth as he stuffed in his shirttail and reached for his hat.

"Let's take a walk over to the Chiricahua camp," Babcock suggested. "Strauss, Carlisle, and a couple of the others are already over there."

"Think that's a good idea?" Norwood spoke around a mouthful of bread. "Might be better to let them parley among themselves."

"Well, they know you, and they know me. It's just a friendly visit. Let 'em know we don't mean them any harm. Strauss is the mayor of Tucson. Maybe he can convince them that the civilian authorities aren't going to press for their arrest and hanging."

Norwood nodded and followed the long strides of the officer with whom he had so recently served. As he caught up, Babcock inclined his head toward the hostile camp several hundred yards distant.

"That old gray fox, Crook, has already sent Kaytennay and Alchise over there early this morning to mingle and try to persuade them to surrender. Some of them are loyal to Geronimo, some to Chihuahua, some to Natchez, even though I think Geronimo is probably their over-all leader. Crook figures if he can get 'em arguing among themselves, he can break down their resolve to stay out. Demoralize and conquer."

They found Geronimo in deep conversation with several of

14

his warriors, along with Kaytennay, one of Crook's trusted Apache scouts. The two white men moved on from one *jacal* to another, nodding to some, passing a word or two of greeting in English to others they recognized from the reservations and earlier negotiations. They passed several young bucks squatting in a circle playing monte. They paused to watch a beautifully muscled Apache using a small rock to pound a Mexican silver peso into a decorative concho.

Farther on was Alchise, the son of Cochise and a close friend of the general's, in earnest discussion with several of the adult Chiricahuas. The men were standing in front of one of the dozen or so *jacales*. These low, round shelters were all constructed of Spanish bayonet and mesquite, covered with pieces of blanket and canvas and whatever cloth was handy. The daggers of the Spanish bayonet were arranged around each dwelling so as to make it a small fortress. The *rancheria,* as the Mexicans called it, was situated on the lip of an extinct volcano so that slabs of lava rock could be used for a breastworks, if necessary.

"Look at the way this camp is set up," Norwood observed in a low voice. "If they were attacked here, with all the guns and ammunition they've got, nothing short of a mountain howitzer could blast them out."

"That's one reason there are hundreds of us chasing a few dozen of them," Babcock replied, looking at the layout. "I'm glad we've got them negotiating."

"Hey, there's the old man now," Norwood nodded. "Reckon he's come over for some informal talks?"

"Wouldn't be surprised. Crook's like that. Hard and intractable when negotiating in public, but he'll probably bend a little in private."

"He can't undercut official Washington policy," Norwood argued.

"Well, all I know is what he told us at officers' call last

15

night. Said Washington had ordered him to get an unconditional surrender and to make no promises, unless it was necessary to secure their surrender. Reckon that gives a little leeway. He said Geronimo and the others would probably want to be allowed to return to the reservations unharmed and with no penalty for all the killing and robbing of civilians. But he'll have to impose *some* penalty. The civilian press has been howling for his hide for being too soft on these renegades."

"What can he do?"

Babcock shrugged. "There was talk of exiling some of them back east for a while. Get them completely out of the territory. Of course, Geronimo may decide to stay on the warpath and fight it out."

They walked along silently for a few seconds.

"You know what I think is the Apaches' most striking characteristic?" Norwood asked.

"What?"

"It's their complete disregard of consequences when they're really riled about something," Norwood said. "They lose all control and reason."

"I guess that's the trait that makes them such desperate fighters when they're cornered."

"It's not very often they let themselves get cornered."

Walking back to their own camp, they continued to discuss the strange twists of the Apache mind — the childish petulance, the superstitions about death and sickness.

"Well, if it isn't Russ Norwood!" a voice called out. "You still traipsing around after the cavalry? I thought the Army had given you the boot once and for all."

The two men turned at the sound of the insolent tone just as Tom Horn spurted a stream of tobacco juice into the dust a few inches from Norwood's moccasins. The scout wiped his mouth with the back of his hand. "Ooops!" he chuckled.

"Get the hell outa my way, Horn!" Norwood said, deadly quiet. He felt his pulse quicken.

Babcock stood to one side, eyeing the sudden confrontation.

"Nobody's in your way, *sir*," came the condescending reply. Horn stepped aside with a bow and made a sweeping gesture with his wide-brimmed white Stetson.

Russ gritted his teeth as he and Perry started to walk past.

"Guess I oughta be grateful you showed the white feather," Horn continued. "Else I might be out of a job as a tracker by now."

Norwood halted and turned around. The lean interpreter was eyeing him with a half smile on his clean-shaven face, slouching on one foot, holding his hat at his side.

"Better quit pushing me, Horn."

"Ooooh! Now he's talking tough. You weren't showing that much sand three months ago."

Russ took a step toward the scout.

"Norwood, you're just no fun a-tall," Horn grinned, backing up in mock fear.

Norwood put his hand on the butt of his holstered Colt.

"Okay, okay, just joshin'," Horn said, hastily replacing his hat. When the receding hairline was covered, his face regained the youthful appearance of his twenty-six years.

Norwood said: "Too bad your old hero, Al Sieber, isn't here. Maybe he could fill those jug-handles of yours with some good advice about staying out of other people's business."

The tall scout reddened at this reference to his protuberant ears and his friendship with the older chief of scouts. Russ had struck his Achilles heel — his vanity.

"You've got a gun, and I'm unarmed."

"Perry, hold this for me." Norwood started to unbuckle his gun belt. He was at least two inches shorter in height and a good twenty pounds lighter, but he was muscular and quick.

"That's enough, Russ," Babcock said, stepping between them. "This isn't the time or the place." He gripped Norwood's arms and pushed him back, adding in a lower voice, "The old man's got all he can deal with right now without the two of you clawing open old wounds in front of these hostiles. If you want to keep your job, let it go for now!"

Norwood's hazel eyes still glared at the tall scout over Babcock's shoulder, but he allowed the tension to go out of his muscles as Babcock guided him away.

"C'mon, I'll get you a cup of coffee."

They walked a few steps in silence.

"You're either gonna have to stay away from that man altogether, or settle your differences by whipping the hell out of him," said Babcock. "I don't think it's worth shootin' each other over it."

"Yeah, you're right. What's done is done, and I have no regrets, even though I got the blame for it."

"You know what I think about *that*." Babcock shook his head. "You know damn' well if that court martial had taken place, the truth would have come out."

"No, Perry, I was in the Army long enough to know how the official military mind works. I was in command of that company, including Horn and his Indian scouts. That makes me ultimately responsible for anything they did."

"Well, Horn was either careless, or he was scared and intentionally let those mules get loose and give the alarm before you could spring the ambush. That was a sure trap!"

"Could have been an accident."

"Not likely. Horn is looking to make himself a reputation without exposing his skin to any hostile fire."

"It wasn't so much the Apaches getting away," Russ said, "but what really bothered me was one of my men getting killed in that skirmish."

"And you took the blame for the whole thing." The disgust was evident in Babcock's voice.

"Even if I had been exonerated, just the fact that I faced a court martial would have stained my record for the rest of my career. I had already been a first lieutenant for longer than just about anyone else. No, resigning my commission before any charges were brought was the best thing I ever did. Thirteen years was enough. I'm still young enough to get into some other line of work as soon as these hostiles are confined for good. Besides," he grinned, "being a courier is a hell of a lot easier than being an officer in the Sixth Cavalry."

"Well, just watch out for Horn," Babcock cautioned.

"I can take care of myself."

"No doubt about that. Just be on your guard. This man thinks nothing of killing. I've seen him in action against the hostiles, and I know you have, too. It's as if . . . as if he were one of the . . . the worst of them. He never takes unnecessary chances and kills without exposing himself."

"He lived with the Apaches for a short time while he was trying to learn their language. In fact, I think he still carries one of those 'medicine bags.' I don't know if he actually believes in its power." Russ gave a short laugh. "I've heard he carries buttons in it."

Babcock stopped walking and turned to face his friend. "I don't mean that he's gone native. What I'm trying to say is that he's a killer. A heartless one. To him, it's like stepping on a beetle. No qualms, no second thoughts . . . at least none that I could detect behind those opaque eyes. Destroying a child or a squaw was no different than shooting a buck."

"Perry, we both know a man can harden himself to killing in the heat of battle, especially if he's afraid and defending his own life."

Babcock shook his head. "It's more than that. Last year I

19

overheard Horn bragging about shooting some prisoners."

"What?"

"Yeah. Said he and Al Sieber were told to do it by some officer. Didn't say who."

Norwood's eyes went wide. "He was ordered to kill prisoners? And you didn't say or do anything?"

"No prisoners were killed," Perry replied simply. "I checked, and none was missing. Either he was talking about some other time and place, or he was just trying to impress his drinking buddies. Knowing what a liar he is, especially when he's been drinking, I'd say he was just blowing a lot of hot air, but I wouldn't put such a thing past him."

Norwood digested this. "I guess there are men that low down," he muttered.

When they reached the cooking fire, Perry tested the blackened coffee pot with his fingers. "Still hot enough." He rinsed out a tin cup with the coffee and then refilled it and handed it to Russ.

Norwood took a good sip, then another, and grunted in satisfaction. "Do you know anything about Horn's background? Where he hails from? What his people are like?"

"Not much. He drifted down here from the Colorado mines. German extraction from somewhere in Missouri, I think. Must have been born about the first part of the war. Could be he saw some bloody border raids as a kid."

"Maybe that's why human life doesn't mean much to him. Or he might have some mental problem."

"You're too kind. Some people are just born mean as the devil himself," Babcock concluded.

They saw no more of Tom Horn the rest of the day. Russ and Perry and the others spent the remaining daylight hours resting and talking and playing cards in the shade. By the end of March, this area of northern Mexico was well into spring and the days were rapidly moving from pleasant to very warm. Several of the men caught up on their personal hygiene by shaving or bathing or washing clothes in the clear, cold creek.

There was no work to be done. It was just a waiting game now to see what Geronimo and his warriors decided to do. Nearly every Chiricahua carried a "medicine bag" of some kind, usually a small buckskin bag on a thong around the neck. The bag contained such things as the feather of a redbird, or of a woodpecker, the head of a quail, the claws of a prairie dog, or some small silver crescents. Only the individual owner of these amulets could decide what effect, if any, this "medicine" would have on protecting him from any danger resulting from this conference.

The next morning, March 27th, the leaders of the hostiles sent word that they wanted to talk. It was nearly noon when the men of both camps reassembled in the ravine. This time Chihuahua spoke first while Geronimo and Kutli sat to one side, under a mulberry tree, their faces blackened with crushed galena. What significance this had Babcock and Norwood were at a loss to explain.

Chihuahua started his speech in the usual roundabout way, praising General Crook in the most elaborate of terms, even indicating that he had the powers of a god to send fruit to the trees, power to make the rain and the wind. Such a one, he asserted, was even greater than his father and mother. Chihuahua and his followers would be glad to surrender to him.

"I now surrender to you, and I want no more bad feelings or bad talk. I am going over to stay with you in your camp. Whenever a man raises anything, even a dog, he thinks well of it and tries to raise it up and treat it well. So I want you to feel towards me, and be good to me, and don't let people say bad things about me. I think a great deal of Alchise and

Kaytennay, and I hope someday to be all the same as their brother."

Chihauhua then paused and shook hands with the two Apache scouts he had just named and stepped forward and shook General Crook's hand. Natchez and Kutli stepped forward and did the same. Geronimo was the last to speak.

"Two or three words are enough. We are all one family, all one band. What the others say, I say also. Do with me what you please. Once I moved about like the wind. Now I surrender to you, and that is all."

He shook Crook's hand.

Norwood caught Babcock's eye as the ceremony was concluding. They exchanged a look of understanding, and Babcock gave a slight smile and nodded. No more fighting and marching under God-awful conditions chasing these will-of-the-wisp hostiles over this rugged country. The white settlers and ranchers would, at long last, have a chance to breathe in peace. It would probably mean the end of his job as a courier, but he hadn't planned to stay that much longer anyway. He might move on to Colorado or Nevada to check on any mining prospects.

But he wasn't done here yet. He wondered about the terms to which the two parties had finally agreed. This would probably not be generally known until Crook reported to his superiors.

George Crook rose from the shady slope, pulled on his gauntlets. The conference broke up, the Apaches drifting away toward their own camp.

Crook went back to where his mule was hobbled and grazing. He pulled a pad, pen, and a small bottle of ink from the saddlebags on the ground, sat down on a nearby slab of lava, and began writing. The steel tip scratched at the paper for several minutes. Finally, he laid the pen down and read over what he had written. He folded the paper and rose.

"Norwood!"

Russ reported quickly. "Sir?"

"I want you to take this dispatch and ride north as fast as you can to the telegraph at Fort Bowie." He handed the message to Norwood. Across one side of the folded paper was scrawled, "Lieut. Gen. P. H. Sheridan, U. S. A. Washington, D. C."

"We'll be pulling out of here early in the morning to follow you," he continued. "Alchise and Kaytennay, Lieutenant Maus and the rest of the scouts will escort the hostiles to Fort Bowie. They have women and children, so they won't be traveling as fast as I will. Any questions?"

"No, sir." Norwood slipped the paper into a flat leather pouch and slid the pouch inside his double-breasted shirt.

"I don't need to emphasize the importance of this. Don't let it out of your hands until you reach Bowie. You should make it by tomorrow evening. Just don't kill your horse getting there."

Fifteen minutes later, Russ swung into the saddle.

"See you back at Bowie!" Perry Babcock saluted him as Norwood turned his bay north and urged the horse into a canter.

As Norwood rode out, he felt good. He was alive and free and doing something useful. It was an almost childish glee. Strange thoughts for a man in his early thirties, he reflected. Especially one who had seem so much blood and death and the conflicts among men. He had been telling Babcock the truth when he said he was happy to have resigned his commission. Some of the lightness he felt was the result of being released from the constant load of command and supervision. Now he was answerable only for himself. He smiled as the wind fanned his face. Discounting the danger, working as a courier was almost fun. Almost like the tales he had heard about the Pony Express a quarter century earlier.

As he slowed his bay to a walk to allow the animal to pick his way down a steep stone incline, the image of the grinning

Tom Horn came to mind. Why did the scout get under his skin so badly? He felt embarrassed for letting his anger cloud his judgment. What more did the man want? After all, Horn had avoided censure for allowing the hostiles to escape a sure trap. And he had successfully shifted the blame to Lieutenant Norwood, the officer in charge.

"Just rubbing it in, I guess," he mused, half aloud. "Hoorahing me for a little entertainment."

But Babcock had a different idea. "He's trying to make himself a reputation as an Indian fighter, a reputation he can trade on for years to come," Perry had stated. "You're a threat to that reputation as long as you're around. You could expose him as a fraud if you decided to press it."

Russ made a mental note to shun Tom Horn, but he also resolved to hit first and talk later the next time something happened. If there was any truth to the killer instinct Babcock was warning him about, he would be ready. In the unlikely event it came to a showdown with guns, he couldn't afford to hesitate or flinch, or Horn would cut him down without a thought.

Once he rode out of the rugged hills, the going was mostly through open, undulating country between ranges of desert mountains. These low ranges, straddling the border, trended north and south for miles. By alternately walking and trotting his mount, he was able to maintain a steady, ground-eating pace.

Around five-thirty he reined up along the bank of the San Bernardino River, climbed down stiffly, and pulled off the light McClellan saddle. He took the precaution of picketing his horse on a long line. Any other time he would have trusted his bay to stay close with a ground rein, but he couldn't take the chance of being set afoot now. The horse gratefully rolled in the grass and then had a good drink before walking a few steps away to graze.

Russ took a long look around before uncapping one of his canteens for a drink. Then he lay down under a cottonwood to rest for an hour, his drawn Colt across his stomach.

Resuming his ride north along the floor of Skeleton Cañon, he saw no one the rest of that long afternoon. He might have been the last person on earth. Yet he was not deluded into relaxing his vigilance by this apparent solitude.

Two hours before sunset some towering thunderheads came billowing up from the west, spreading, blotting the sun and gradually massing to form a black, solid base.

"Maybe those hills will catch most of it," he muttered to himself, eyeing the ominous sky. He pressed on without pausing for food or water, riding for a time, and then walking and leading his horse to give both of them some relief. He did not stop when twilight came and then darkness shrouded the land.

The fresh fragrance of rain over the dusty earth was carried to his nose on the breeze. Intermittent flashes of lightning gave him enough light to guide his bay along an uneven valley floor, cut up by shallow washes and shrubbery. Heart-stopping bolts of approaching lightning, followed by crashing thunder, finally forced a halt. They were in open country with no shelter anywhere. As nearly as he could judge, they were on a slight rise of ground, covered with sparse grass.

He jerked the saddle off the skittish horse and dumped it on the ground. Then, using a rock, he drove the picket pin deeply into the soil, hoping it would hold. At every flash, the animal's head jerked up. For an instant, the horse was frozen in sharp relief — ears forward, eyes walling, nostrils flaring, and black mane flying in the rising gusts. Then the stark image blinked out and a black roar of thunder smothered them.

Russ fumbled his way to the saddle and unstrapped his bedroll from the cantle. Always cautious, he carried it about a hundred yards away, dropping it under a big mesquite bush. He flinched at another brilliant flash of lightning. Then, with a ground-shaking boom, the storm was on them. He huddled down on his blanket, using his slicker for a cover from the downpour that burst out of the heavens.

A gusting wind drove the storm before it across the broad valley, whipping the branches of the bush. Every sound, every sense was drowned in the roar of continuous cannonades. In spite of the flapping slicker, rivulets of water quickly began to soak his blanket and then his moccasins and pants. The leather case was still dry and secure inside his shirt.

In less than an hour, the storm passed, rumbling and grumbling into the distance, leaving a few stars showing. Russ dragged his wet bedroll into the open and lay down to rest. He had forgotten to pull any jerky from his saddlebags, but he was too tired to go after it. He finally dozed off, wet and miserable, between pangs of hunger.

By the earliest light, he was retrieving his horse that had jerked the pin loose and was a half mile away, peacefully grazing. The picket line was tangled in a clump of creosote bush.

A piece of jerky and some water from his canteen was breakfast, and then he was in the saddle and making time northward toward the Dragoon Mountains. A few hours later, he looped around the base of these mountains, bore east into Apache Pass, and then south down a desert wash, past the ruins of a stage station to Bowie.

By midafternoon, saddle chafed and weary, he rode up the lazy short incline to the quadrangle of adobe buildings and corrals that was Fort Bowie. It was cupped in a hollow among some steeply rising desert mountains. Swinging around the back of the sutler's store, he rode across the parade ground, stopped at the adjutant's office, dismounted, and reported. The officer acknowledged his arrival.

"So the general's got him again. That's good news. Better get that report on the wire." He pointed toward an open door to the next room where a corporal wearing the crossed flags of the Signal Corps was handling the telegraph key. "Then get yourself some sleep. You look beat."

Russ delivered the report but lingered as the soldier began tapping the message over the wire to Washington. Casually looking around the telegrapher's shoulder, he managed to read enough of the General's scrawl to see that Crook had accepted surrender on the terms that Geronimo and his renegades would be exiled for two years, with or without their relatives, before returning to the reservations in Arizona.

So the Indian wars of almost three hundred years were finally over, Norwood thought, retreating toward his quarters at the end of the long adobe building that served as the officers' quarters. His job was done. Now for a good wash and some food.

Reveille had just sounded the following morning when the door to Norwood's room burst open and slammed back against the wall. Russ jumped and instinctively clawed for his gun that hung on the bedpost.

Perry Babcock stood there, trail worn, dirty, and out of breath. "You heard the news?"

"What news? What're you talking about?" Norwood shoved his Colt back into place and swung his feet to the floor.

"Geronimo's escaped!"

"What?"

"You heard right."

"What happened?" Norwood couldn't seem to get his mind functioning.

"Some damned trader named Tribollet sold them a few jugs of whiskey and then commenced to plyin' them with lies. Told 'em they were being tricked into surrendering and, as soon as they crossed the border, they'd be arrested and hanged. Really spooked 'em. That slippery old bastard lit out in the storm the other night. Took over twenty braves, thirteen women and six kids. Probably headed back to the Sierra Madre. Natchez went with him. Only seventy-nine hostiles are being brought in."

"Oh, no!" Russ leaned forward, holding his head in both hands.

"Yep. He's about as trustworthy as a rattlesnake . . . and just as vicious."

"Damn!"

"Looks like the chase is on again."

Chapter Two

Although only about a day and a half's ride from Fort Bowie, Fort Huachuca bore little resemblance to the other. It looked more like the military installations on the plains with its large, two-and-a-half story frame buildings lined up in two rows, facing each other across the parade ground. The blacksmith shop, corrals, and other outbuildings were scattered around the perimeter of the quadrangle. This post, at the foot of the Chiricahua Mountains, was only twenty-two miles from the Mexican border. It had been used most recently as a staging area for troops pursuing Apaches across the international boundary, in accordance with the so-called "Hot Trail" treaty.

"Damn that Nelson Miles for an arrogant fool!" Perry Babcock yanked off his gauntlets and slapped them across his leg as he sank into a wooden chair in the barracks room.

"Shhh! Keep your voice down!" Russ cautioned, moving quickly to close the barracks-room door. "Anybody hears that, you could be reported for insubordination."

"I don't really care," Babcock continued, angrily tugging at the top button of his uniform blouse. Rivulets of sweat had traced grooves in the coating of dust on his face. His hair was plastered to his forehead. "In all my growin'-up days in north Alabama, I never saw a fighting cock preen himself the way that man does." He bit at his lower lip, a habit that always revealed his agitation, even when he was quiet. "I'm beginning to think you made a wise move when you resigned your commission. I'm considering doing the same thing."

"You can't be serious. You're an academy man. Don't throw

away your future just because of one bad officer."

Babcock didn't reply until he had stripped down to his sweat-soaked undershirt. Then he rose and went to the window and threw the sash all the way up. The parade ground of Fort Huachuca was deserted at the moment, shortly after noon. The colors were snapping in the breeze at the top of the flagpole. The wind was the only thing that was saving the June heat from being intolerable. Babcock spread his arms to the hot air that fanned in the open window.

"Whew! That feels good!"

"Well, we've got General Miles, and there's no use cussing about it," Russ said. "We'll just have to put up with him."

"I don't know how much longer I can do that."

"I know, I know. I wish Crook was back, too. But he's been gone for more than two months. If he hadn't asked to be reassigned, we'd all be better off."

"I can understand how frustrated he was."

"We've got to think about dealing with what's going on now and forget about Crook," Norwood insisted.

Babcock turned back from the window and mopped his face with his shirt. "Miles has been here since the first week of April, and he's not one bit closer to catching Geronimo than the day he arrived. First thing he did was request two thousand more troops. That made five thousand altogether — about a fourth of the entire U. S. Army! Ye gods! Five thousand men chasing about two dozen warriors and a few women and children."

"And that's not counting the Mexican forces who are after them," Russ added.

"Right. Then he takes a map and divides the territory into big squares and posts a troop at every water hole and pass along the border, figuring the hostiles will have to pass by there sooner or later. Not only that, but he sets up heliograph stations on every mountain top so mirror signals can keep all the commands in touch with each other. Sounds good on paper, doesn't it?" Babcock asked rhetorically. "The only problem is there are gaps in that chain thirty and forty miles wide. When he saw that didn't work, he ordered my company and several others out after the hostiles. For the past month we've done nothing but run 'em back and forth across the border. Except for Captain Lebo's men, who had a brush with them in early May, nobody's seen hide nor hair of them." He slumped back into the wooden armchair.

"Nobody's seen them except those two or three dozen ranchers and prospectors they've butchered in the past few weeks," Russ said. Through his mind flashed a vivid image of a ranch family they had come upon a few hours too late. The man had been shot down; the woman had been tied to a tree upside down, with a fire built under her head. The brain inside that blackened skull had been roasted. A small child had been hanging by a meathook pushed through the back of her head. Somehow, the small child, a little girl, had been still alive, but she had died within the hour. "The tigers of the human race," Crook had called them. But that was doing an injustice to the jungle cats who had no capacity for torture. It wasn't enough to steal horses and ammunition and shoot down terrified ranchers. They were exacting revenge on all whites.

"Well, you can bet that bunch of business men in Tucson will do all they can to keep the pot boiling," Babcock was saying.

"You mean that group the papers are calling the 'Tucson Ring?' "

"Yeah. Apache wars are good for business. They can sell the Army food and supplies and remounts. The longer this trouble drags on, the richer they get. Miles is fool enough to play right into their hands by changing Crook's strategy, and all it will do is prolong this mess. I guess he was so anxious to show everyone that Crook's methods wouldn't work, he dismissed most of the Apache scouts. He even made the statement that the 'right sort' of white men could run down those renegades. Now, I ask you, is that arrogance, or vanity, or what? The man has no experience in this terrain against Indians like this."

"If nothing else," Russ said, "this just proves Crook was right . . . it takes an Apache to catch an Apache."

"Damned small consolation for Crook and for the rest of us, I'm sure."

Norwood let the sarcasm pass. "I have to look on the bright side of Brigadier General Nelson A. Miles," he said seriously.

"There's a bright side?"

"Sure. Miles not only dismissed most of the Apache scouts, but he got rid of Tom Horn, too."

Babcock grinned. "That's one less problem you've got," he agreed. He seemed to be cooling down, both physically and emotionally.

"Wonder where he went?"

"A couple of my men who were on leave mentioned they'd seen him hanging around the saloons over in Tombstone."

"Not surprised," Russ replied. "Never struck me as the kind to go looking for honest work."

"Rumor has it that he's got an interest in one of the silver mines over there."

"I'd bet it's not a *working* interest."

"Good to be rid of him, in any case," Babcock said, stretching. "I've got to get into a clean uniform. Miles has issued an officers' call for one o'clock. He's down here from his plush digs at Fort Bowie. Probably has some new hare-brained scheme in mind to tell us about."

"Well," Russ said, sliding off the bed and walking to the

door. "you know the old Irish saying, 'Never shake hands with the devil 'til you meet him in the road.' Miles may have something good to say."

Babcock rolled his eyes upward. "There's another old saying, 'Blessed is he who expects nothing, for he shall never be disappointed.' "

"*Touche!*" Russ laughed. "But just keep a poker face. I don't want you getting into any trouble. See you at supper. If you're not too tired, we'll have a beer at the sutler's afterward."

Russ stepped out onto the porch of the barracks, as Perry clumped down the wooden steps and angled across the parade ground toward his room in the officers' quarters.

It was after eight o'clock, but the lingering June twilight still lighted the windows of the sutler's store.

"Well, let's have it," Norwood said, leaning back and propping his feet on a nearby chair.

Babcock set his pewter mug of beer on the stained, round-top table and sat down. He took a deep draught of the beer and wiped the foam from his mouth before replying.

"General Miles has decided to put together a picked group of one hundred of his best men, headed up by Captain Henry W. Lawton. He's signing on some Apache scouts. This force, traveling light but supported by a pack train, will strike south into Mexico after the hostiles. You will be part of that group as a courier to keep the soldiers in touch with the pack train and to perform any other duties Lawton can think of for you and a couple of other civilians."

"How soon?"

"As soon as all the supplies can be collected and packed, and the men can get their equipment in order. At the earliest by the end of the week. Most of the men and supplies are here or at Bowie."

"Sounds like he's back to using Crook's methods."

"Not entirely. He's still got this idea in his head that the best white men are at least equal to the Apaches in physical endurance and stamina and savvy when it comes to tracking and chasing around these mountains and deserts."

Russ shook his head in disbelief.

"There's one more thing you should know about. Al Sieber is too stove up with rheumatism and old wounds to hold the saddle on this kind of campaign. So Miles has sent to Tombstone for Tom Horn to come back as chief of scouts."

Chapter Three

By the time Russ Norwood was ordered south five days later, he had forgotten all about Tom Horn. The scout had not shown up at Fort Huachuca, and Russ was too busy even to bother watching for him.

Perry Babcock had been wrong about one thing. Most of the troops who were to make up this hundred-man force of the best cavalry soldiers were not at Fort Bowie and Fort Huachuca. They had to be gathered from field duty. The commander, Captain Henry W. Lawton, had a troop with him and was near Patagonia. He and his men had been in the field for more than a month. The men, the pack train, and all the supplies were to be assembled at Calabasas, a town about forty miles southwest on the Santa Cruz River, just north of the border with Sonora.

"Last call for the Atchison, Topeka, and Santa Fe!" Lieutenant Babcock grinned as the private who was driving pulled the team of mules to a stop. Norwood handed up his bedroll and rifle, then accepted a hand up into the spring wagon.

"No sense walking to the depot when you can ride," Russ said, settling into the wooden seat beside his friend. "Hello, Doc," he added, nodding to Doctor Benjamin Sutter, the young contract surgeon who twisted around from his seat in front. "Glad to see we've got a medical man along."

"I hope no one needs my services." Sutter had a twinkle in his blue eyes. He had a ruddy complexion, a sweeping, light brown mustache, and looked a little more fleshy than fit.

The private slapped the reins, and the mules started toward

the open end of the quadrangle.

In the confusion of orders being dispatched, supplies being gathered by the quartermaster, horses being shod by the farriers, Norwood had only caught a glimpse or two of General Nelson Miles, and those from a distance. Now, as the wagon cleared the parade ground, he saw the commanding officer standing on the porch of the adjutant's office, conversing with General George Forsyth who was stopping over at the fort. Forsyth, a handsome, black-haired man, had risen from the rank of private since the Civil War and was a veteran Indian fighter who carried in his body at least three pieces of lead from hostiles.

He and Miles glanced up as the spring wagon passed, but neither made any sign of recognition. To Russ, General Miles seemed to be giving them a haughty stare as they went by. Then he turned back to his conversation. But Russ had had his first really good look at the man who had replaced the beloved General Crook. Miles was tall and straight in his blue uniform, with an imperial tilt to his head. He had wavy brown hair and a thick, pointed mustache, both tending to gray. Beneath the belted coat, Russ thought he could detect the slight growth of a paunch.

Babcock gave Norwood a significant look but said nothing in deference to the other two men in the wagon. Russ was a civilian and under no such restrictions, so he spoke for both of them.

"If that were General Crook, he'd be down at Calabasas, overseeing the organizing of this expedition."

Perry evaded the comment by replying, "You'd better enjoy this trip. It'll be a long time before you get to plant your butt on a spring wagon or the velvet cushions of a railroad-coach seat."

"Well, I am glad to get ze order to go down by train,"

Doctor Sutter nodded, his German-Swiss dialect showing through.

"Same here," Russ replied. "I was mighty tired of sitting a saddle. And my bay was about done in. Turned him in to the post stables. He'll be well cared for until I get back."

"You'll be issued a horse when we get to Calabasas," Babcock assured him.

"Actually, I may try a mule this time, if I have a choice," Norwood said.

"Couldn't be better for stamina," Babcock agreed. "'Course, if this past month is any indication, we'll be doing as much walking as riding. But, since you're a courier, that may not apply to you."

"The pack train's already forming up there?"

"Right. In fact, the packers should already have all their supplies. They were shipped down by train the past two days."

The train pulled out at ten after four in the afternoon, and they arrived in Calabasas just before dark. Norwood and Babcock discovered that most of the pack train was formed up and ready to go, but that Captain Lawton was already in Mexico, rather than in the Patagonia Mountains, as they had been told. A telegram had been sent directing Lieutenant Babcock to take command of the pack train and any cavalry there and to catch up to Captain Lawton as soon as possible at Ojo de Agua.

The two men went to the Hotel Santa Rita, the regular stopping place for railroad passengers and the best hostelry in town. Although Calabasas had a reputation as a wide-open, rip-roaring place, the two men contented themselves with a good meal of boiled mutton at the hotel and then retired to the billiard room.

"Seems like a special expedition like this would have been a little better planned," Norwood observed, chalking his cue and bending over the green baize.

"I know it looks like total chaos," Perry admitted. "But you know, yourself, that these campaigns are organized confusion. It'll sort itself out. Probably better that we don't all start out together. Keep the hostiles watching all directions at once. We'll catch up to Lawton in a couple of days."

Babcock replaced the curved pipe in his mouth and leaned over the table. The balls clicked together. "Damn! Can't believe I missed an easy shot like that!" He straightened up, and the aromatic tobacco smoke curled through the yellow light of the hanging oil lamp.

"How is the Sierra Madre for forage in summer?" Russ asked.

"So, so. Not good until you get into some of the higher valleys. We'll buy about eight hundred and fifty pounds of dry alfalfa for the animals at the Martmnez ranch just south of here."

"How many animals?"

"We've got forty-nine mules and twelve horses just now, not counting the cavalry and the packers' mounts. We'll do okay. Don't concern yourself about that. Anybody'd think you're still in charge of a company."

"Old habits . . .," Russ muttered, draining his beer glass. He pulled out his small, gold-plated Waltham. "Past my bedtime," he yawned.

Perry lined up his shot and proceeded to sink the winning ball. "Ha! That's a dollar you owe me."

"That's my last game," Russ said, replacing his cue in the rack. "Time for some clean sheets and soft pillows." He had a premonition that this would be his last touch with civilization for many a long day to come.

Even though the sun had not yet peeked over the eastern mountains, there was plenty of light by five o'clock the next morning for Russ to select a mule from the remuda. The mule he picked was caught and bridled by one of the Mexican herders.

"Good choice, *señor*," the man said, leading up the mule. "He have plenty bottom." He grinned at his use of American slang.

Russ checked the mule's teeth and hoofs and felt the leg tendons. The gray did not appear to be over five years old and had no pack or saddle galls. It remained to be seen about his wind and his disposition.

"He'll do," he said shortly and proceeded to throw an Army-issue McClellan saddle on the animal. The mule was a reasonable size so the light saddle fit perfectly over his withers. He cinched it up and strapped his duffel behind the cantle. Lastly, he shoved his .44-40 Marlin carbine into the saddle scabbard.

"We'll be marching with stripped saddles," Babcock said, coming up as Norwood finished.

"Yeah. I figured as much."

"Stripped saddles" for the cavalry was officially "light marching order" and meant carrying rations for only four days, one change of underwear, one hundred rounds of ammunition, and one blanket. Any additional gear, food, and ammunition would be carried on the pack mules.

"Just like serving under Crook again," Perry said.

"No change a-tall," Russ agreed. "But damned if I'm going without my slicker. Nothing worse than being wet all the time."

"Hope you brought some extra cartridges for that Marlin."

"A thousand rounds. Already packed on a mule. They'll fit my Colt, too."

Just as Babcock turned to leave, a dark-skinned Mexican came up to him. He had coarse black hair and a huge black mustache.

"I am called Rolando Vasquez. I am ready to start when you are, *señor*," he said.

"Good." Perry replied, glancing at the pack train where the *aparejos* were all in place and the packs lashed atop them. "You're to guide us to Lawton."

"*Si.*"

"Isn't that Captain Lawton's mule, Dolly, that Indian's holding?"

"*Si.* She got away again and was heading home. He sent this man to catch her and bring her back."

Babcock nodded. "We're forming up now. Be ready to move in ten minutes."

The Mexican packer mounted and rode away.

"I've never met Lawton," Russ said to Perry out of the side of his mouth as he adjusted the length of his stirrup. "But, if a man can't hang onto his mule, what chance does he have of catching Geronimo?"

Babcock looked around to be sure he was out of earshot of anyone else. "Henry Lawton's a good officer. Steady and true, but plodding. The bulldog type. Not innovative. Give him an order, and he'll carry it out come hell or high mountains. My guess is that Miles selected him because he's a giant of a man . . . six feet four at least and all muscle. He's Miles's idea of the strong, enduring white man who will wear these savages down."

Norwood halfway hoped that this first day on the trail would be a relatively easy one to give him a chance to get accustomed to his new mount and to toughen up his backside after about ten days out of the saddle. He was disappointed.

The column rode out at five-thirty, and the Mexican guide took them down the valley to the southeast then started up over a series of hills that led to the backbone of the Blue Mountains. They were strung out in single file, the cavalry in front led by Lieutenant Babcock followed by a sergeant and perhaps fifteen troopers, then Norwood and Doctor Sutter, several civilian packers, and the mule train. At first it was a long, gradual climb out of the valley in the fresh, clear air of early morning.

About noon, when Russ thought they might get over the Blue Mountains by this easy trail, they struck a huge cañon and began a perilous descent. The trail was narrow, steep, and twisting. Even though his mule seemed sure footed, Russ finally dismounted and led him. Hardly a minute later he was thankful he did. One of the troopers' horses ahead of him slipped and rolled down the hillside. The soldier managed to leap clear and was uninjured. His mount rolled over once and came to a sliding halt on the grassy slope before scrambling back up, none the worse for the fall.

Before the column reached the bottom of the cañon, two of the mules behind Norwood suffered the same fate, one of them crushing the wooden boxes on its back and scattering hardtack and sacks of beans everywhere. The packers were kept hard at it, rescuing the braying, kicking animals, reloading the damaged packs, all the while filling the air with a blue haze of profanity in both English and Spanish.

This descent was only the beginning. Next it was up another long hill and down the other side where the column halted in midafternoon for a brief rest and some food. A number of the soldiers and experienced packers gathered twigs from the abundant scrub brush and had a few small fires going. Coffee was boiling almost before Russ could loosen the saddle girth and hobble his mule. There was a clear stream running through the hollow but no trees for shelter from the sun. The surrounding heights blocked any breeze.

"Good water," Perry Babcock remarked, strolling up, gnawing on a piece of jerky. "But an ugly hole to get caught in if there are any Indians about." He glanced uneasily at the steep hills. "We've only got a few guns."

"Just keep a sharp eye. We'll be up and out of here in thirty minutes," Norwood said. The heat had taken his appetite, but he sipped tepid water from his large, blanket-sided canteen.

Babcock turned away, obviously preoccupied. "Sergeant Burke!" he yelled at a nearby non-com. "There will be no cooking now. If the men are hungry, they can eat whatever's in their saddlebags. We'll be pulling out of here very shortly."

Russ squatted in the scant shade of his mule, removed his sand-colored campaign hat, and wiped a sleeve across his brow.

"The lieutenant is unusually nervous this early in the campaign," a clear, cultured voice remarked.

Russ swiveled to see a small man sitting, cross-legged, on the ground a few yards away.

"Yeah, I guess he is," Russ answered distractedly when he realized the man was speaking to him.

"But he's a good officer," the little man continued. "He'll settle down before we get to Lawton's outfit."

"You've served with Lieutenant Babcock before?" Russ asked, more to have something to say than for information.

"Several times. Smart. A good southern boy."

Russ struggled to reconcile the appearance of this scruffy, leathery man with the voice that was coming from him. He took the initiative, rose from his crouch, and extended his hand. "Russ Norwood."

"Stratford McGee," the man replied, taking his hand in a strong grip. "I go by Mac."

The man wore fringed, leather breeches that had seen much hard usage, moccasins, a red flannel shirt, and a brown hat with a wide, straight brim. His beard was a mixture of gray and black, and the eyes that peered from the weathered face were a startling blue.

"Pardon me for not getting up, but an old man needs his rest," McGee was saying as Norwood appraised him.

"Didn't I see you with the packers earlier?"

"That's right," McGee nodded. "In my younger days I roamed the Rocky Mountains a free man. But of late I've been reduced

42

to nursemaiding a bunch of damned contrary Army mules. Actually, these southwestern mules are not your ordinary cross-grained Army mules. These are smaller, more sure footed. A cross with a Mexican jack."

"They really looked sure footed today," Norwood snorted.

"They're a lot better than the bigger mules," McGee insisted. "And they're smart. Why, you saw those animals fall and roll downslope a hundred yards. But did you notice they climbed right back up and found their proper place in line?"

Russ hadn't noticed. "I was too busy watching the trail, myself," he admitted.

"And you'll never see one of these critters try to walk between two trees where his pack won't fit. Smarter than a lot of men in this outfit, I'll be bound." He eyed the gray over Norwood's shoulder. "That's a good-lookin' ridin' mule you got there. What's his name?"

Russ was taken aback. "Doesn't have one. I just got him." He realized he had never named his bay, either.

"Looks like a smart one."

As if he knew they were talking about him, the animal raised his head and looked at them, his long ears twitching forward and back. Then he resumed grazing.

"Gotta name him something befitting his wise looks."

Norwood scrutinized McGee. Was the man a little "tetched," or just stringing him along? All he saw were humorous creases around his blue eyes.

"How about Socrates or Diogenes?" the packer suggested.

"Too long."

"Plato, then?"

Russ considered it in spite of himself. "That'll work. It sure beats the name Dolly . . . Lawton's mule." Norwood's curiosity was piqued. He came over and hunkered down near the packer. "Where you from?"

"Everywhere and nowhere."

"I mean, where do you hail from originally?" Russ made a practice of never prying into a man's background, but this time he couldn't help himself.

"South Carolina. Father was a schoolmaster. Mother brought up six kids." He paused, staring off at two men trying to lash up a broken pack. "On the whole, I'd say she had the tougher job," he added reflectively.

"What brought you west?" Russ asked, still squatting on his heels and chewing on a stem of grass.

"I got all those foolish notions about prospectin' for gold, or trappin' beaver, or fightin' Indians. Once I hit seventeen and was out of school, there was no holding me. Besides, I saw all those damned politicians stirring things up and figured we were about to get into one helluva scrap. I had nothin' to gain in an argument like that." He shook his head. "Anyway, I've done a little of everything from driving a six-horse hitch to running a saloon. Even lived with the Indians once, but I had too much civilization in me to be happy there. On the other hand, I couldn't stand to live in white man's towns, either. Just wanted something I could make a living at and stay out in the open."

Russ nodded. He knew the feeling.

"Even tried reading for the law, but it didn't take me long to see that it was just more of the same . . . trying to untangle all the snarls people get themselves into . . . you know, the whole mishmash of broken-down human nature? So now, instead of reading for the law, I just read whatever books I can find for my own pleasure. It's amazing how much a man can learn on his own. Almost wish I hadn't lit out so soon. I might have been able to go to college."

"Hey, Mac! Get over here and gimme a hand with this!" an exasperated packer yelled.

"Duty calls." The older man pushed to his feet. "'Course, if I'd've stayed home, I'd've been bones and dust long ago."

"What makes you think so?"

"The war got my whole family. It probably would've got me, too."

He walked away.

Russ stood up to stretch his legs as he watched him go. Most would likely dismiss the packer as a garrulous old man, but Russ resolved to plumb the mind of Stratford McGee at some future opportunity.

"Saddle up!"

The packers jumped to get their fires smothered, their gear packed, and girths tightened. In ten minutes the command was strung out and pulling up a trail over the divide. The trail, if it could be called that, was steep and nearly impassable in places.

Just about dark, they crossed the main divide, noting numerous dead horses rotting along the trail where the Indians had killed broken-down stock in their flight. Russ tried to hold his breath against the stench as they passed.

Instead of camping on the divide, Babcock ordered the column to continue down the other side in the dark. They were fortunate that they had good moonlight. Norwood felt more secure on his own two feet and led Plato most of the way. The packers didn't favor it at all, Norwood judged by their comments. But they had no choice. Their remarks turned to the worse cursing he had ever heard as the descent became treacherous. The trail in several places was rock covered with leaves and pine needles. By the pale moonlight, these dark spots appeared to be perfectly safe. But, as the mules stepped on these patches, their feet shot out from under them as if they were on ice. The poor animals went rolling and sliding to the bottom, crashing and banging, bringing forth more curses from the packers. The two-hundred-and-fifty-pound packs probably cushioned the falls, preventing many mules from being killed.

They finally reached the bottom and went into camp near a small stream about ten o'clock. After seventeen hours on the trail everyone was exhausted, but Norwood took his turn at herd guard. It appeared to him that the Indian scouts and the packers did the lion's share of the guard duty.

Just as Norwood was finally retiring to his blanket, about one-thirty, he heard hoofbeats and a shout from the perimeter, "Hello, the camp!"

There was a challenge by someone on herd guard and a quick, clear reply. "Sergeant Cabaniss and Private Eastman from Captain Lawton's camp!"

The two men rode into the firelight, leading a pack mule. The sergeant dismounted as Lieutenant Babcock came up and identified himself.

"Got orders from Cap'n Lawton to bring some rations on ahead. We're out of everything, sir."

"How far is Lawton from here?" Babcock asked.

"No more'n fifteen miles, sir. But up and down, it's at least twice that. We had a tough time finding you."

Babcock ordered their mule to be loaded with flour and bacon. The mule was hurriedly packed, and the two men departed.

Norwood didn't know how long he had been wrapped in exhausted slumber when he was jarred awake by pounding hoofs and the braying of mules. He rolled over, reaching for his rifle. Men were yelling and running, trying to head off the animals' stampeding through the camp. He jumped out of the way just in time to avoid being trampled by a mule that ran, kicking, across his blanket.

"Get hold of him, gawdammit, before he wrecks the camp!" someone yelled. No shots were being fired, so Norwood quickly realized they were not under attack.

46

It was over nearly as quickly as it had started. In a few minutes, all the mules had been caught and were being returned to a new rope corral. Everyone was awake.

"What's all the ruckus, Mac?" Russ yelled. McGee paused, wearing only underwear and moccasins, his hair wild in the firelight.

"That mule we loaded up a couple hours ago came tearing up the trail and stampeded our stock."

About ten minutes later Sergeant Cabaniss and Private Eastman rode in, apologizing.

"Got away from us and threw his pack, sir."

They quickly repossessed the rebellious mule and led him away, followed by the disgusted comments of the packers.

Lieutenant Babcock cautioned the guards to stay alert, and everyone else returned to their bedrolls. To Russ Norwood, at least, it was a very short night. They were up, breakfasted, saddled, repacked, and on the trail again by six.

It proved to be almost a repeat of the day before, if not a little worse. The trail was very steep, rocky, and narrow. At one stretch the trail traversed the side of a dangerous cañon. One mule slipped, tried to recover, bumped its bulky load against the rock wall, and went over the side, falling sheer for at least two hundred feet before striking the bottom of the gorge. Norwood peered over and saw the body of the poor beast split open on the rocks far below. Its cargo was badly broken up and scattered around. Norwood had no particular fear of heights, but he found himself sweating profusely as he pulled back against the rock face, keeping a good grip on Plato's bridle.

Shortly after noon the trail took a very steep dropoff of about forty feet. Babcock halted the column and, one at a time, the horses and mules were forced over the edge, some sliding down on their haunches, some stumbling and rolling over and over. Norwood counted as one of the mules made a dozen turns before reaching the bottom and staggering to this feet, pack askew. Somehow, none of the animals was killed or seriously injured.

About two o'clock they came on one of Lawton's old camps with good water and grass, and the column stopped for an hour to regroup and have a bite to eat. Rolando Vasquez, the Mexican guide, pointed out the ruins of an old mine nearby which he called the Santa Teresa. Obviously, it had not been worked for many years.

"*Oro,*" he remarked.

"I guess the gold played out long ago," Norwood said.

"No, *señor,*" Vasquez replied. "Apaches."

"A man of few words," McGee said, walking up at that moment and hearing the exchange.

"Not much else need be said," Norwood replied. "They've depopulated whole sections of northern Mexico and southern Arizona. Killed all the people or run 'em off."

Stratford McGee nodded solemnly and moved away.

An hour after they had resumed the march, Vasquez, who rode about three hundred yards out in front, came galloping back and slid his horse to a stop near Lieutenant Babcock. Norwood could hear him talking excitedly and pointing ahead. Word filtered back along the column that several horsemen had been spotted in a bend of the cañon.

Babcock called several of the Indian scouts up and sent them forward to have a look. When they all reached the point a half mile beyond, the rest of the command halted while the lieutenant conferred with the scouts.

Norwood rode up alongside as Babcock remounted. "What's up?"

"Apparently some Indians, according to the sign the scouts are reading here. My guess is a few hostiles cut in behind Lawton to see if there was a chance they could catch us napping."

"Reckon they'd love to get their hands on the food and ammunition that's on this pack train."

Perry nodded, then motioned for the column to move forward. Vasquez rode out front again but stayed less than a hundred yards in advance this time.

Lawton's trail was now fairly easy to follow — many hoof marks of shod horses, piles of manure, and old camp sites — so the column continued on after dark. The trail passed through beautiful timbered country with plenty of grass in the open spaces. In places the trail could be followed in the moonlight by those walking in advance. In others it was possible to see it from horseback.

During one stretch, the column passed along the side of a mountain. Again, the smooth rock was covered with leaf mold, the entire surface slanting downward into a pocket, or gully, In a matter of seconds, three mules slipped and piled up, one atop the other. The packers outdid themselves in inventive cursing.

The mules and their cargo were untangled and retrieved, and the command finally camped in a shallow cañon. Norwood dismounted stiffly and eased his crotch. Then he pulled out his Waltham and popped the case. In the moonlight the hands pointed at one-ten. They had made a distance of about thirty miles through some very hard country.

The next day was June 16th by Norwood's calculation. Word had been passed that they were to make a late start and give the stock a chance to rest and graze. It was eleven o'clock when they finally pulled out. The marching was through very rough, but beautiful, country that was alive with game. Deer bounded away at their approach, and Norwood stopped counting after he had spotted eighteen of them. In this rough country their only natural enemies were wolves, or mountain lions, in addition to an occasional hunter.

After a march of eighteen miles, they finally reached Lawton's camp at seven o'clock. It was in a rocky cañon, and there was no more room for the newcomers who had to camp about a mile away. There was not much water in the small stream that trickled through the declivity, and the approach to the water was difficult due to piles of boulders. But the animals managed, a few at a time, to pick their way down to it.

"Now you can see why Geronimo and his band take to these mountains," Perry Babcock said, raking a match across the boulder he was seated on and touching it to his pipe.

Norwood propped one foot on a large rock and leaned both elbows on his knee. "As few as they are, they could hide out here indefinitely. And I understand we're not even out of the foothills yet."

Babcock nodded. "I've been deeper into the Sierra Madre than this. These mountains are magnificent works of nature, or the work of the devil, depending on your point of view."

"I'm sure the packers believe the latter."

"These mountains range from desert to tropical forest, from low foothills to sheer barrancas that are hundreds of feet deep." He puffed on his pipe and chuckled. "Two hundred years ago one of the Spanish *padres* rode up unexpectedly to one of these precipices. He wrote that he was so frightened he couldn't dismount but actually fell off the opposite side of his mule, sweating and trembling."

The sun was long gone and the cañon in deep shadow. Cooking fires were crackling into life, and the men were settling into camp.

"I'm damn' glad to finally catch up with Lawton," Norwood said. "Maybe we can rest up a bit."

"Not likely. When I reported to him, he indicated he was very frustrated by not being able to cut the hostiles' trail. Then he had to halt his command for lack of supplies until we could

50

catch up. Once he and his men get their bellies full, we'll be out of here. He's got one eye on Miles. The rest of Lawton's career may depend on his success, or failure, in running down these hostiles. General Miles is not a man who accepts excuses." He stood up and stretched. "Let's get some victuals."

As he walked past Norwood, he said over his shoulder, "Whatever happens, our work is just beginning."

Chapter Four

The next morning Lawton surprised them by sending out the Apache scouts to comb the mountains for any trails of the hostiles, while the cavalry and the pack train lay in camp, resting and allowing the animals to graze. Norwood and Babcock took advantage of the opportunity to get some fresh meat. They took their rifles and set off into the surrounding woods after deer. They were quickly out of sight and sound of the camp, seemingly swallowed up in the vastness of the pine-covered slopes.

"Let's split up," Perry suggested after two or three deer had been spotted bounding away through the sparse undergrowth. "If either of us hears a shot, the other will come running."

"Agreed."

Some time later Russ got a clean shot at a small buck in a clearing a hundred yards away and dropped him. The explosion of the rifle sounded like a cannon in the stillness, echoing off the rocks. Norwood gutted the animal and then waited. Babcock did not appear.

Late that afternoon, after a hike of several miles, Norwood staggered, exhausted, into camp, packing two hind quarters and a fore shoulder. Babcock showed up an hour after dark.

"Got lost," he mumbled to Norwood as he slumped down on his bedroll, setting his rifle down beside him. "This is the damnedest country to find your way. My pocket compass was useless. Nobody could travel in a straight line. Mighty humbling experience, I can tell you."

"Want a piece of venison?" Norwood asked, cutting a slice from the meat that was sizzling on some willow spits.

Babcock glanced sharply at him.

"I'm not rubbing it in," Norwood assured him with a straight face. "Just thought you might be hungry."

Babcock filled the rest of his plate with beans from a pot and sat down, cross-legged, to eat. His face was drawn and weary in the flickering firelight.

"I'd appreciate if you didn't mention this," Perry said, glancing around at the indistinct forms moving about the other campfires.

"Don't worry," Russ said. "But if you hadn't shown by daylight, I was going to take a couple of Indian scouts and try to track you."

"Did the scouts have any luck striking a trail today?"

"Spotted a few hostiles on horseback, but they scattered on sight. Otherwise nothing."

The two men ate silently for a few minutes, and Babcock had filled and emptied his tin plate a second time before he spoke. "You know, it *is* pretty ridiculous that a company commander of cavalry with all those years of experience couldn't find his way back to camp from a one-day deer hunt." A bemused smile was stealing over his features, and the corners of his eyes crinkled.

"Hey, nobody will hear it from *me*," Norwood replied. "Besides, these mountains have probably swallowed up better men that either of us. What was that you were saying yesterday about the Sierra Madre being 'magnificent works of nature?' "

Norwood rocked sideways as a friendly fist slammed his shoulder.

The whole command pulled out early the next morning. The twenty-five Apache scouts were out front under First Sergeant Dick. Russell Norwood and Perry Babcock rode ahead of the command and a half-mile behind the scouts. The column advanced in good order southwest, angling along the side of a cañon.

About noon, three of the scouts came running back, excited and gesturing. "¡Mejicanos! Soldiers!" They pointed ahead.

"How many?" Babcock demanded, reining up.

An Apache held up all ten fingers five times.

Babcock sat for a moment in deep thought. "Just what we don't need right now," he said to Norwood. "I'd much rather deal with hostiles than with these Mexican troops. They resent us being down here in spite of that treaty. Hell, they're liable to start shooting right off. We don't want another incident. Some of those Mexican irregulars shot poor Emmett Crawford in the head a few months ago when he was trying to parley with them."

The rest of the scouts came crowding up.

"Sergeant Dick, take your scouts and get up into the rocks on each side, here and there," Babcock ordered the Apache sergeant who repeated the instructions in his native tongue. The scouts scattered.

Captain Lawton, who had ridden up just then, took command. "Let's ride down to meet them. Just be cautious and ready for anything." He slipped his revolver out of the holster and kneed his mule into a walk.

In five minutes, the three of them rounded the next bend in the cañon. They could see another half mile ahead. There were no troops.

"Where are they?" Lawton asked.

"The scouts indicated they were right close," Babcock answered.

"Probably turned tail when they saw our scouts," Norwood said.

"Let's go after them," Lawton said. "We need to make contact."

54

They spurred their mounts and rode as hard as the broken cañon would allow. Dodging rocks, they splashed across the shallow stream in the bottom one last time and followed the many hoof prints up over a rise where the cañon flattened out. Just then they spotted the last few riders of the fleeing horsemen another half mile ahead.

"What the hell are they running for?" Lawton panted. His head snapped down and up as his mule stumbled and nearly fell with the big man. Nobody answered as hoofs drummed in a steady rhythm. They rode up and over another low hill.

The Mexican riders, seeing their pursuers were gaining, slowed, leapt from their horses, and pulled them into some rocks. Norwood saw rifle barrels flash in the sun as the men prepared to fight.

The three Americans reined in about a hundred yards away, their mules circling and snorting.

"*Se llamo Capitán Henry W. Lawton de los Estados Unidos,*" Lawton boomed at the top of his voice. "*¡Americanos!*"

Norwood was sweating. They were within easy rifle range. He had visions of Captain Emmett Crawford's tragic shooting in just such a situation only a few months earlier. Lawton walked his mule a few yards closer and shouted again. Finally, a few men cautiously emerged from cover, rifles ready. One rangy, dark-skinned man mounted and rode slowly toward them. The rest of his troops followed.

"I am *Capitán* Antonio Lopez," the mustachioed leader announced, walking his lathered horse up to Lawton, "and these are my men. We saw your Indians and thought you were the Apaches, *señor*. My apologies. We just fought with them and were not ready for another engagement so soon," he said in heavily accented English, removing his hat and wiping sweat from his brow.

"I'm Captain Henry W. Lawton, United States cavalry. Where

are the hostile Apaches?" he asked hurriedly.

Lopez shook his head. "I do not know, *señor*. Our fight was yesterday."

"Any casualties?"

"We suffered four men killed." He shook his head sadly. "But my men killed one Indian woman and wounded several others," he added proudly. "And we captured a white girl from them," he stated, turning in his saddle to point out the child who was riding double with one of his soldiers.

"The Peck child," Lawton commented. "I recognize her from her picture."

Norwood edged his mule sideways and back as the Mexicans closed in around them. Except for some semblance of green and red uniforms that most of them wore, they were as villainous looking a group as any *bandidos* he had ever seen. There were at least sixty-five of them, and they were all heavily armed. Norwood was wearing his Colt, and his rifle was in its scabbard, but he dared not make a move for either of them. For some reason the Mexicans hated the gringos, even though the Mexican and American governments had officially agreed to allow each other's troops to cross the border when in hot pursuit of their common enemy — the hostile Apache.

"We have some friendly Apache scouts with us," Lawton was saying.

"We were hunting for the bodies of our dead when we saw them," Lopez replied. "We thought they were the main body of those human *tigres*."

"We must return to our men," Lawton said, pulling Dolly's head around. *"Buena suerte."*

"Adios, señor."

The three white men rode back the way they had come, leaving the Mexican troops staring after them. Norwood felt a prickle of fear up his back, and sweat was running down

56

inside his shirt until they had topped a hill and were out of rifle range.

The American column moved on down the cañon a short distance and went into an early camp on the opposite side from the Mexican forces. Babcock's thought was to get as far as possible from the Mexicans, but Lawton overruled him with the idea that they must maintain at least an appearance of friendly relations.

"Besides," Lawton added, glancing across the shallow stream, "it's not likely they will start shooting at us if we're staring right at them. They like to attack from cover."

The Mexicans found their four dead and the dead squaw and buried them all in the sandy soil. The little Peck girl, a child of about ten, was given to the Americans to be returned home to her parents in Arizona. She was wearing a ragged cotton shift and was badly bruised. As Norwood got the story, she was being carried by an Apache brave when the Mexicans fired their first volley, killing the horse of the brave. The girl was dropped among the rocks as the horse fell. The men cleaned her up as best they could, and gave her the best food they had in camp.

The next day, as the command pulled out marching south, the Peck girl was sent back toward the border in the care of one of the civilian couriers. Norwood thought he would be assigned the task, but Lawton answered his inquiring look with, "Not this time. You're a former officer. I might need you for other things."

The command marched only eight miles that day over some very rough and broken country. The trail wound down toward Saracachi Creek, and they made an early camp near the ranch of a *Señor* Valenzuela. Lawton sent Stratford McGee to see the weathered old rancher and purchase some green forage for the animals. Lawton, Babcock, and Norwood all paid a courtesy call on the old man in the evening. He spoke no English but, with Lawton's limited Spanish and many signs, the visit went amicably. The old man treated them to a shot of fiery mescal before they departed.

The next day Lawton moved the command a few miles away to a position with better wood and water. The animals were badly used up and needed rest and forage. As they lay in camp, Russ and Perry and the rest of the men, including the packers, had an opportunity to take a refreshing swim in the clear creek and to wash clothes stiff with old sweat, wood smoke, and trail grime.

Russ paid one of the Apache scouts six dollars to make him another pair of moccasins to replace his own that were worn out. Toward evening, Perry gave money to one of the Mexican packers. He said: "I hear there's a little town just over this mountain that has a lot of good fig trees. Here's something extra for you if you ride over there and bring some fruit back." The Mexican courier departed at dark to avoid any Indians and returned before morning with twenty pounds of fresh figs which Perry shared among the men.

Lawton decided to remain one more day in camp, but sent Lieutenant George Finley, First Sergeant Dick of the Apache scouts, and fifteen of the cavalry out on a reconnaissance toward the Sonora River with instructions to proceed on to the town of Sinoquipe to investigate any Indian rumors. The Apache scouts were also sent out in many directions to search for trails.

"Mighty damned frustrating," Norwood remarked, popping a fig into his mouth. "If they follow their usual tactic, those hostiles that the Mexicans had the brush with will split up into twos and threes and scatter like chaff in the wind."

"Yeah," Babcock agreed, pulling his shirt out of the shady pool and wringing it out before spreading it on a rock to dry. "But if we and the Mexicans can run 'em back and forth between us enough, we may wear 'em down. I think we just have to keep 'em on the run."

"Maybe it'll come down to Miles's idea of who're the better athletes. We may wear out first."

"The Mexicans are none too friendly," Babcock continued. "You saw that bunch the other day. And to top things off, Lawton got a message this morning by Mexican courier from the prefect of the District of Montezuma ordering Lawton not to proceed farther into the state of Sonora. How's that for gall? Afraid the Americans are going to upstage him, I reckon."

"What's Lawton going to do?"

"Ignore it. Didn't even send a reply."

"Good idea."

Norwood reached for his razor and a small bar of soap on a flat rock in the shade. He stood, waist deep in the cool water, and proceeded to work up a lather on his growth of stubble. He had hardly taken three strokes with the razor when he became conscious of a thudding of hoofs and looked up under the overhanging trees to see five men ride into camp on Mexican mules. They dismounted in a swirl of dust, and Norwood recognized Billy Long, a civilian courier, and three soldiers from the troop. Then he lowered his razor and stared, his stomach tightening. The fifth man was lean and tall and had a familiar, swinging walk. It was Tom Horn.

Chapter Five

"Your old nemesis," Perry remarked, squinting into the bright sunlight.

"I saw him," Russ answered, rinsing his razor and taking another careful stroke.

"Why are they riding those Mexican mules?" Perry wondered.

The mules were picketed on some fresh grass, and the riders dispersed. A few minutes later, Russ finished his toilette and climbed, naked, out of the water. Being careful to stay in the shade and off the hot rocks, he looked around for his still-damp underwear, shirt, and pants. Just as he picked up his white cotton drawers, he saw Horn striding toward the creek, swinging his canteen, his big white hat shoved back on his head. He stopped short as he caught sight of Norwood stepping into his underwear.

"Well, I'll be damned if you don't look like a plucked chicken," he grinned at Norwood's white, naked body. Russ had already lost several pounds since the beginning of the march and was down to a lean, muscular hardness. He did not reply.

"And there's your old buddy, Perry Babcock," Horn continued. "Howdy, Lieutenant."

Perry grunted a greeting.

Horn went on down to the creek, lay down on his stomach, removed his hat, and thrust his whole head in the water. He came up blowing and sputtering. "Whew, but that feels good!" He stood up and ran his hands through his wet and thinning hair.

"Where'd you get the Mexican stock, Tom?" Perry called.

"Aw hell, our horses were stolen last night. We stopped at Pesquera's ranch, and the Apaches got 'em from a field near there. We got some hands from the ranch and followed this morning, but only found some worn out nags they left behind."

"That the only sign of Indians?" Perry asked.

Russ paid no attention to the reply as he finished dressing, took up his razor and soap, and walked off.

Lieutenant Finley and his patrol returned from Sinoquipe the next day, reporting no definite news of the Indians, so the whole command pulled out and moved up the cañon about twelve miles to camp.

That afternoon Norwood noted smoke blowing down from the surrounding hills and then saw dry summer grass burning along the slopes far above them. He borrowed Babcock's field glasses and focused them on the flames. As the irregular line of flames crept down the hillsides, a small pine now and then erupted into a resinous torch.

"As if it wasn't already hot and dry enough," Perry said.

"But it's an old trick. The hostiles are firing the grass every chance they get to slow us down and destroy the forage for our animals."

"They must not be too far away, then."

"I'm sure they're miles from here. That fire's probably been burning since yesterday." Russ handed back the glasses.

The next day the command marched to the Sonora River Valley where there was a fairly good supply of grass and forage. They camped not far from the small Mexican village of Sinoquipe. Russ and Perry went into the village which consisted of a few adobe buildings. At one end of the dusty street was an adobe church with a short bell tower.

Russ noted that the townspeople were more Indian than Spanish in their physical features. It had been over three hundred years since the *conquistadores* arrived from Spain, but these people

61

on the remote western slope of the Sierra Madre had retained a strong strain of the ancient Aztecs.

Russ and Perry paid a visit to the church. The inside of the building seemed much smaller due to the thick adobe walls, but it was these walls that also kept the interior relatively cool. The flickering candles of the red vigil lights reflected dully from the golden door of the small tabernacle on the wooden alter. A large crucifix with a grotesquely twisted and suffering Christ hung from the ceiling behind the simple altar. The floor was dirt and had been packed hard and smooth by many bare feet. Two native women, their heads covered in red and blue scarves, knelt in prayer in the handmade wooden pews. In the dim, cool quiet the two men automatically went to their knees. Rather than turning to prayer, Russ's mind wandered, taking in details of this peaceful refuge. It was a welcome relief from the hot sun, the hard marches, the heartbreaking spectacle of newborn babies left to die along the trail by the fleeing Apaches. There had to be a God looking down on all of this. What did He think of one people fighting and conquering another, some in His name, some for gold, some for land? Did the God whom he believed resided in that tabernacle under the appearance of bread really play any favorites? Or were people only judged as individuals with the free will to choose right or wrong, regardless of mass political movements and the wars of nations? Such were his thoughts — or his prayer — before he made the sign of the cross and rose to return to the harsh sunlight of a world that held his immediate problems and concerns.

This world came back to him with a vengeance as some two dozen of the soldiers and packers ventured into the village that night. They were welcomed at first by the townspeople who gathered at the *cantina* to help celebrate the fact that these *Americanos* were here to protect them and make war on their terrible scourge, the Apaches. But the festive atmosphere soon turned ugly after too much *bacanora* and mescal. Fights broke out and, as Russ got the story later, Tom Horn stabbed Private Jason Lowry after the two got into some sort of argument. Those who were sober enough to remember indicated that it was a fair fight, but Horn was just bigger, stronger, and quicker than his adversary.

Lieutenants Finley and Babcock were out most of the night trying to round up their men and herd them back to camp. Doctor Sutter bandaged up Lowry and indicated he would live, provided he didn't try to travel for at least two or three weeks. He would have to stay in the village and pay someone to look after him when the command moved on.

Captain Lawton decided that he wanted no disciplinary action taken against the men for the incident since the whole affair had started out as a good-will gesture, and the strong liquor had caused it to get out of hand. "We'll need every man we've got," was the way he put it to his two lieutenants. "Just make sure it doesn't happen again."

"I'm glad you weren't in town the other night," Perry Babcock said as he and Norwood shared a bite of lunch in the shade.

"Why's that?"

"The fight."

"I know. I'm glad I decided to go to sleep early. Saved me a lot of wear and tear."

"I don't mean just the drinking and fighting. I mean you could have been in Lowry's place."

"Stabbed?" He dismissed the idea with a shake of his head. "No, I wouldn't have let it come to that."

"I don't know what happened between the two of them, but I've seen Tom Horn in action before," Perry persisted. "He gets talkative when he's drinking. Starts bragging. Anybody crosses his path, he gets belligerent. I'd be surprised if he didn't goad Lowry into it."

"Jason Lowry's a hothead, too."

"Maybe. But it wouldn't be above Horn to deliberately use that situation on you. Push you into a fight so he can use a knife or gun and then claim self-defense."

"I may have something to say about that."

"Just be alert at all times. I'm convinced the man means to eliminate you if he can."

"I can't figure out why. He won. I'm out of the Army."

"I hear he's got his eye on Buffalo Bill's Wild West Show. He couldn't parade himself as a hero of the Apache wars if his reputation could be shattered by the likes of you. As long as you're around . . . in or out of the Army . . . you're a threat to him."

"I'll watch my step," Russ assured him. "In the meantime chasing down Geronimo is our main problem. I know Lawton didn't want to pull out of here yesterday because so many of the men were hung over and banged up after that night in town. But why are we sitting here again today?"

"For one thing Lawton doesn't have a clue as to where to start looking for the hostiles," Perry replied. "He's got the scouts out searching for sign but, until he can get something firm to go on, there's no sense marching back and forth in these mountains with no idea of where the Apaches are."

"Seems like what we've been doing so far."

Perry nodded. "Sometimes you have to go with rumors and hunches and a few splintered trails."

"I'd hate to be in Lawton's shoes when he has to report to General Miles."

"I think Miles has a pretty good idea that we're not getting the job done because he's sending down a detail of infantry from Fort Huachuca. We're waiting for them here. That's another reason Lawton's not moving."

64

Russ got to his feet. "Think I'll walk into town and mail these letters. Want to come along?"

As the two men were returning from the village early that afternoon, the infantry detail arrived, accompanied by Lieutenant R. A. Brown of the Fourth Cavalry. There were also ten Apache scouts to replace an equal number whose enlistments were up. It was a peculiar sight. Brown was the only one of the group mounted, and he was leading a soldier by a rope fastened to the soldier's neck. The man's hands were tied behind him, and his rifle was lashed across his back.

Brown dismounted and saluted Captain Lawton.

"What's all this?" Lawton demanded, returning the salute.

"Acting First Sergeant was insubordinate, sir. Insolent. Refused to take orders from me since I am assigned to the cavalry."

There was a general grumbling among the infantry who had fallen out of ranks without orders. Some of them were sitting on the ground, resting, while three or four had removed their shoes and socks and were examining their feet.

"Where's the officer assigned to these men?" Lawton asked.

"There isn't one, sir. Apparently there was none available on short notice, so I was asked to escort them south and put them in your hands." Brown dropped the reins of his horse and stepped a few yards away from the infantry toward Lawton and Babcock. "Truth is, there's not a man among 'em who's not insubordinate, sir," he said in a lower voice. "They feel they've been badly used . . . poorly fed, poorly equipped, and ordered to march in this summer heat." He paused. "Truth is, sir, their shoes *are* in bad shape. The new footgear is already falling apart after only a few days on the trail."

"I know," Lawton replied. "Damned things are cheaply made at Fort Leavenworth prison. Well, maybe we can supply 'em with some Mexican leather, or some Indian moccasins. These trails will cut up the best footgear."

"The men are in an ugly mood, sir. Bad discipline, low morale. I had to make an example of this acting first sergeant just to keep them in line."

"Don't worry about it, Brown," Lawton said, eyeing the men who were milling about and sitting on the ground. "They're my responsibility now." He turned away. "Lieutenant Finley, see that these men are fed and then assemble them in that grove of trees over by the creek. I want to talk to them."

Russ and Perry moved away, neither speaking for a few minutes. Finally Russ voiced his thoughts. "We're going after Geronimo's band with that bunch?"

"I know," Perry replied. "It's a scary thought."

"What happened to General Miles's idea of a hundred picked men . . . the 'right sort of white men,' the athletes of our race who were going to run these Indians to ground?"

"Like most of Miles's other ideas and plans . . . a lot of hogwash," Perry rasped.

Russ took a deep breath of the heated air and squinted up at a hawk soaring on rising thermals high above the flank of the mountain. "Lawton needs a bird's eye view like that if he ever hopes to locate these renegades."

"And wings to reach them," Perry added.

At seven o'clock the next morning the command pulled out, heading south with the Indian scouts leading the way. Lawton had decided to move, even though he had only the vaguest idea which way the hostiles had gone. According to rumors and speculation, and the evidence of a few scattered trails, he guessed they were heading south, deeper into Mexico and the Sierra Madre. They followed the valley for the time, avoiding the hard marching in the mountains.

It was nearly the end of June and, as the sun rose higher in a cloudless sky, the full force of summer came down on the valley like a hammer on an anvil. The column maintained a slow, steady pace, not pausing for lunch. Shortly after noon, Perry Babcock pulled an encased field thermometer from his saddlebags and hooked it on a buckle. A half hour later, he held it up to Russ who rode abreast of him.

"I can't read it from here."

"A hundred twenty-seven degrees in the sun."

"Damn! I didn't really need to know that." He looked ahead at the shimmering heat waves rising from the baked earth.

They rode on in silence, the patient Plato plodding ahead tirelessly. Once or twice Russ turned in his saddle and surveyed the infantry detail as the command forded the shallow river. Several of them were cursing. Lieutenant Finley had been assigned the unenviable task of leading the infantry, so he walked ahead of them, leading his horse. Their invective seemed to be directed at him. The second or third time they had to ford the stream, several of the infantry became so insubordinate and abusive they were disarmed and their hands tied to their sides as a precaution against their becoming violent.

Perry shook his head. "Can't really blame 'em for raising hell about their footwear. The more those shoes get wet, the faster they're gonna fall apart. But discipline has to be maintained."

"It's tougher to do in the field," Russ commented.

"Yes, but they've got to learn they can't drink all the water in their canteens the first hour and then expect to refill them right away. They go to drinking the water in this river, they'll have dysentery right quick. And a man with dysentery isn't fit for duty."

"I've had a touch of the runs, myself," Russ said. "Been forcing myself to eat in this heat, but I feel like I've lost weight."

Perry eyed him critically. "Yeah. You look a little leaner. You keep that up, you'll be as skinny as I am."

"But not near as ugly," Russ grinned. "Damn! Split my lip."

He uncapped his canteen and moistened his mouth.

"We won't have to worry about eating much bacon from now on," Perry continued. "The heat has been melting the fat right off it. Couple of slabs I saw yesterday were down to the lean and the rind."

The command halted for only a brief rest near the good-sized town of Banamachi. Captain Lawton, Perry Babcock, and Russell Norwood paid a quick visit to the *presidente* of the town, a gracious old gentleman who wished them well in their quest. Norwood noted that the town was much larger than the village they had just left. Banamachi had a paved main street, many of the buildings were of stone instead of adobe, and part of the town was even walled, evidence of the precarious existence these people had led for centuries.

Later that afternoon the command camped a few miles south at a place called Las Delicias Rancho. Here the grass and firewood were plentiful, but the water was almost undrinkable since it was drawn from a hot spring and had to be cooled before it could be used for anything except coffee. Even then, the foul taste indicated the presence of impurities.

This ranch was owned by a Doctor Blaine, an American who had been in Mexico since 1868. Whether he was a medical doctor was never disclosed, but he was more a mine operator than a rancher. He took the officers and Doctor Sutter to see his mine, the Santa Helena, where there was a sixty-stamp mill in good working order. He indicated he was extracting, with the help of much Mexican labor, gold, silver, and lead from this operation. Doctor Blaine was an excellent host, happy to have someone to practice his long-unused English on, and kept the men at his ranch house, sipping some excellent port and regaling them with stories of his past until almost midnight.

"Thought we'd never get away from there," Russ remarked as they finally made their departure and walked back to their camp in the dark. "But it's nice to escape for a few hours into an atmosphere of culture and refinement."

Perry stifled a mighty yawn. "That wine will really put me away for the night . . . as if I needed anything to help me sleep."

"Did you notice Blaine didn't say anything about his life in the States? All his tales were of his life in Mexico . . . mining, working, fighting duels, and so on."

"Yeah. I suspect he came down here after the war. Maybe one of those unreconciled southern boys who couldn't accept defeat and go on. Had to make a new life somewhere else."

Chapter Six

The next day was notable for two things. First, Lawton decided to change course from following the Sonora River Valley south to starting back northeast into the mountains to see if he could find some sign of the hostiles. Consequently, the column started at seven o'clock in the morning, filled their canteens at the mill, and then pulled up into the mountains, Babcock and Norwood riding out front with the thirty Apache scouts.

The second occurrence was that Stratford McGee was riding with the scouts as well. Much to Mac's chagrin, Lawton had overheard him talking to one of the scouts in his native Apache dialect and immediately promoted McGee from packer to interpreter.

"Why the long face, Mac?" Russ chided him as the two rode along, side by side. "The pay's better as an interpreter than a packer. Even if you had been *chief* packer."

"Maybe so, if I live to spend it," he grumbled. "That's what I get for trying to bum some tobacco off one of those scouts."

"You never told me you could speak Apache."

"Didn't want anybody to know it."

"You did say you lived with the Indians for a time, though I didn't know it was with the Apaches."

"It wasn't really by choice. I was captured from a freighting outfit where I had hired on when I was seventeen. It was after I first came to the territory. Thought I was a goner for sure, 'cause they usually kill the men and take only the women and children captive. I reckon they kept me 'cause I was so slight of build and looked a lot younger. They kept me for nearly

70

a year and a half before I was able to slip away from them. I reckon they had about given up trying to make a warrior out of me."

"Right up ahead here is where we found 'em." Jack Frisbey, an American employee of Doctor Blaine's, had ridden up a few miles with the column to point out where the bodies of three Mexican mine workers had been found slain by Apaches the day before. "They were lyin' right about there." He pointed to the ground. Dark splotches showed where their life blood had stained the rocks and soaked away into the earth. "They were out hunting deer," Frisbey continued. "When they didn't come back, we came searching. The sign indicated they'd been cut down from ambush. Indians took their rifles. Helluva price to pay for tryin' to bag some fresh meat." He glanced around at the silent pine growth apprehensively, as if the hostiles might still be close at hand. He wheeled his horse around. "This is as far as I go, gents. Good luck." With that he urged his horse to a trot and started down the backtrail.

This bloody sight put a damper on the white men's conversation for the next few hours and seemed to confirm the ever-present danger to which McGee had referred. Norwood, however, could hardly imagine the hostiles attacking a force as large as this. Their tactics were always to hit and run, taking weapons, ammunition, horses, food, or whatever else they wanted. Besides, he assured himself, he was with the hunters, not the hunted. It was the Apaches who were fleeing from *them.*

The heat did not abate. Any breeze that might have reached them was cut off by the trees and surrounding hills. As the day wore on, the men shed articles of clothing until all but their hats, underwear, and footwear were rolled up and strapped across the pommels of their saddles. Rank had no meaning. Looking at the column from a distance, an observer could not have distinguished an officer from a mule packer. Heat and exertion had pounded the insolent members of the infantry into submission. They plodded along, rifles slung across their backs, uniform blouses off and hanging through their canteen straps or from their rifle barrels. No word passed between them, except an occasional curse when one man accidentally stepped on the heels of another.

Tom Horn, in sweat-soaked cotton shirt and pants, rode back and forth along the line of march, occasionally stopping to confer with Tony, the San Carlos Apache who was now designated the first sergeant of scouts. Tony had a rudimentary grasp of English so no interpreter was needed. The first sergeant had been dubbed Tony by someone due to his unpronounceable Apache name.

Norwood kept an unobtrusive eye on the rangy chief of scouts, but Horn ignored him. Tony had his thirty men break into small groups, fan out, and go ahead a mile or more to scout for recent sign. On impulse, Russ said, "Come on, Mac, let's go with these three scouts."

McGee shot him an alarmed look.

"Hell, nothing's going to happen. You've lived a lot of years in this country, and you're still kicking."

"That's because I don't take unnecessary chances," he replied.

"Okay, if you want to stay here and melt down into your moccasins, that's your affair." Norwood, with a wink at Babcock, pulled his mule out of line and urged his forward.

"Hold on, I'm coming," McGee said, mumbling something under his breath as he kneed his mule forward to catch up.

The three scouts started off at a lope on foot, cutting away from the column up through the pine trees toward the top of a ridge. McGee reluctantly turned his mule over to one of the civilian packers along with Norwood's mule, Plato. As Norwood started on foot at a jog after the Apache scouts, he had second thoughts about having goaded McGee into following him. He had forgotten the man was probably in his mid-forties and possibly could not keep up, but he needn't have worried. Stratford McGee was as fit as any man he had ever seen. The wiry little fellow was at his side and past him before he had run fifty yards.

When they gained the top of the ridge, the Apache scouts were hardly breathing hard, but Norwood and McGee were panting and sweat was streaming from their faces.

"I must be out of my mind for letting you talk me into this," Mac gasped as he stopped and leaned forward, hands on knees.

"You okay?" Russ panted, putting his hand on the older man's back.

"Yeah . . . just gimme a minute to get my wind."

The scouts were trotting on ahead, and the two white men trailed after them.

"Apaches are trained from childhood for this," McGee grunted as he jogged along. "They make the boys get up at daybreak and jump into ice-cold streams. To test their endurance, I've seen them run as hard as they could go to the top of a hill and back and, to make sure they only breathed through their noses, they had to carry a mouthful of water."

The three scouts ahead were running partly bent at the waist, scanning the ground. Twice they halted, peered closely at the ground, and said something to each other before moving on at a ground-eating pace. Once they stopped still and glanced warily around, as if sniffing the air. Norwood and McGee halted and made no sound for the half minute the scouts were sensing the rocks and woods around them.

The scouts trotted on for another hundred paces before halting again. This time, as the two white men came up, Norwood saw they were examining some droppings. One broke a pile of manure apart and raked through it with his fingers. Stratford McGee watched intently and listened as the Apaches conversed in their native tongue. Then the three Indians separated and began scanning the area within several rods of the manure. One spoke to another in a low voice and pointed at some hoof marks. They moved on, following some less than obvious trail as the ridge began to bend downward.

A quarter mile farther they halted again. Russ and Mac watched and listened as the scouts carefully examined some patches of grass. One of them moved to one side and broke off several blades and held them close to his face. Then they conferred briefly with each other, nodded and, ignoring the white men who were trailing after them, took a left turn and started down the steep ridge toward the bottom of the cañon so as to come out ahead of the column.

"Did you catch any of that?" Russ asked, as they followed at a more leisurely pace.

"Most all of it."

"What'd they find?"

"That manure had maize in it, which means the horse was recently stolen from the Mexicans."

"Why not Americans?"

"The horse wasn't shod. Most of the poor Mexicans around here can't afford to have their animals shod."

"What else?"

"Apparently from the freshness of the manure, the horsemen passed here no more than a day and a half ago. There are three sets of tracks, and the horses were tired because their heels were bumping together."

"That time would make it about right if they killed those Mexican deer hunters."

"They confirmed the time of passage back there. The hostiles got off to walk their tired horses and crushed down some of

74

that grass with their moccasins. That scout broke off some sprigs of grass to compare how much juice was in the fresh grass against how much was left in the crushed grass. So now we know there were only three hostiles, riding tired Mexican horses, and they passed here going northeast less than two days ago."

"I know they do this routinely, but it still amazes me."

"This was easy. I've seen 'em track over slabs of solid granite. A really good tracker will make you think he's performing magic."

"Are they headed back to the column now?"

"Yeah. They'll get down into the cañon bottom and return where the going's a little easier."

The two men slipped and slid down a shale-covered section of hillside before they regained their footing. Russ stopped to look and listen, uneasy that they had made so much noise. The scouts were already out of sight somewhere below. Even as they talked, his eyes were roving everywhere, and his ears were automatically tuned to catch any sound that seemed out of place. He was no Apache, but he had ridden with them and chased them long enough to know better than ever to let his guard down in hostile country.

"They've been using the same tricks for years, and they seem to work," he said.

"What's that?"

"The hostiles split up into small groups of two or three and ride for miles and then reassemble at some pre-determined place."

Mac nodded. "Helps to know the country."

"And it helps to be a native."

The two men were completely soaked with sweat when they finally reached the column, and each of them drank nearly a quart of water from their canteens before mounting their mules and rejoining the march.

Lawton pushed the column deeper into the mountains, halting just before sunset to allow men and animals to rest in place while they gnawed on some beef jerky and hardtack from their saddlebags or haversacks. Some of the men in the infantry, who had thrown away the burdensome packs and had failed to slip any dry provisions into their blanket rolls, were forced to borrow or buy something from their more experienced companions.

The march resumed. The sun disappeared, twilight came, then faded to darkness, and there was no sign of a camp being made.

"Lawton must think he's on some kind of a hot trail," one of the infantrymen grumbled.

"The only thing hot about this trail is the rocks we been marching over. My feet must look like raw beef by now."

"Hell, you been complainin' we didn't get any fresh meat," the first man guffawed.

"Aw, shaddup!"

The moonlight illuminated the face of Russ's watch when next he glanced at it, showing the time as twenty-five minutes past nine. Five minutes later, ragged, swift-moving clouds shut out the moon over the roof of the widening cañon. Flickering lightning told them what was coming, and Russ unstrapped his slicker from the cantle of his saddle and slipped it over his head.

Lawton still did not call a halt. Lightning cracked and thunder boomed, echoes rolling down the cañon.

"Here she comes!" Norwood yelled at Babcock who was riding somewhere to his left. But his words were drowned in another crash of thunder as the rain and wind came whipping down the cañon onto them. It was every man for himself as the packers struggled to secure the mules and keep them from stampeding in the blinding flashes of lightning. Any shouted orders went

76

unheard in the confusion and the thunder reverberating from the cañon walls.

Russ and Perry took what shelter they could find under bushes and some projecting rocks, but they needn't have bothered. They were soaked to the skin in a matter of minutes. No one had any supper. To drink they had only what little water was left in their canteens or rainwater they could catch in their hats.

The soaking continued through most of the night, and it was a miserable-looking group that started out at daybreak. The command marched about three miles before they were able to find some badly needed drinking water for themselves and the animals. They paused to get something to eat and began drying their soggy clothing and gear in the sun.

Before anything could get more than moderately dry, they were on the move again and, shortly, came to an area where no rain had fallen in weeks. Brush fires, set by the Indians or lightning, were burning in many places, sending white smoke billowing through the trees and adding to the misery of suffocating heat. The trail was twisting and narrow and very difficult for the pack mules.

During the afternoon they passed many small rock tanks but, since they were at the end of the dry season, they were either dry, or the ones still containing some liquid were almost gelatinous in consistency, covered with scum and leaves and bird feathers.

Toward evening someone in the party shot a deer which was quickly divided among the men and buoyed up their spirits. It was a much-needed lift for supper because, shortly after dark, another terrific storm blew up and drenched the camp with a downpour of rain that drowned all camp fires.

"This feels good for a while," Perry said between thunderclaps. He and Russ sat on the ground in the dark, the water streaming from their hat brims. "I remember that in Alabama we used to call one of these a 'frog choker?' "

"At least it gets the sweat out of my clothes for a while."

A bolt of lightning struck a tree a hundred yards away with a sizzling crack. Both men jumped and scuttled for some sort of shelter next to a large boulder. Here they huddled for the next several hours, as the rain continued unabated. In spite of the conditions, Russ dozed off several times, leaning back against the rock, his hat tipped over his face.

In one period of wakefulness, Russ looked over at Perry. "Well, one sure thing," he said, the rain drumming steadily on his sodden hat, "if this keeps up every night, I'll have the cleanest-smelling mule in all of Sonora."

He saw a spot of white as Perry flashed him a grin.

When there was barely enough light to see the ground, the order was given to move out. It was three-thirty in the morning, but everyone was glad to be on the march — anything to take their minds off another sleepless, wet night. They followed the trail the scouts had located the previous day until about ten o'clock when they stopped for their first food of the day — fresh deer meat and salt. Then they went on until they struck the trail that connected the towns of Cumpas and Sinoquipe. Here they made camp in midafternoon.

Captain Lawton came up to Babcock and Norwood as Babcock was trying to coax a flame from some damp pine needles.

"I wanted Stratford McGee and five Apache scouts to go into Sinoquipe to find out if there has been any news of the hostiles since we left there," he stated with no preliminaries. "But now the scouts are refusing to go unless the whole command goes in." The frustration showed in his voice.

"Reckon they're afraid they'll be mistaken for hostiles and shot on sight," Babcock commented, blinking tears from irritated eyes as smoke finally curled up from the tiny blaze.

"Knowing how nervous these Mexicans are about any Apaches, I can see their point," Lawton conceded. "The problem is, I can't very well force them to go without most of them deserting."

"I'll go, Captain. I'm supposed to be a courier anyway," Norwood said.

Lawton's face brightened. "I was just about to suggest that."

"I should be back sometime in the morning."

"Thanks, Norwood. You might want to take McGee with you."

"I think I'd rather go alone."

"Suit yourself. Just be careful." Lawton moved away.

Russ took his time and drank two cups of steaming coffee and had some hardtack softened in water and bacon grease before checking his rifle and hand gun. Just as he was throwing an almost-dry saddle blanket on Plato, Stratford McGee came up.

"I hear you're going into Sinoquipe," he said.

"That's right. You want to go?"

Mac shook his head. "Not without some of the troops or the scouts. And I don't think you should go alone."

"Somebody's got to do it."

"It's too risky for one man."

Russ shrugged as he settled the McClellan in place and reached under the mule for the straps.

"Keep your head about you. If you see anything suspicious, don't take any chances. Just go into hiding and lay low until nightfall."

"Thanks for the advice." Russ hefted his canteen, looped it over his shoulder, and swung into the saddle.

He left camp about four in the afternoon and had hardly been on the trail twenty minutes when he was doused by another rain shower. The rain passed on and, as he was crossing a low mesa about a half hour later, he pulled Plato to a sudden halt and stared down at the muddy trail in front of him. Crossing the trail from south to north were the fresh moccasin prints of about eight men. They had apparently been made since the rain, so it was plain the Indians could not be far away.

He urged his mule forward but, as he crossed the trail, Plato evidently caught a scent, threw back his head, and brayed loudly. Russ's heart began to pound as he urged Plato off the trail a hundred yards into some rocks where he tied the animal out of sight. Then, taking his rifle, he crawled up between two tilted slabs of rock where he could watch the trail, and waited. If the hostiles had been within earshot of the mule's bray, they wouldn't be long in returning.

Fortunately, he waited in vain. After nearly an hour, he began to relax and finally slid his rifle back into its scabbard, climbed aboard Plato, and went on to Sinoquipe.

He found the townspeople on edge. The prefect told him a man had been killed nearby hardly an hour before.

"Probably the hostiles whose trail I crossed coming here," Russ told the prefect. "Has there been any other news of these Indians since the American troops were here?"

"No señor. None. I wish I could point them out to you. But they come from nowhere and strike swiftly, and then are gone. *¡Madre de Dios!*" He shook his head. "The Apaches are the avenging angels of God who come to punish us for our sins."

Russ had other ideas, but he kept them to himself.

"Are your men coming back this way, *Señor* Norwood?"

"I'm not sure. Captain Lawton has been trying to get a firm lead on these hostile Indians. It depends on where the hostiles are leading us, and what Captain Lawton decides to do."

"How long will you stay with us?"

"I have to start back as soon as it gets completely dark."

"Then rest and refresh yourself. Won't you join me and my

family in some food and perhaps a glass of wine?"

"*Gracias.*"

It was about midnight when Norwood arrived back in camp after a forty mile ride and reported to Lawton the little news he had obtained.

"One man killed near the village by a party of eight hostiles heading north on foot this afternoon."

Lawton sat up on his blanket, scrubbing his fingers through his thick, brown hair as he received the news.

"Good work, Norwood. We're headed in the right direction, then. We'll keep going north for now." He rubbed his eyes wearily. Russ could not help but notice how gaunt the big man looked.

"Good night, sir."

"'Night."

Perry roused up sleepily as Russ settled in on the opposite side of the glowing coals of their camp fire. "Any news?"

Russ told him briefly what had happened.

"A long ride for nothing, then."

"No. I picked up a few fresh bruises and cuts. Plato took a wrong step in the dark coming back and both of us rolled down the side of a steep hill."

Perry turned over and pushed his wadded shirt back under his head. "Builds character," he said, and went to sleep.

Chapter Seven

The next day was the first of July. At five o'clock in the morning Norwood and Babcock went on ahead with three Indian scouts. Even though they were in dangerous country and subject to ambush by hostiles at any time, Norwood felt more relaxed than usual.

"Maybe you're still tired from that long ride and only four hours of sleep," Perry remarked when Russ mentioned how he felt.

"Could be. But maybe it's because the weather's not so damned hot today."

High, white, drifting clouds kept the sun somewhat at bay, and there was a good breeze as they rode along.

"And look at this beautiful country," Russ continued, drawing in a deep lungful of the fresh air, redolent of pine. The landscape was green and picturesque, rolling and covered with old lava formations in places but with enough pine trees to keep the terrain from looking barren.

"Yeah," Perry agreed, glancing at the widely spaced scouts who were loping ahead on foot, "there are some compensations with this job."

Around noon they each bagged a deer with their rifles and left the carcasses for the packers to pick up. Fresh meat was always needed and welcome. The trails they were following were numerous but scattered, purposely intended to confuse any trackers as to which would be the main body of hostiles.

The last few miles of their twenty-mile ride led down into a large cañon with a small stream that had formed many pools of deep, clear water. They pulled up and made camp near one of these pools. Babcock scribbled a note to Lawton and sent the freshest of the scouts back to let the rest of the command know where they had stopped.

While they waited for the column to come up, the two white men went downstream a short distance to another large pool and took a refreshing swim. By the time they had dressed and returned to the upper pool, the rest of the command was arriving. The mules were unpacked and hobbled to graze on the bench grass. Camp fires were quickly started and coffee put on to boil as everyone had pretty well settled into the routine of march and camp, march and camp, fatigue having knocked off the rough edges.

"Got an extra cup of coffee?" Stratford McGee asked, sauntering up to where Perry was leaning back against a boulder, smoking his pipe.

"Sure. Help yourself," Russ answered, digging into his saddlebags for a small skillet.

"Never thought I'd complain about having fresh meat to eat every day," Mac said, tossing his hat on the ground and sitting down, cross-legged, with a steaming tin cup. "But I'm about to get tired of fresh venison for every meal."

"You sound like one of our infantry. Nothing pleases you."

"Well, if you're up to a little change of diet, I've got a treat for you," Mac said, a glint in his blue eyes.

"And what might that be . . . plum pudding?"

"Not quite. I happened to mention to one of the packers a while back that there were a lot of wild turkeys in these mountains."

"You shot a turkey? I didn't hear any shooting."

"Nope. Didn't have to. One of the scouts heard me and asked if I wanted a turkey. I told him, 'Sure.' So he sees one heading into the trees and takes off after it. He was gone for a while but, before we even got down into this cañon, he comes jogging back with this big turkey hen slung over his back."

"He ran it down?"

"Sure did. And he wasn't even breathing hard. And this was after he had walked nearly twenty miles."

"Is he going to share it with you?"

"Share, nothing. He gave it to me. Apaches don't eat turkeys because turkeys eat snakes. I dumped the bird over there with my stuff. Want me to get it?"

Russ and Perry looked at each other and chorused, "Yes!"

"I'll let you boys pluck the thing," he stated, lugging the big bird up by the feet and setting it by the fire. "Sorry there's no mashed potatoes and dressing."

"Those scouts don't know what they're missing," Russ declared. "They're probably eating deer meat again."

"A few of them aren't," Mac said, pointing up the cañon.

Several of the long-haired Apaches had gathered near a pile of brush that had caught on a rocky ledge in a bend of the cañon during some previous flood.

"What are they doing?"

Even as they looked, one of the scouts thrust a bundle of burning reeds into the base of the brush pile.

"If they're lucky, there will be a few rats in there," Mac said. "When they run out, the scouts will catch 'em and kill 'em and then boil 'em whole in a pot. When they're done, they'll fetch 'em out on a pointed stick and the hide and hair will sluff right off. They'll disembowel 'em with a knife, and the feast will be ready."

"I think I've lost my appetite."

"To each his own," Mac replied. "They're pretty particular. Usually like only one species of rodent. Unless they're really hungry, they don't bother with gophers or ground squirrels."

"Very fastidious," Russ remarked, dryly.

"Really, they taste pretty good," Mac insisted. "When I was their prisoner, I had to eat rat a time or two. Kinda reminded me of tender chicken or frog legs."

Perry had gone somewhat pale and laid his pipe aside. "Can we stop talking about eating rats before I lose what little I've got in my stomach? I've lost enough weight already."

"Sure," Mac grinned into his beard. "Here, lemme help you pluck that thing. It'll take you the rest of the night. Too bad we don't have a big pot of boiling water. It'd be a lot easier."

The next two days were spent marching northward down the cañon. Because of the terrific heat, Lawton had the column rousted out each morning between three-thirty and four, as soon as there was barely enough light to see the ground. They marched seventeen to nineteen miles each day but, to the weary men, the distance seemed more like fifty.

They passed near Cumpas. The *presidente* of the place, being cautious, refused permission for the Apache scouts to pass through the town. While the command was camped a few miles from Cumpas, nearly a hundred sick people came out to ask for assistance from Doctor Sutter. He treated their various ailments as best he could, using quinine and what little else he had for medication. Sometimes it was a matter of cleaning out infected wounds, dispensing stomach powders, or lancing a boil. When he had nothing to give a patient but good advice, they still reacted to his rosy-cheeked smile and Tom Horn's translation as if the good doctor was some sort of miracle worker.

After a three-hour march, the column arrived at Oposura, sometimes called Moctezuma. It was eight in the morning on July 4th — the hundred and tenth Independence Day. No one felt like celebrating. In fact, Captain Lawton seemed not only frustrated, Russ thought, but mildly depressed.

"I think maybe it's because we're back in Oposura. He probably feels like we're going in circles and not getting anywhere,"

Perry observed in his easy-going manner.

Camp was set up about four miles from town and, when the pack train caught up about two hours later, Captain Lawton, Perry Babcock, and Russ Norwood went into town to talk to the Mexican officials. In broken English and what little Spanish Lawton knew, the men conversed concerning their common problem — the hostile Apaches. The meeting, in a large, thick-walled adobe building, was cordial but, besides good relations, the meeting did little to add to knowledge of the whereabouts of the hostile bands. Mexican troops from the local district were out searching also, but their success, or lack of it, was unknown since there had been no word from them for several days. A toast was drunk to the health of all concerned as the meeting broke up. Norwood sniffed the clear liquid, discovered it was tequila, and merely touched the drink to his lips in token gesture, since he hated the taste.

"I don't think I've ever felt heat like this," Russ declared as he and Perry stepped into the glaring light of the street.

"Not even in San Antonio?"

"Texas is downright cool compared to this place. Maybe you have to grow up in it."

"You've spent a lot of time in the Arizona desert, too," Perry reminded him.

"It still doesn't hold a torch to this. It must be a hundred and twenty in the shade."

"Well, you see how the natives handle it," Perry said, gesturing at the deserted street.

They heard the slow clopping of hoofs and looked up to see Doctor Benjamin Sutter riding his mule languidly down the street from the other direction. The mule came to a halt, swishing his tail at some biting flies. Doctor Sutter was in his undershirt, and his rosy cheeks were beet-red under the straw hat.

"You gentlemen are done vith your meeting, yes?"

"Sure are, Doc. Time to get into the shade and get something to drink."

"You might vish to accompany me to see ze *padre*."

"Is this a professional call?" Russ asked, noting the small black bag strapped to the cantle.

"I am told zat ze *padre* has been sick for a goot many years. His niece rode out to camp and asked me to look in on him."

Russ looked at Perry and nodded. "If that's an invitation, then we'll join you. I don't relish the ride back to camp just now."

They followed the mule to the end of the block and around the corner. Three houses up, next to a stone church built of lava rock, was a good-size adobe house that apparently functioned as the rectory.

Doctor Sutter dismounted, retrieved his bag, and rapped with the wooden door knocker. To Russ's surprise, the door swung inward to reveal a black-veiled nun. She silently ushered them into a dim hallway that led into a spacious room. A bookcase covered one wall, floor to high-beamed ceiling. Some of the ornate, darkened volumes appeared to be very old. The wide-planked floor was polished and partially covered with red and black rugs of Mexican design. The whitewashed walls gave the room a bright, airy appearance, even though it was lighted by only two windows, and they were partially shuttered against the noonday glare. A beehive fireplace was plastered into one corner.

All this Russ took in at a glance as the nun inclined her head and, in heavily accented English, invited them to be seated. Then she disappeared.

As Russ sat down on the cushions of the wooden couch, he was struck at how much cooler it was inside. The temperature was probably still above ninety, but it seemed like the recesses of a cool, damp cave by comparison to the sun-blasted street outside.

"Doctor Sutter, it was so kind of you to come," a female voice said.

The three men rose instinctively as a young woman entered from an adjacent room. Russ caught his breath at the sight of her. She was a stunning beauty. About five feet, three inches tall, she wore a starched white shirtwaist and a full skirt that reached almost to her ankles. As she stepped forward to take Doctor Sutter's hand, Russ saw that she was wearing sandals. A portion of her shoulder-length black hair was swept back from her face on either side and tied with a small piece of red ribbon.

"And who are these gentlemen?" she asked, her sparkling black eyes taking in Russ and Perry. Even though she was obviously not American, she spoke English with only a trace of an accent.

As Russ was being introduced, he became immediately conscious of his own scruffy, unshaven, sunburned appearance, the knee-length moccasins turned down and tied around his ankles. He clumsily moved to take her hand, and the Colt at his hip bumped against a chair. Her slim hand felt surprisingly rough and callused to his touch.

"Elena Maria Calderón," she said, fixing him with a quick look that went through him like an Apache lance. "I'm happy to meet you."

Judging from the smooth light skin and delicate features, Russ guessed her age at around twenty, give or take two years.

"Ma'am" he managed to acknowledge.

"It's not madam. It's just Elena," she said with a smile. "Doctor, my uncle is in his bedroom. If you will follow me? You gentlemen make yourselves comfortable. We will have some refreshments shortly."

When they had gone, Russ stepped to a window and pushed open a shutter. The house was built in the old Spanish style — a rectangle enclosing an interior courtyard. Fringing the courtyard were beds of orange caltrop Russ had seen growing wild on the Chihauhuan grasslands to the northeast. It was in full summer bloom. Several large date palms partially shaded a circular pool of water cupped in stone blocks about two feet high. A statue of the Blessed Virgin Mary stood on a pedestal in the center of this pool. The pool was probably fed by some sort of stone aqueduct and very likely the source of water for the whole house. The moving shadows of the palm fronds over the stone paving and the clear pool gave the courtyard the appearance of an oasis in some burning desert.

As he turned away from the window, Russ saw Perry examining some of the books in the tall case.

"These are all in Spanish."

"What did you expect?"

"No, here's one in Latin . . . and here are a couple of Dickens's novels in English."

Russ joined him to examine some of the volumes. As nearly as he could make out from some of the titles and subtitles, there were even a few books written in the late 1600s and early 1700s, reporting in detail the state of the missions in various provinces of New Spain.

About ten minutes later Doctor Sutter and Elena reappeared, helping between them a frail old man who appeared to be close to eighty. He had a full head of white hair, and his skin was nearly as fair as his niece's although splotched and wrinkled. He was wearing a collarless white shirt and a pair of faded black pants.

They seated him in a worn armchair, and Elena introduced him as *Padre* Juan Miguel Calderón. When the old man greeted them, Russ could see that, though his body was declining, his spirit was still youthful.

While the priest regaled them with tales of the town of Op-osura, Apache raids, oppression by past dictators, and the steadfast faith and endurance of the townspeople, the nun who had answered the door brought some food and set it on the heavy wooden table that stood in the center of the room.

Father Calderón said the blessing but remained where he was as the other four sat down to a simple lunch of *carne seca*, peppers, and a bowl of fairly fresh figs. It was washed down with some sort of mild home-made red wine poured from a crock jug. Elena set a cup of water on a stand beside the priest's chair.

"How old is that church, *Padre?*" Russ asked, helping himself to another fig.

"It was erected in sixteen hundred by Indian slaves." He gestured with gnarled hands to indicate the shape and scope of the building. "They build with rock of the volcano." He paused to clear his throat and take a sip of water. "It was many times a fortress when the Apaches came. And the bells . . . they ring now for almost three hundred years."

"And probably will for another three hundred," Perry added, wiping his mouth with a napkin and sliding his chair back. "Amazing how this town has endured."

"The people here are strong," Elena said.

"How do you get along?" Russ asked. "This place must require a lot of upkeep."

"Not so much," Elena said. "Two nuns live here and see to the church and the house. The three of us can do the cleaning and washing and prepare the food." She glanced at the *padre* who had his eyes closed and seemed to be dozing. "Uncle Juan . . . really he is my grandfather's brother, my *tío grande* . . . he has been sick for a long time now. I am worried that he will not be able to say Mass much longer. When that time comes. . . ." She shrugged. "I do not know what we will do, since there is no other priest. Perhaps the Church will send another *padre* from Mexico City, but that is many miles away over the mountains. And Oposura has no wagon roads in or out. Everything that is not produced in this valley must be brought in by mule back. If something happens to Uncle Juan, I am afraid that *los Hermanos Penitentes* will take over. Most of them are good-hearted men, but they are too . . . too. . . ." She groped for the correct word.

"Extreme?" finished Russ.

"Yes . . . extreme. I don't want to see them take over if we have no priest."

Russ nodded, thinking of the Penitentes of New Mexico — the self-flagellants who went to extremes of penance. These were nearly all men of Spanish descent who had brought the practice from Europe where it had existed in some form since medieval times. The organization had recently been publicly condemned by the Bishop of Santa Fé, but he had succeeded only in driving the Penitentes underground. They usually existed only where no priest was available to serve their spiritual needs with the sacraments.

"We very much appreciate your hospitality," Doctor Sutter said, giving them all a cue. "But I must get back to camp. Zere are some soldiers I must attend."

"Thank you for everything," Elena said, encompassing them all with a gracious smile. "It is not often we have visitors from outside."

Doctor Sutter said something in an undertone to the *padre*, patted him on the shoulder, and joined the others as Elena showed them down the hall to the door. Russ was enraptured by her charm and graceful movements as she told them good bye once more and let them out into the brightness of the dusty street.

"Pretty girl," Perry remarked, replacing his hat.

"An understatement," Russ responded and then asked as Doctor Outter mounted his mule: "Did you get the *padre* fixed up?"

"*Padre* Calderón is an old man vis rheumatism. Zere is little I can do to cure ze infirmities of age. He also has ulcers that make him very veak from slow loss of blood and lack of food. I have given him some powders and ordered a bland diet. That should help him some."

He guided his mule around and started back toward camp. Russ and Perry walked toward the hitching rail around the corner where their mules drowsed in the heat.

Chapter Eight

"Norwood, I want you to take charge of the infantry," Captain Lawton said in a rather abrupt fashion as he dismounted from Dolly. Russ tried not to let the surprise show on his face. He started to reply, but Lawton held up his hand. "I know. You're no longer an officer. But you're the same man who was a company commander for a dozen years. I know it's illegal, but you're the only one I can turn to. Hell, this whole campaign is an irregular operation." He tilted his hat back and rubbed a sleeve across his forehead as he squinted off into the distance.

Russ took advantage of the pause. "What about Lieutenant Finley? I thought he was leading them."

"I guess you heard about Finley getting drunk and raising hell in town last night."

"Yes."

"Well, it's not the first time he's been drunk on duty. I had to put him under arrest. He's a good man when he's sober . . . one of the best. But I can't depend on him staying that way. Anyhow, he's to be sent back for court martial. Lieutenant Brown will escort him, since he's an officer. I won't demean him any further by sending him in the custody of a sergeant. Also, Doctor Sutter is ordering three of the men back for medical reasons. I think one of them has malaria." Lawton paused and appeared deeply in thought. "Anyway, that will leave you and me and Babcock in charge of this campaign. I believe you'll find the infantrymen have settled down considerably since they joined us. Their morale has improved since they've been getting fresh meat every day, and they haven't been asked to do any more than the rest of us are doing. We've been able to provide most of them with new shoes, and the cobbler in town was able to fix the rest." He gave Norwood a tight smile. "Sometimes performing under stress pulls a group of men together. Gives them a sense of *esprit de corps!*"

Russ nodded. "Fine. I'll be glad to help out."

"Oh, one other thing," Lawton said, pausing as he started to lead his mule away. "I just had a talk with the prefect today, and he's agreed to provide us with a couple of guides who know the local area well. They'll be able to help the scouts for a few days."

"I saw Mexican troops coming in a while ago. Any news?"

Lawton shook his head. "They confirmed the reported killing of people by the hostiles over toward Bacadehuachi. That's all."

When the command marched the next afternoon at three o'clock, the cavalry was left behind in camp near Oposura. The country they were entering was too rough for horses to be of any good use, according to the local guides. The three in command, along with Doctor Sutter, Tom Horn, and Stratford McGee, rode their mules, stuffing their saddlebags with as many items as they thought might be needed. In addition, the infantry marched with fairly full packs.

When they had made seven miles southeast toward the town of Tepachi, a courier from Oposura overtook them with the news of fresh Indian attacks thirteen miles due east of Oposura. The command immediately swung east to cut the trail that would take them to the mescal ranch where depredations were reported.

"It is only about four miles from here, *señor,*" one of the local guides said to Captain Lawton as the Apache scouts, with Tom Horn leading, started down the trail toward the ranch.

Shortly, they were marching over a broken lava bed. The black rock seemed to suck up and intensify the late afternoon heat. Those who were riding were forced to dismount and lead their animals over the hard, broken surfaces. Russ saw in places where the lava had cracked that the rock varied from three to fifteen feet deep. A few bushes straggled up through these splits where a little soil and moisture had manage to collect.

Lawton quickly saw that the pack train could not make it far over this kind of terrain and ordered them to take the other local guide and go around by a longer detour to the ranch. The rest of the column continued onward, slipping and sliding over the thick lava flow. The sharp edges were like knives, gashing the footgear at every misstep. The iron shoes of the mules rang on the hard stone, their legs often slipping into the cracks.

"How much farther, Ramón?" Russ panted, the bottoms of his feet burning through his thick-soled moccasins. "Seems like we've come more than four miles already." He wiped the stinging sweat from his eyes.

"Four miles, *señor?* No, no. I meant four leagues. We have a good way to go yet."

"Aw shit!" said one of the infantrymen, hauling up short. There was murder in his eyes as he glared at the guide.

"Keep moving, Roberts!" Russ snapped.

The private uncapped his canteen and drained the last few drops before giving one more hard look at Ramón. He plodded on.

At last, shortly before dark, the column reached the ranch. One Mexican had been shot the night before. It was not a dangerous wound, and Doctor Sutter cut the bullet out of the man's shoulder and bandaged it. While the doctor was attending the wounded ranch hand, the exhausted men were trying to get some drinkable water from the spring, but the water was so hot it had to be cooled before anyone could drink it.

"Helluva chase for one wounded man," Perry complained

under his breath to Russ as they flopped on the ground near the rest of the men. Kettles and pans and buckets from the ranch house were cooling the hot spring water as the men looked at it longingly with thick tongues.

"Yeah, the men are about dead, and their shoes are torn up."

"The pack train's not even here yet."

About a half hour later one of the Apache scouts came trotting back and reported they had found the trail of the hostiles who had done the shooting. There were three of them.

"And they're long gone," Lawton remarked in disgust. "That was about the hardest four miles I ever marched."

"More like twenty," Babcock said.

"That'll teach me to ask for any local guides again."

A rumble of thunder cut off the conversation, and the men glanced at the thickening black clouds that were darkening the long twilight.

"I think I know what's going to be cooling that spring water a lot faster," Russ said.

It was barely fifteen minutes before the rain hit them, and the downpour lasted most of the night as the men found what shelter they could. A few of the men who had been most affected by the heat merely lay in the open and let the rain pelt them for hours, oblivious to the lightning bolts all around them.

The next morning at five o'clock they were on the march again, tired, wet, and stiff with no breakfast due to the lack of dry firewood. The ground was muddy, sloppy, and covered with cactus, making difficult going for the infantry and the Indian scouts. After only five miles of this, the Indians located a cold water spring and recommended to Lawton that the command halt there until the scouts could go on ahead and work out a trail.

While they waited, the men managed to get a little something to eat, mostly cold jerky and coffee. The Indian scouts returned about noon and reported a trail of two horses and a mule headed almost due south.

"Norwood, I want you to take fifteen Indians and follow that trail," Lawton said thoughtfully, after he had received this news. "Keep going tonight, and tomorrow, and follow it as long as you can. The rest of us will come along slowly and will camp on the first good water we find this afternoon. Send back a runner with any news. Then I'll decide if I want to drag the whole command along. Tom Horn will also go with you as chief of scouts."

When Norwood didn't reply for several seconds, Lawton looked at him curiously. "Understand?"

"Let me take this scout, Captain," Babcock said quickly. "I need to get out of camp for a while, and Norwood has his hands full with the infantry."

"Well . . .," Lawton hesitated, looking from one to the other, "I guess it really makes no difference, if it's agreeable to both of you. Be ready to move out within the hour."

As Lawton walked off, Norwood glanced his thanks to Babcock.

"I just jumped in there," Perry said. "Didn't think you'd mind."

Babcock, Horn, and the scouts rode out shortly thereafter, while the rest remained camped on the spring, finding what shade they could from the burning sun and resting. Shortly before dark, the rain descended again. It poured all night. Instead of cooling them, this deluge only succeeded in turning the air suffocatingly close from heat and dampness.

They marched at five o'clock sharp in the morning, following the trail due south for four miles and then swinging a little west for two more miles where the trail led into a cañon. Russ walked and led Plato now more than he rode, not only as an example to the infantry, but because of the treacherous, muddy footing. His high moccasins were soaked and caked halfway to the knees with a yellowish brown clay.

Stratford McGee moved up alongside him in the midmorning. His doeskin breeches were in the same condition. He had shed his red flannel shirt and had it tied around his waist by the arms, the rest of the garment hanging down behind. He trudged along in silence for a few minutes, sweat running down his face under his hat and into his beard.

"Where's your mule?" Russ finally asked.

"Turned him in with the pack train. No point in leading him if I can't ride."

Russ nodded as they picked their way around and over the rocks that formed the sandy cañon bottom. The swollen brown stream rolled along beside them, carrying its load of silt.

"Damnedest country I ever saw," Mac opined. "And I've seen some country in my time. But this beats all. Too hot, too dry, too wet, too steep, too slippery, too rocky, too full of cactus. Shit!" He coughed and spat into the swollen torrent a few feet away.

"That's why the Indians like it," Russ concluded. "Did you ever hear the story of B'rer Rabbit in the briar patch?"

"Nope. What's that?"

"Never mind. It'd take too much effort in this heat to tell it."

The cañon gradually broadened out, and stretches of grass appeared. A mile farther along Russ saw that large patches of the grass were blackened by recent burning. The column went into camp that afternoon in an area that had fairly good grass and water but was dry from no recent rains.

Lieutenant Babcock rode in shortly after camp had been set up.

"Horn's still out with the scouts," he said as he dismounted near Lawton and Norwood. "Those scouts did one helluva job trailing today. For miles there was no trail at all, as far as I could tell. Washed out clean by the rains. I'm sure they lost it for a while, but somehow they instinctively knew where to go and were eventually able to pick it up again."

"I wonder if those scouts are completely trustworthy?" Lawton mused aloud. "They *are* Apaches and former hostiles. Some of them are even related to the men we're chasing. It would be no problem for them to deceive us into believing they were tracking when they're really just leading us around in circles."

"Possibly, sir," Babcock said, "but not likely. These scouts have proven many times in the past that they are loyal."

"Yes, yes, I suppose you're right. But it seems odd that they are forever finding trails, but we never catch up with the hostiles."

Perry and Russ glanced quickly at each other, but there was nothing to say.

Finally, Babcock added, "We have no choice but to trust them, Captain. We wouldn't be even this close without them."

"Very well. Babcock, you go back out with the scouts, and we'll follow just as we did today. Our only hope is to wear them down. They've got to be getting as tired as we are. And they're encumbered with women and children. I think it was a good idea to leave the troop at Oposura. We have no use for horses in this terrain. In fact, I'm considering sending the pack train back, too. We'll draw ten day's rations for the infantry first. Our mules are thin, but they'll survive on what grass we can find. And we can probably buy some corn for them at one of these Mexican villages."

Lawton followed through on his plan and instructed Rolando Vasquez, the head packer who had functioned as their guide down from Calabasas, to prepare the pack train for the return to Oposura the next morning. Lieutenant Babcock, after some rest and food, mounted up and rode back out to join the Indian scouts, about fifteen miles in advance.

Except for the fact that they were not in hot pursuit of the hostiles, as he settled down at dusk on the blanket he had finally managed to dry, Russ felt reasonably satisfied with things so far. The infantry had reconciled themselves to the situation and were performing very well. Most of them had even stopped grumbling. Russ, himself, had ceased losing weight and was hardening up to the trail. Except for the lack of fresh vegetables, the food was passable. The fresh air and exercise had apparently increased his appetite for meat, and venison was in abundance. Just this afternoon the men had killed eight deer not far from camp, and nearly all the meat was being eaten voraciously since there was no means of preserving it except drying and smoking, for which they had no time. Yes, things, as far as he was concerned, were not going too badly. Even Tom Horn had given him no trouble since coming back to the command. Now, if the weather would just cooperate — and give them all a good night's rest.

He peeled off his undershirt and pants and spread them over a nearby bush, facing the small fire to dry. Then he stretched out on his back, his hands behind his head. Drifting into that twilit state between wakefulness and sleep, he felt something tickle the skin of his thigh. He sleepily brushed at it and immediately felt something sting him sharply.

"Aahh!" He jerked awake and his eyes flew open just in time to see a hairy black Tarantula spider scuttle away into the darkness. "Damn!" His heart beating faster from fear as much as the searing pain, he twisted around to the firelight to examine the burning spot on his naked thigh. "He got me good," he muttered.

He washed it off with water from his canteen and tried to think if there was anything else he should do. There was no whiskey in camp, and he doubted that Doctor Sutter had anything that was an antidote for spider bite. He shook his blanket and moved to another spot, away from any rocks or bushes but knew of no other precautions. One of the hazards of the country, he thought as again he settled down. This time, as the pain gradually subsided to a dull ache, he was nearly an hour relaxing sufficiently to doze. Finally he slept.

The next morning they didn't get underway until about eight o'clock due to issuing rations to the men, packing new loads on the two mules they were keeping with them, while Vasquez and the civilian packers prepared to return. The heat became intense by the time they were on the southerly trail only an hour. Even without the pack train, the pace was slow due to the rough terrain and the enervating heat. After experimenting with several methods of dressing, Russ had finally hit on one that was not terribly suffocating yet protected most of his skin from the burning rays of the sun. He wore only his high moccasins, his underwear bottoms, his long-sleeved cotton shirt, and his campaign hat that had been soaked with sweat and rain and dried in the sun so many times that it had almost lost its shape. Even so, as he trudged along leading Plato, he felt as if he were walking in an oven. The stones were burning his feet through the thick-soled moccasins, and the sun was reflecting off the rocky cañon walls. He had rid himself of all extra weight by looping his gun belt over the stock of his carbine in the saddle scabbard and even tying the two-quart canteen to one of the rings on the McClellan saddle for Plato to carry.

By early afternoon he was in a heat-induced stupor, plodding numbly, placing one foot after the other, his slitted eyes on the hoofs of the mule in front of him, but his mind was elsewhere — drifting, dreaming. He was clean and shaved and lolling in the breezy shade of the courtyard where waters splashed in a fountain, and the palms rustled overhead. Elena Maria Calderón was there, her black hair shining, smiling, teasing him, tempting him with those black eyes and those languid movements. She was wearing a white blouse that concealed little of the full breasts that strove to escape. She beckoned to him as she seated herself on the stone parapet of the fountain, sliding the full skirt up over shapely thighs. He started to move toward her but caught his toe and fell face down on the hard flagstones. Suddenly, he was on his back, looking up into the sun. Someone was calling his name, but he had trouble responding.

"Russ! Russ! Are you all right?"

The voice was familiar, but he couldn't place it. Then a wide hat brim blocked the sun from his eyes, and he could make out the fuzzy face of Stratford McGee, bending anxiously over him.

"Here, take some of this."

Norwood felt the tepid wetness as McGee dribbled some water from his canteen over parched lips. He allowed McGee to raise his head sufficiently for him to swallow. After a few sips, Mac poured some of the water down Russ's face. "Can you get up?"

"Yeah, Mac. Thanks. I'm okay now." Russ rolled over and pushed himself to his feet as Mac retrieved his hat, slapped the dust off, and handed it back. "Guess I just got overheated," he apologized.

He felt somewhat lightheaded. This was not like him. He had thought he had become accustomed to the heat. As he turned to grasp Plato's reins, he felt the tightness of swelling in his left thigh. And then he knew. It was the spider bite. He didn't know how much poison had gotten into his blood, but that, combined with the heat, had caused him to pass out. He motioned for McGee to help him mount.

"Think I'll ride a while," he muttered. The smaller man

helped him lift his left leg to the stirrup and boosted him into the saddle. "Thanks again, Mac. I'll be okay now."

As the infantry again fell in behind them, Russ took a long drink from his canteen, poured a little into his hat and placed it back on his head, reveling in the fresh coolness as the water trickled down his face and neck. If the bite wasn't better by the time they camped, he would have to look up Doctor Sutter.

By the time they camped on a large plateau on what appeared to be the top of a mountain range, he felt much better. For one thing, the weather had cooled as another storm threatened. The grass was thick and lush for their remaining animals, and the wind was sighing in the branches of the pines around them. A stream, that appeared to be permanent water, flowed through the camp.

McGee joined him in getting a cooking fire going before the storm broke. The coffee had just come to a boil, and the remains of some melted bacon was heating with the beans in the frying pan when Tony, the first sergeant of the scouts, loped into camp and looked around for the big figure of Captain Lawton.

Russ walked over to get the news just as the scout finished his report and headed toward the rest of the Apache scouts to get some food.

"Tony tells me the scouts are on a fresh trail that's leading over that big mountain just to the east of us," Lawton said as Norwood came up. A grim smile stretched his thick mustache. "We need to keep pressing them. By God, we need to show them we are stronger than they are. If we can break their spirit, we've got them."

"Yes, sir."

A rumble of thunder made Russ forget anything else he intended to say. He hurried back to his fire for supper before the tempest struck. He was just cooling a second cup of coffee with canteen water to get it down quickly when the rain started.

Just a few drops at first, but they quickly increased to a downpour, snuffing all the fires into hissing steam and plunging the camp into blackness. The blackness was only temporary. Sizzling bolts of lightning lit up the area in brief glares of brilliant light, followed by crashing cannonades of thunder.

The metallic taste of fear was in Norwood's mouth as one lightning bolt struck a tall palm tree hardly fifty yards away. He and McGee made a simultaneous dash for the partial shelter of a huge boulder, passing mules that were squealing and kicking on their picket line. They slid, breathlessly, against the smooth face of the curved granite. The next flash showed them that Captain Lawton was already there

"Here, get these rifles away from us!" Lawton shouted, thrusting his carbine at Norwood. "We don't want anything metallic near here."

"Gimme those!" Stratford McGee grabbed both rifles and darted away into the darkness. He was back shortly. "They're safe and dry . . .," he announced, the rest of his words smothered by thunder.

The fireworks continued for nearly an hour, and several pine trees were struck and set afire in spite of the rain, their resin-filled needles flaring up briefly.

The next day's march proved a living hell for Russ Norwood. His upper thigh had become so swollen the skin was about to split. A large area around the bite was red and feverish, and the skin chafed with every step. As usual, the night's storm clouds had dissipated with the dawn and provided no protection from the blazing sun that rose high to suck up all the moisture into a suffocating vapor.

"Damned if I don't think I'm gonna mildew before this trip is over," Stratford McGee grumbled as he and Norwood plodded down the trail that led off the plateau into another cañon. "Ain't a damn bit o' breeze down here, either. But, I reckon those hostiles aren't gonna make it easy for us to follow 'em."

He glanced aside at the flushed face of Norwood. Just then Norwood stumbled and had to catch himself on McGee to keep from falling.

"Here, now! I know you're sick. Hold up a minute. You should be riding. You're sure not in any condition to walk."

Norwood didn't object as McGee checked the cinch on Plato and then helped him into the saddle. He felt nauseated and dizzy. Without his own weight and the constant motion of walking, the thigh didn't pain him as much. But he didn't want to faint again in front of his men. They didn't know what was causing it and probably assumed he just couldn't stand the pace and the heat.

About six miles into the march, the trail they were following in the cañon bottom dropped off about fifteen feet. Russ and the others had to climb around the drop on foot then coax and push their mules, stumbling and sliding, down the side trail that was hardly passable for a single human. Once over this hurdle, a fairly even trail led on down the cañon toward the Yaqui River. They came to the river and waded, knee-deep, to the opposite side. Here they plunged into a dense thicket of cane, following an obvious trail made by the hostiles. As they forced their way through, several of the mules were cut by the sharp edges of the cane leaves. In his feverish state, Russ found his mind dwelling on these wounds.

"Hafta treat all those cuts as soon as we can, or the blowflies will get in there and maybe kill 'em," he muttered to McGee who was walking just ahead of him.

"Don't worry, we'll take care of 'em as soon as we camp," McGee nodded, a concerned look in his eyes.

The men and mules came to a halt as a runner reached the front of the column with the news that Babcock and the scouts were camped about a mile ahead through the canebrake. The column again waded the river and finally came up with Babcock, Horn, and the scouts on a low, rocky ground near the river.

Babcock took one look at Norwood and quickly sent for Doctor Sutter.

"You should haf called me sooner," the doctor admonished as he examined the grievously swollen thigh.

Sutter took a scalpel from his case and walked to the nearest camp fire that was already blazing and held the blade in the flames for a few seconds. Then, with Russ sitting on the ground, he made a small, slicing cut through the spot of the bite. Blood and pus immediately poured out, and he pressed gently on the thigh. Then he soaked up the blood with a cotton cloth, swabbed the area with carbolic, and deftly wrapped and tied a clean bandage around the leg.

"I vill maybe haf to lance it again to ease the pressure," the doctor said. "For now, I vant you to take zis."

"What is it?"

"Quinine. Thirty grains for now." He handed Russ his canteen to wash down the medicine.

"Hey, Norwood, we're gonna take a little swim in the creek. You coming?" Tom Horn asked in mock seriousness as he passed and took in the scene.

It was a measure of how badly he felt, Russ reflected later, that he hardly even glanced up as the chief of scouts went by, chuckling.

But Doctor Sutter took Horn seriously. "You vill *not* bathe in zat filthy water!" he stated flatly to Russ. "And ze other men should not also."

"Hell, as grimy as *I* feel, I'm not getting in that stagnant, greenish stuff," McGee said.

Russ watched with dull eyes as several of the men stripped off their clothes, leaving them in the shade and then waded into the waist-deep pools. One soldier cursed as he hopped barefoot from rock to rock where the sun had turned the flat stones as hot as a stove top. To Norwood, the splashing of the algae-covered water looked cool and inviting. But he allowed himself to be helped to his feet by Babcock and McGee then walked gingerly to a blanket spread on the hard ground.

"Russ, I hate to leave you like this, but Lawton has ordered me to take two day's rations and pull out of here by two-thirty this afternoon. We've got a hot lead on the hostiles' trail, and we can't slow down now."

"That's okay. I'll be fine. Just need a little rest and some food. I can't believe how hot it is, though."

"You've got a fever. The quinine should start working soon."

"I'll watch after him, Lieutenant," McGee said.

"It's probably no consolation, but you're not the only one. Private Reynolds fell out on the march today, and Captain Lawton had to fetch him into camp on his own mule. And he wasn't bitten by any spider."

"He's one of my men, and I didn't even know it," Russ moaned. "Helluva leader I am."

"Get well," Perry said, rising to his feet. "I'll see you in a day or two. If this trail's as hot as the scouts seem to think, we'll need you."

Chapter Nine

After a fitful and feverish sleep, Norwood forced himself up with the rest of the men for a five-thirty start the next morning. He felt terrible, but he was careful not to let on, especially when he thought Doctor Sutter or Captain Lawton might be looking his way. As he saddled and mounted Plato slowly and with great difficulty, he uttered a silent prayer that the trail today would be easier. His prayer went unanswered.

As the column marched up the river, winding its way along the sides of the cañon wherever there was a passable trail, Russ found himself walking as much as he was riding. After about five miles of this, they reached a spot where another cañon branched off. Babcock and the scouts had left sign that they were to follow the branch to the left. Mountains rose sheer on both sides as they picked their way along.

"Did you ever see such god-forsaken country?" McGee asked, glancing at the splintered rock of the steep cañon walls. "Great place for an ambush, if the Apaches were so inclined."

The statement didn't seem to require a reply, so Russ saved his strength. It did seem to him after nearly five more miles of walking that this twisting side cañon was leading them into a hole that they would require them to backtrack in order to get out. Yet there must be a way out since Perry and the scouts were still ahead of them. Russ's thigh felt tight under the bandages, and the buzzing in his head could very well be the quinine working. His strength did appear to be returning slowly as he kept up a steady pace.

He jerked up suddenly as the flash of a red headband announced the silent arrival of an Apache courier. After a short exchange with the scout, Lawton reined Dolly around and rode back to them.

"Babcock sends word that the scouts have located the hostiles' camp. Wants us to come ahead as fast as we can. This courier will lead us back."

Russ felt a surge of energy he had not felt in days.

"This may be our chance," Lawton said. "So, if you've ever wanted to cover some ground in a hurry, now's the time to do it." His professional restraint barely concealed the excitement in his voice.

"Get a grip on those rifles and canteens," Russ barked to the double column of infantry behind him. "The hostiles' camp is up ahead, and we've got to make tracks to get there. Double quick time! Let's go!"

He led them off at a fast trot, barely keeping the mounted Captain Lawton in sight as they followed the tireless courier. Every quarter mile Russ slowed the men to a walk for about a hundred paces before picking up the trot again. Mile after slow mile passed under their thudding feet. The surge of adrenaline they had all felt at the prospect of imminent combat began to fade. One by one the foot soldiers began to stagger and fall by the wayside. Lawton impatiently circled his mule back to urge them along.

Russ estimated they covered nearly eight miles this way, but they were paying the price. He counted twenty men who had fallen out of ranks. They would have to fend for themselves and eventually catch up as best they could, he thought as he paused, panting heavily, and looked back.

The cañon had shallowed and broadened, and the courier led them on a trail to the right out of the cañon and up a mountainside. The Indian indicated the hostiles were camped on a river on the other side of the mountain.

When the slope became too steep to ride, those who were mounted, including Doctor Sutter and Captain Lawton, dismounted, and the men looked to their arms. Wooden ammunition boxes were unloaded from one of the two pack mules. The boxes were nailed shut and had to be pried open. But nothing metal could be handled without blistering the hands because of the searing sun.

"Here, give me that," Lawton said, hefting one of the heavy boxes in a bear-like grip. He carried the box to a sharp outcropping of rock on the hillside. He raised the box and let it fall. The lid splintered and the cartridges spilled out. While the men crowded around, scooping up the shells, filling their cartridge belts and putting handsful into their pockets, Lawton broke open a second case the same way.

"Make sure anything that could rattle or make a noise is tied up or left behind," Russ cautioned his men as he moved among them, checking their equipment. "Everybody have a full canteen? It's going to be a hot climb. All right, let's go."

The command started up the trail at a fast pace, the only sound the soft thudding of feet, an occasional grunt, and the rasp of harsh breathing from many throats. They were less than half way to the top when Captain Lawton pulled up, gasping. Russ stopped to help.

"Can you make it, Captain?"

"Yeah . . . yeah. . . . Give me a few . . . seconds," he panted. "Shouldn't have drunk so much water. I realize . . . you men have . . . been marching hard . . . all day." The big man took a deep breath and visibly pulled himself together. "Let's go."

The column started again. It was the hottest, hardest climb Russ had ever attempted. They were on the lee side of the mountain in the full rays of the sun, without a breath of air. They were soaked with sweat when they finally reached the summit and carefully worked their way forward. The scout held up his hand for caution and then pointed to a crack in an outlying ledge of rock. Russ could see the Indian camp far below them on the Yaqui River. The camp was situated on a ledge, or small plateau, hemmed in on two sides by the steep mountains that came down to the river both upstream and downstream of the camp. Fires were burning, Indian ponies picketed, and a good many Indians — men, women, and children — were moving about in all directions.

Russ backed away for others to have a look. He knew by the signs that they were on the trail the Indians had taken to reach the camp below.

"What do you think?" he asked Babcock who had come over as soon as he saw Norwood.

"Looks from here like there's no outlet, but Geronimo would be the last one to put his people in a trap."

"That's what I think. There's got to be another way out."

"How's the leg?"

"It'll do."

"This all your men?"

Norwood shook his head. "Left the ones who played out to guard the mules and a couple of packers."

After surveying the situation, Lawton came over to the two men.

"Here's what I plan to do. Babcock, you and Horn take the Indians and make a flanking march to the left. Be very careful to stay below the ridge and out of sight. Work your way down to the river well above the camp. Norwood and I will stay here with the infantry. We'll give you time to get into position, then we'll start the attack and drive them upstream toward you."

"The terrain is really rough. There are plenty of hiding places for them," Babcock said.

"I know. It's going to be an ugly fight. But it's the best we can do. Just be careful. This is our best chance yet of getting these Indians we've tracked for so long. Any questions?"

Babcock shook his head.

"Then get to it."

It was a nervous wait, but finally Lawton decided that enough time had elapsed. He took one end of the line of infantry, Norwood took the other, and in loose, open order they began working their way down toward the camp, utilizing every rock and bush as cover.

Suddenly heavy firing began on the upriver side.

"Come on, men! Get down there, quick!"

Norwood and Lawton and the infantry went plunging down the steep slope, sliding and bounding from rock to rock. Breathless, they reached the bottom and charged through the brush toward the camp site, rifles at the ready.

Russ burst out of cover, holding his Marlin carbine, ready to see fleeing hostiles. Instead, bullets began whining off the rocks around him. He hit the ground instinctively and began firing toward some unseen foe in the foliage across the camp site.

"Hold your fire, dammit!" Lawton yelled. "It's us!"

Another volley crashed from the trees. Lead hummed past them like bees.

"Hold it!" Lawton roared above the cracking of gunfire. A few scattered shots and the volley ceased as Babcock and the scouts crept out of cover.

Russ rose to his knees and started to stand. A rifle cracked and he felt a tug at his pants leg. A slug whined off the rocks behind him. He jumped back and was vaguely aware of some angry voices coming from across the clearing. This time he waited several moments before he advanced into the open again.

The Indians were gone. The fires still smoked, and the ponies jerked at their picket lines. Blankets, food, and some clothing were scattered about. But the Indians were gone.

As the two groups advanced toward each other across the camp site, Russ stole a look at Captain Lawton. He looked as if someone had kicked him in the stomach.

"What happened, Babcock?" Lawton asked, sounding very depressed. "I thought I told you we would start the attack from this end."

"I don't know, sir. They must have spotted us. *Something* alerted them. We were still a long way off, but we had to start firing when we saw them start running."

"Then why in hell were you shooting at *us* just now?"

"Horn and a couple of the scouts saw the Apache courier with you and mistook him for one of the hostiles."

"Shootin' at each other while the hostiles slip away!" Lawton lowered his rifle and shook his head in disgust. "Round up those Indian ponies. We'll take them with us. Then take what food and blankets are usable. Burn the rest. We'll camp here tonight."

After the adrenaline ebbed and the bitter disappointment of losing their quarry set in, Russ realized just how sick he really was. While Stratford and Perry prepared some food, Russ found a quiet place where the water was fairly still near the river bank and sat down on the sandy bottom with the water up to his armpits. He declined an offer of food when Babcock came to check on him an hour later. He had no appetite. His slight buoyancy in the water seemed to take the pressure off his leg, and the relatively cool water eased the fever in it.

Twilight came, then night descended, and still he remained in the river. Sometime near midnight he heard three packers come in with the mules and the stragglers of the infantry who had not been up to the march.

He heard someone approaching in the dark.

"You okay?" It was Perry's voice.

"Yeah."

"Anything you want me to do for you before I turn in?"

"No. This water feels good. I think I'll just sit here for a while."

He heard Babcock slide to a sitting position on the grass nearby.

"Tough about the hostiles' escaping."

"I thought we had 'em for sure this time."

"If we'd trapped them, that might've ended it."

"Was Geronimo with them? This might not have been the only bunch."

"I don't know," Babcock said. "Didn't have any field glasses with me. The scouts didn't know, either."

"Lawton is really disappointed."

"Huh! That's an understatement."

Neither man spoke for a few seconds. The soft night sounds made themselves heard — the gurgling and sucking of the nearby current, someone coughing in the camp, the clink of a metal pan.

"Something happened today that you need to know about," Perry said in a more serious tone.

"What's that?"

"I wasn't going to mention it until you were feeling better, but I think you need to know now."

Russ waited.

"Tom Horn tried to shoot you today. If I hadn't bumped his arm just as he started to fire, he probably would have drilled you."

"That was probably the bullet that went through my pants leg. Was it just as most of the firing had stopped?"

"Yes. I saw him raise the rifle, and I realized he had to know at that point you were not the hostiles."

"Thanks. I owe you my life."

"I don't think Horn knows I saw him aiming directly at you. But it was no mistake, I'm convinced of that."

"He could have claimed it was a mistake, but I'd be just as dead."

"Don't let down your guard. The man is dangerous. Just when you think he's paying no attention to you, he'll try something."

"As soon as I feel better, maybe I should take the initiative and put him out of action somehow."

"I don't know what you could do that wouldn't make you look like the aggressor."

"I know. And I'm not a killer. Maybe I could break his leg so he would be sent back."

"No. You'd be fired, too. Just bide your time and never turn your back on the man. The situation today couldn't have been prevented. I'll provide an extra pair of eyes for you. Between the two of us, we should be able to keep him in check until this campaign's over."

"Good enough."

Russ heard Perry's knees pop as he gathered his long legs under him and stood up. "I'm about done in. I have to get some sleep. See you in the morning. Don't fall asleep in there and drown, or Horn won't have to bother with you."

Norwood could almost see his friend grinning in the dark. Nothing was ever totally serious with Babcock.

"You bet. And thanks again. I owe you a big debt."

"Forget it. You'd have done the same." Babcock hesitated. "You know, I wouldn't be surprised if Tom Horn didn't have something to do with planting that Tarantula near your blanket."

"H-m. It's possible, I guess. I never considered that. But I think that's probably a little too subtle for Horn. Besides, they're

115

probably *some* troublesome things in this life we can still chalk up to chance."

The command stayed in camp the next day, with only the Apache scouts out trying to pick up the trail of the fleeing hostiles. Russ Norwood spent most of the day in the soothing river water, nursing his infection, watching Stratford McGee and several of the soldiers fishing from the river bank. Their efforts were rewarded with a number of good-size catfish which they cooked and ate immediately as a welcome change to their diet. McGee brought Norwood some hot, cooked catfish and a piece of hardtack softened in coffee about mid-afternoon.

"Mac, you're a life saver. How'd you know this is just what I've been hankering for?"

Norwood climbed out of the water and accepted the food, served in a frying pan.

"Feeling any better?" McGee asked.

Russ nodded, biting into the fresh fish. "Quite a bit. I think I can make it if we pull out of here tomorrow. I wonder if the scouts are finding anything."

"Don't know. They went without any white men with them."

"Why? Where's Tom Horn? And Babcock?"

"The lieutenant's sleeping. I think Horn's over there some-where, cleaning his gear. I guess the captain just thought the scouts could probably move faster on their own and didn't need anyone else along. I guess he's learned to trust them."

Russ nodded, chewing thoughtfully and squinting toward the camp, some fifty yards away. "Do me a favor, will you, Mac? Bring me my gun belt."

"Sure. What are you going to do with that?"

"In this country you never know when you're going to need a gun. There are probably snakes around here, and I don't aim to get bit by any more critters if I can help it."

116

"I know what you mean. When I'm in the desert, I make a habit of shaking out my moccasins every morning. It's the scorpions and centipedes I hate."

The next morning Doctor Sutter had to lance the swollen thigh again then disinfect and wrap it in a clean bandage. Norwood was grateful that Lawton didn't move the command until two-thirty in the afternoon. They marched up the river about five miles. For Norwood, every step was jarring pain, and the five miles seemed more like twenty. That night he was taken by chills and a fever, and McGee wrapped him in an extra blanket, and slept close by.

The following day Russ was able to force himself to start off on foot with the column. But, after a march of five miles, he felt so sick and dizzy, he was stumbling and falling and was forced to take to his mule. They marched only a mile or two farther before Lawton, out of deference to Norwood, went into camp on top of a small divide.

Russ ate no supper, and toward evening his fever shot up alarmingly. He lost all interest in his surroundings and drifted in and out of consciousness. He tried to stay awake so the fearful nightmares would not overtake him, but it was impossible. During one of his periods of wakefulness, he was aware of Doctor Sutter at his side.

"Here, take zis."

The doctor slipped some quinine into Norwood's mouth and held his head while he drank from a canteen. Russ swallowed the cool water gratefully. He closed his eyes and lay back. Apparently Doctor Sutter thought he was asleep again, but Russ heard the doctor speaking to someone else.

"If he does not come out of zis soon, ve may lose him."

In spite of his somnolent state, Russ fought to stay conscious. If will power could insure his survival, he would not die. But the fever of the infection overcame him, and the next thing

117

he knew Doctor Sutter was again coaxing more quinine down him.

"That is sixty grains of quinine, all told," he said to someone out of Russ's vision. "Now ve can only vait and see."

At some time during the night Russ drifted back to consciousness long enough to hear thunder booming and to feel a cold rain falling on him. He was grateful for the delicious coolness. He awoke at dawn, drenched with rainwater and sweat, but his fever was broken.

"By God, I thought we were going to have a corpse to shovel under," McGee greeted him upon seeing that he was awake.

"Thanks, Mac. I appreciate your confidence."

"Feeling better?"

Russ nodded. "Pretty weak, though."

"Hungry?"

"I could eat a little something."

In short order the small man brought him some bacon and beans with a piece of hardtack soaked in the grease. While Norwood ate slowly, McGee fixed him a cup of steaming black coffee.

"What's going on, Mac? Why aren't we moving out?"

"Lawton decided to lay over today. He's got the scouts out hunting trail, but it's tough to follow in this kind of terrain."

Doctor Sutter came over just then to check on his patient and to change the dressing on his leg.

"The swelling's beginning to go down already," Russ observed with relief when the doctor removed the wet bandage.

The morning sun was increasing its weight on the camp, so Doctor Sutter and Stratford McGee helped Russ into the shade where he reclined on a blanket to finish his breakfast. The ground grew so hot that no one could sit on it. Norwood stayed in the shade all day resting, and McGee kept his head bound in wet cloths.

"This water's just lukewarm," Mac apologized, wringing out the cotton cloth.

"Feels great to me," Russ said, smiling weakly.

That night the fever left him completely, and he slept an exhausted but restful, eight hours.

The next morning he was able to mount Plato and move with the command. He was still weak but made the day's ride without much trouble. However, he was ready to camp when Lawton called a halt about two hundred yards from the Arros River, a tributary of the Yaqui. They were on a bench land, with high cliffs rising from both sides of the river.

As soon as they settled into camp, Captain Lawton went down to the river to bathe. Driftwood and brush were gathered, and cooking fires were lighted. Suddenly, two deer bounded through the camp, headed for the river. Several of the men grabbed for their rifles. Both deer pitched down, riddled with lead, as the blasting of the shots echoed off the nearby cliffs.

Captain Lawton came running, naked and dripping, up from the river. "What's going on? What's the firing about?" By the time he reached Russ and Perry, he limped to an agonized stop. "Aaaarrgghh!!" He gritted his teeth in pain and hobbled to a nearby blanket where he collapsed, cursing.

Russ and Perry looked at each other and then saw that the commander's feet were bristling with tiny cactus needles. Most of the ground beyond the immediate camp site was covered with what the men had been referring to as "baby cactus" that stuck up only a half inch to an inch above the ground. Lawton was in pitiful shape.

"Don't say anything," Babcock warned Norwood as the two of them, along with others, went to help. "He's hotter than a rifle barrel!"

It was an extremely painful and time-consuming process, but several of the men, including Stratford McGee and three of

119

the Indian scouts, finally succeed in pulling all of the nearly transparent barbs out of his feet.

"No wonder he was startled," Norwood said to Dabasah as the two of them left the finishing touches to Doctor Sutter. That volley of shots, echoing off those cliffs, must have sounded like we were under attack from all sides. Poor fella."

Perry looked at him, and his long face broke into a grin.

"I can't help it," he chuckled. "That was the funniest thing I've seen in a long time."

Norwood returned his laugh, making sure his back was still to Lawton as they walked away. "The sight of those long legs high stepping through the cactus . . . !"

"And him naked as a jay-bird and yelling at the top of his voice . . . !"

The two of them nearly choked trying to stifle their laughter.

"One good thing about it," Perry said, trying to catch his breath, "we've got plenty of fresh deer meat in camp."

Deer meat there was. Along with the rest of the men, Russ and Perry and Mac feasted on steaks that night.

Lawton, none the worse for his experience, had the command up and on the march by five-thirty the next morning. They traveled along the Arros River for a time, fording it once or twice to get a better trail. Tom Horn and a few of the scouts were out front, but the majority of the Apache scouts had been doing nothing but driving the captured Indian ponies since the abortive raid on the hostile camp. As a result, many of them were behind the infantry and straggling everywhere, trying to keep the herd moving through the rough, cut-up terrain.

When they finally camped about two miles from the river, Horn and the few scouts who were with him rode into camp. In order to cover more ground quickly, the half dozen scouts had been mounted on captured ponies. Horn reported that the trail had become indistinct, and the scouts were no longer able to determine which way the hostiles had gone.

Lawton received this news tight-lipped then dismissed Horn and went over and sat by his own fire for a long time, staring into the flames. The lingering twilight gradually faded, but the commander still sat, cross-legged, apparently oblivious to the weather, supper, or anyone around him.

"I believe he could cry, just out of sheer frustration," Mac said as he ate with Russ and Perry at their cooking fire a few yards away.

"The weight of command," Russ said, pouring himself another cup of coffee. "Any more sugar?"

"Huh!" Perry snorted. "Any sugar that hasn't been dissolved by all of this rain is with the rest of the pack train back at Oposura."

"Do you reckon one of us ought to go over and say something to him?" Russ asked, glancing toward the captain.

"No. Whatever it is, he'll work it out alone. If he wants to confide in any of us, he'll do it in his own time and his own way," Perry said.

Chapter Ten

It was the following morning when the captain revealed his next move. Babcock and Norwood were slicing thin stripes of venison to fry for breakfast when Lawton approached.

"Some coffee, Captain?" Babcock offered.

"Yes, thanks." The big-boned commanding officer accepted the tin cup Babcock handed him and hunkered down near the fire. For several seconds he did not speak as he tentatively sipped the scalding brew. Lawton was not in the habit of paying social calls, so Norwood knew he had something on his mind. But, uncharacteristically, he was not taking his usual straightforward, blunt approach. Norwood couldn't help noticing how gaunt and hollow-eyed the big man looked. This campaign had been hard on him, both physically and mentally, and it was not over yet.

"First of all, I want to thank you two for helping pull those cactus thorns out of my feet the other day," he began. Apologizing and thanking someone for a favor were two things that did not come easy to Lawton. He hated making mistakes or putting himself in anyone's debt.

"Think nothing of it," Babcock said.

"Could've happened to any of us," Norwood added, placing some strips of meat in the frying pan and setting it over the flames.

Lawton paused again, sipping the coffee. He was unshaven, and his sandy hair had obviously been combed only with his fingers. His heavy mustache was untrimmed and was growing down over his mouth. His tan canvas pants and uniform shirt looked as if they had been slept in.

"We've lost the trail," Lawton said abruptly, coming to the point. "The command will stay in camp until I decide where to go from here. I'll send a few of the scouts out to see if they can cut some kind of trail. I'm sending a courier to Oposura to let the pack train know we are short of supplies. In the meantime, the rest of us will stay here a couple of days, resting and repairing our gear and drying some of the deer meat to take with us." He paused and set his cup on a flat rock. "How are you feeling, Norwood? Have you recovered from that spider bite?"

"Yes, sir. I'm feeling fine."

"Do you feel up to riding into the town of Sahuaripa? It's about thirty or forty miles. The map we've got isn't much account, so it's hard to say. Anyhow, the way I've got it figured, the hostiles lost everything except their guns when we jumped them in that cañon on the Yaqui the other day. They've got to resupply themselves with horses, blankets, food, and ammunition. The quickest and easiest way to do that is by raiding some Mexican village. Sahuaripa may be a likely place for them to hit. Even if they haven't headed that way, I still want you to ride there and see if you can find out any news they may have of the hostiles."

In truth, Russ had not recovered his full strength, but he doubted he would until he was back in the States, eating and sleeping properly.

"All right, then, take what supplies you think you'll need and start whenever you're ready. It would be safer traveling at night, but it's not likely you could find the place in the dark. There are no roads that I know of. Copy part of this map on a sheet of paper to give yourself a rough idea of where the valley lies. The town is in a wide, fertile valley, I've been told." He stood up and stretched. "You may want to take one

123

or two men with you. This ride will be hard and dangerous."

Norwood nodded. "I'll give it some thought. I may prefer to go alone."

"Suit yourself. I was just thinking that if you run into trouble, there would be a better chance of one of you getting through or getting back here."

"Yes, sir."

"We'll probably move before you get back. Sahuaripa is south-southwest of here. If we move, we'll either go north or east of here. We'll leave plenty of sign for you to follow." He turned to leave, then paused. "Thanks for the coffee."

When Lawton was out of earshot, Perry said, "You're not going alone, are you?"

"I wish you were free to go."

"So do I. But you know he wasn't referring to me when he said 'one of the men.' He'd never turn both of us loose at the same time. I wouldn't be surprised if I didn't have charge of the infantry while you're gone."

"Hell, I may just go alone."

"That's really not a good idea in this country. You may disappear, and we'd never see you again. Take at least one man. Somebody you can trust."

Russ thought for a moment. "Well, with Lieutenant Finley gone, that leaves only one man I can rely on to watch my back and who won't panic in case of trouble. If anything, he's overly cautious."

"Who's that?"

"Stratford McGee."

"The old man might be the one at that . . . if he'll go. He's trail wise and tough and he speaks Apache." Perry gave a tight grin. "In case you run into any, that is."

To his surprise, Norwood found McGee willing and ready to go.

124

"I'm getting mighty sick of plodding up and down these cañons day in and day out, not knowing where we are, or where we're going."

"This won't be much different," Russ said. "And probably more dangerous."

"Well, we can pick our own terrain and move at our own pace. With any luck, we can follow some ground where we can ride rather than walk all the time."

"Good. Do you have a gun?"

"Hell, yes. I'd never come on an expedition like this without one."

"What is it?"

"Pistol. Remington forty-four."

"Okay. With my rifle and Colt that should be enough firepower. Bring extra cartridges, full canteen, deer meat, hardtack, and anything else you can scour up to eat."

McGee tied off the leather thong he was relacing on a moccasin and looked up. "Don't worry about me. I've been packing for trips like this since before you were born." The amusement in his blue eyes belied the gruffness in his voice.

The two men rode out of camp a few minutes after nine. Norwood knew the exact time because he had just handed his Waltham watch to Babcock to keep for him.

"You act as if something is going to happen to you on this trip," Perry had said, accepting the timepiece and its heavy chain.

"I won't need it, and I don't want anything to happen to it," Russ had replied. "It's already been wet so much, I'm surprised it hasn't rusted up and stopped running."

"I'll keep it safe and dry."

Norwood swung into the saddle and rode off with McGee without a backward glance. For the first two miles, they backtracked the column's route of the day before. Then they struck off, cross country and, using both the sun and a small pocket compass borrowed from Babcock, they attempted to head south-southwest. But, from the start, the terrain did not co-operate. Most of the cañons seemed to run diagonally northwest to southeast, so they were constantly detouring, changing directions, sometimes riding five miles out of their way before they could come back onto their approximate course.

But, generally, it was good to be cut loose from the command and on their own. After the first few miles their conversation flagged and communication became only an arm indicating direction, or a short, "Watch that dropoff," or "Let's try that river bank. It looks easier."

The two men were not conscious of it, but the power of the mountain wilderness was enveloping them and smothering conversation the deeper they penetrated the vastness of the Sierra Madre. Norwood was vaguely aware that much rougher and wilder country existed to the south and east of them — barrancas with sheer rock walls hundreds of feet deep that were impassable, even on foot, huge vertical, unexplored caves, home to millions of bats, much higher mountains often enveloped in cloud-mist where tropical birds and plants throve year around, not dependent on the rainy season as was this lower, drier section of the western Sierra Madre. It was a good thing for the U. S. Army that the hostiles had not taken refuge in the deeper, wilder portion of the mountains, or Lawton and company would not even be as close in pursuit as they were.

By Norwood's estimation, they had traveled nearly twenty-five miles when they halted for a short rest in midafternoon. They loosened the cinches, slipped out the bits, and let the hobbled mules graze while he and McGee rested, gnawed on some dried meat, and drank water from a clear stream they had stumbled upon. Lacking any kind of grain for weeks, Plato with so much hard work had lost weight, but the gray mule still seemed to have plenty of energy and stamina. Much to Norwood's relief, the animal had never balked nor given one minute's worth of trouble since he had selected him at Calabasas.

In less than an hour they were back in the saddle and pressing onward, angling up and down over low ridges, several of them looking nearly the same. Coming down the side of the one of these ridges, the men had to dismount when the mules began to slip and slide on the steep, shale-covered slope. They picked their way carefully around the short barrel cactus and hedgehog cactus.

Norwood, who was leading at the time, reached the bottom of the cañon first and heard the welcome gurgle of a running stream. He parted the thick growth of willows, stepped out onto the long sand bar, and froze. There, clearly imprinted in the sand, were the prints of many moccasined feet. He led the eager Plato upstream several yards to drink so as not to disturb the tracks.

"Look here," he pointed to the marks as McGee pushed through the willows behind him.

"How old, do you reckon?" Mac asked, tethering his mule to a snag of driftwood near the water.

"Hard to say. Made since the last rain, that's for sure."

"When did it rain last?"

"Last night. Hell, it rains every night."

"But not everywhere. We were a good twenty-five miles from here last night."

"That's so. It might not have rained here. I've seen no sign of it the last couple of hours. But I'm sure this little creek is just an arroyo in the dry season."

The two men carefully examined the tracks.

"How many would you guess?" Russ asked.

"Eight or ten. They're all mixed up. They did a lot of tramping around. Notice they're all adults."

"No hoof prints or manure, so they're afoot."

They looked at each other.

"Can't be far away," Mac said.

Russ instinctively slipped the safety loop off the hammer of his Colt and loosened it in the holster as he looked around.

"Let's fill our canteens and get out of here as soon as the mules are watered," Mac said. "I don't like this."

Russ, too, was feeling a chill at the sight of the tracks. The silent, willow-bordered stream had taken on an ominous aspect.

He retrieved Plato's reins and prepared to mount. "Let's move."

"Hold up," Mac said. "Maybe we should scout around to see which way they headed, so we don't just run right into them."

"Good idea."

"Here's where they started downstream," Mac said, leading his mule. "Probably looking for a place they can cross without soaking their moccasins."

They followed the obvious trail about forty yards before the tracks bent away from the stream, past a huge cottonwood, and started up the ridge the two men had just descended.

"Going the other way," Mac concluded.

"Maybe they were heading northwest and just detoured down here for water," Russ speculated.

They stopped, staring at the spot where the tracks disappeared onto harder ground. Norwood's eyes ran a line straight up the hill from where the tracks disappeared. There were rocks, brush, and small varieties of cactus. Otherwise the empty hillside told him nothing.

"Well, at least they're not headed in our direction," Russ decided, the relief sounding in his voice. "Let's get on."

McGee mounted, and they splashed their mules across the stream, pushed through the bordering foliage, and started the climb up the other side. The animals slipped a time or two but finally lunged to the top. The men eased the mules below the ridgeline and paused to let them blow a minute while Norwood checked his compass and the westering sun, studying the lay of the land ahead.

They started again, silently. The sight of the tracks had dampened the thought of any unnecessary conversation. In fact, Norwood caught himself thinking that Plato was making a lot of noise, iron shoes clanging on rock ledges and loose stones rattling down the slope ahead of them. He rode with a loose rein and his rifle across his saddle, keeping Plato generally on course with his knees. His gaze swept back and forth and around, noting potential ambush sites, his ears attuned to any unusual sounds.

Once or twice, he glanced over at McGee. The wiry frontiersman's eyes, under the low-crowned hat brim, were darting here and there, his concentration never wavering from the terrain around them.

"Whoa!" Mac's quiet command also brought Russ and Plato up short. Mac pointed to a clump of trees about a hundred yards distant. A flock of crows had been startled into flight, and they flapped away, cawing raucously. "Don't know what scared 'em, but let's bend around to the south. Stay well into the open that way."

Norwood nodded and urged Plato forward. The mournful cawing of the crows gave the late afternoon an even gloomier and lonelier aspect. Unnoticed, the sky had become overcast and the air sultry. Norwood reached for his watch and then remembered he had left it behind. He estimated the time at somewhere close to six o'clock, and his stomach was grumbling. He began looking for a potential camp site. The thick clump of trees gradually passed to their right, nearly out of effective rifle range.

Their vigilance never relaxed. Finally, a light breeze into their faces brought the fresh smell of rain.

"Might be a good time to camp while there's still light enough to see, and before the rain starts," Russ suggested.

"Probably ought to go for some high ground," Mac answered.

A quarter mile farther, they found what they were looking for. It was not on a skyline, but was on a small level spot along a hillside. The spot had no running water, but there was plenty of grass and several sheltering trees. With the water in two extra canteens, the mules could be watered enough to get them by.

"Think it's safe to make a fire?" Mac asked as he dismounted.

"Yes. Even after dark, it should be okay, if we keep it sheltered. The breeze is upslope, so nobody will smell the smoke unless they're above us."

The mules were unsaddled and hobbled. While Norwood watered them from his hat, McGee gathered brush and some pieces of dead mesquite for a small cooking fire. There were plenty of loose rocks lying around to make a fire ring.

The long summer twilight was closing down quicker than usual as dark clouds massed in the west. Thunder was rumbling by the time McGee struck a wooden match to the twigs and dry grass, and a cheery flame began to blaze up. He set a frying pan over the tiny fire so the flames got air between the stones but were hardly visible fifteen feet away.

Norwood took his carbine and walked away from the fire about fifty paces then made a slow circuit completely around the camp site, listening, looking, and sniffing the air. Finally satisfied, he returned, propped the rifle against a tree, took off his hat, and hunkered down near the fire. A delicious aroma began to fill the air as bacon popped and sizzled in the pan.

"How much farther do you reckon this town is?" Mac asked, pouring some water into the coffee pot.

"Not much telling. We've probably traveled thirty-five to forty miles today, but a lot of that was up and down and sideways. This map is pretty vague. Even if we don't hit the town directly, we should cross the valley at right angles and be able to find it."

"Surely we'll be in there by noon tomorrow."

"I'd guess so, if we get an early start."

A flash of lightning lit up the darkening sky.

"We'd better get a move on with supper, or we're going to get wet."

"Coffee'll be ready in less than five minutes."

Thunder rumbled closer. Just then Plato raised his head, curled back his upper lip, and brayed loudly. Startled, Norwood reached for his Colt. Another flash of lightning revealed the forms of several Apaches standing no more than a dozen paces from them, carbines leveled.

"Ahh!" Norwood jumped, involuntarily, cold chills sweeping over his whole body. He looked quickly around him and saw movements of others in the dim light.

One of the Indians said something and immediately Norwood heard the loud clicking of several hammers being drawn to full cock.

"Holy shit!" McGee breathed.

Even in his sudden panic, Norwood tensed to throw himself to the ground a second before they fired. But they didn't fire. For several heartbeats he stood there, unmoving, his hand on the butt of his gun, wondering why he didn't hear the crashing of gunfire and feel hot lead slugs slamming into his body. But then his mind began to function again, and he realized the Apaches were holding their fire because they had formed a rough circle around the camp site and would be firing at each other. He let go of the pistol grip and brought his hands to shoulder height.

The Apaches advanced, holding their carbines at waist level, and motioned the two white men to move toward the oak tree where Norwood had propped his rifle. The Marlin was gone; one of the Indians was holding it. Norwood noted that all five of the Indians were carrying single-shot Springfields.

An Indian spoke to another and then yanked the frying pan of burning bacon off the fire. He threw the rest of the extra brush that McGee had piled on the ground onto the fire, knocking over the coffee pot. The dry brush caught and flared up, revealing the faces of their captors, all adult males. Norwood recognized two of the faces from the reservation at San Carlos, but he didn't know their names. All five were painted for war — a single yellow stripe across the bridge of the nose and the cheekbones. A raiding party. Loot and revenge was what they were after. The firelight, wavering in the rising wind, highlighted the broad faces, and Norwood thought he had never seen such hate and cruelty. The hostiles wore various items of white man's garb. One had on a white shirt, another a vest over a bare torso. Yet all had on the traditional loin cloths, two wore the high desert moccasins, and each man's shoulder-length black hair was bound with a colorful strip of cloth around the head.

Norwood absorbed all this at a glance. He knew that he and McGee had only seconds to live. These Apaches were all business. They would kill without a thought and steal anything they wanted. Maybe the two whites hadn't been shot immediately because the Apaches were going to take their time to enjoy a little torture.

Damn the luck! And he and Mac had been so careful! About the only other precaution they could have taken was to travel at night. But that would have been extremely difficult at best. In any case, it was too late now.

The Apaches were talking among themselves as they rifled

the saddlebags and began saddling the mules.

"What's up?" Russ whispered to Mac.

"One of them was saying that your mule would feed the whole camp with fresh meat. The other said these mules would be used for riding."

"They're going to kill us," Russ whispered. He could barely keep from trembling as the shock of sudden fright began to wear off, and he realized their predicament.

A brilliant flash of lightning lit up the sky, and a crash of thunder immediately followed, causing the mules to jump and jerk away from their restraining ropes. Plato pitched off his loose saddle. Three of the Indians were yelling something to each other and trying to get the animals under control. The sparks of the dying brush fire were scattering in the wind.

"We've got to try something, or we're dead," Mac mumbled out of the side of his mouth. The two Indians guarding them were distracted by the oncoming storm and their companions' problems.

"I'm going to act crazy," Mac whispered. "They won't hurt a crazy man. When I get their attention, make a break for it."

He didn't wait for an answer. A bolt of lightning struck a tall palm tree some twenty yards away with a sizzling crackle, and McGee pitched himself onto the ground, screaming. But the high-pitched wail was lost in the ground-shaking boom of thunder that burst around them. The startled Indians apparently thought McGee had been struck by the bolt. Yet he continued to wail and shout gibberish. The camp was almost totally dark.

The next starkly white flash revealed a bearded man, rolling on the ground, wild eyed, tearing at his clothes and foaming at the mouth. The two Indians with the carbines backed off several quick steps at this appalling sight.

When the lightning blinked out, momentarily blinding the human eye, Norwood was gone. He ran like he had never run before. A frightened deer would have been pressed to keep up with him as he leapt and bounded down the hillside, sliding and tripping in the dark, bushes and cactus spines ripping at his clothing and legs. A flash of lightning gave him a quick look at the brushy hillside, and he imprinted the scene on his mind's eye, darting and dashing confidently for several seconds after blackness reclaimed it.

A solid curtain of rain swept over him, the wind-driven drops stinging his face. He thought once he heard a rifle shot but couldn't be sure over the dull roar of rain pounding on the hard earth, the thunder, and his own harsh breathing. His whole mind and effort were focused on escape — getting away at any cost.

Suddenly there was nothing under his running feet and, for a half second, he felt the sickening sensation of falling as he pitched forward in the blackness. He struck hard on his right forearm and somersaulted into water. He caught his breath as head and shoulders went under, and water was forced up his nose. Floundering to his feet in the knee-deep creek, he groaned aloud from the sickening pain in his arm where he had hit the ground.

Gasping, he staggered to the opposite bank and, grasping the bushes, pulled himself out with one hand. He would have to slow down and start picking his way. Running in a blind panic was almost as likely to kill him as any pursuing Indian. He felt his forearm. Nothing broken. The intense pain was ebbing.

Thank God for the rain! he thought. That and darkness would cover his flight better than anything. The storm continued unabated as he attacked the unseen slope, wet moccasins slipping and sliding in the mud. He was on the lee side of a hill so the wind seemed to have died, but the heavy rain still fell in torrents.

As he swung his right arm at his side, it bumped something on his hip. He paused, put his hand to his belt, and felt the butt of his Colt! He couldn't believe it — he still had his gun! Unbelievable good fortune. The Indians, in all the confusion, had not disarmed him. Since the Apaches had been in control and about to kill them, maybe they hadn't thought it necessary for the moment. Surely they had seen that he was armed.

He checked the weapon for damage. Except for being wet, it was in perfect working order. By some miracle it had gotten jammed into the deep holster, and the wet leather had gripped it tightly enough to keep it from falling out. The loops in his canvas cartridge belt were full as well. This changed the situation somewhat. Instead of running from these armed savages like a frightened jackrabbit, he now had the means to do some damage himself.

He took a deep breath and tried to slow his wildly beating heart. He went to one knee next to a big mesquite bush and looked back. A few seconds later a lightning flash gave him a glimpse of the terrain. In the brief flare of light, he was unable to pick out the camp site on the opposite hillside. But neither did he see any movement of pursuit.

He gave himself several more seconds to get his breath and then went on up the slope, over the top of the ridge, and started down the other side. He had only a general idea in what direction he was going. The wind was blowing in his face now, and the storm had come up from the west, so he assumed he was bearing westward. He had no illusions that he was safe from pursuit. The Indians had an almost supernatural bond with the land and everything on it. If they had a mind to come after him, nothing would discourage them — not

135

weather, not darkness. It was just a matter of how badly they wanted him. With any luck, they were interested in the mules and guns and would entertain themselves with torture and murder only if it was convenient. What had they done to poor McGee? The little man had risked his life to give him a chance. McGee had probably been gunned down as soon as they discovered Norwood was gone. But he had heard only what he thought was one rifle shot.

His mind revolved back to his own plight. He had to be careful he didn't travel in a big circle, so he slowed to a walk and anticipated the lightning flashes. Each time one came, he took a quick reading on a tall tree, or some jutting ledge of rock, or a notch in the next ridge top and plodded toward it. The next flash would reveal if he was still on course. The weight of his Colt on his hip was a comfort he never expected to have. It served to calm some of the terror of what he could only assume were pursuing Apaches.

When his labored breathing and his heart rate had slowed somewhat, he started jogging, unmindful of the cuts and bruises and cactus barbs that had not yet really begun to hurt. Time lost its meaning. He didn't know if he had been fleeing for twenty minutes or an hour. It was all one blur of fear and physical exertion. Could he finally afford to relax — to fall down under a bush in the pouring rain and rest? Exhausted as he was, the fear and uncertainty drove him onward. In the less frequent lightning flashes, the terrain was becoming more broken. His recently infected thigh was aching which caused him unconsciously to seek the trail of least resistance. And this trail led downward. Unless he wanted to climb over one of two steep hills, it was the cañon down the middle or nothing. His way into that yawning black crevice led diagonally down across a slope covered with brush and cactus.

The way the rain was sluicing down, he didn't think there

was an Indian alive who could track him, once daylight came. Yet, there was a seed of doubt. Their own Apache scouts had done some trailing after rain storms that was nothing short of magical. *Never underestimate the enemy,* he thought, trudging grimly ahead.

Just as he expected, when he reached the bottom, he could hear a small stream rushing along. He guessed it was flowing directly into the mouth of the cañon. He turned to parallel it, thinking that it probably carried little or no water during the dry season, but now it was gathering the runoff from the surrounding hills and, no doubt, was rising. How fast he couldn't tell. If luck stayed with him, he could traverse the narrow cañon before the water got too high.

He wiped the rain from his eyes and turned to scan the darkness of his backtrail before he dropped down the last incline to the stream bank. A wavering flash lit up the sky between the two hills. He froze and his heart nearly leapt into his throat. A human figure was coming at a fast trot down the hillside through the cactus and brush a quarter mile behind him. Before the light flickered out, he knew from the long black hair that it was not Stratford McGee.

Chapter Eleven

The sudden surge of fear lent him a reserve of strength he didn't know he had. Following his first instinct, he ran down the slope and, moving carefully in the dark, found and slid over the lip of the four foot dropoff that landed him on the gravel bank of the stream. He started toward the cañon but, after a few steps, paused. Had the Indian spotted him? Or was he just pursuing in the same general direction? The Apache had to have caught sight of him at some point. Otherwise, he would have not continued so blind a chase for so long. *Do I stand and fight it out, or try to slip away unseen and take on the unknown dangers of that cañon?* He hesitated, knowing he had only a minute or two to decide. *Why not do both?* He yanked his Colt, shook and blew the excess water out of it. Then he flipped open the loading gate, slipped a cartridge from his belt, and loaded the sixth chamber on which the hammer had been resting.

The rain was still falling steadily, but the lightning was now less frequent. Without the aid of nature's illumination, he would have no idea where his pursuer was. But that worked both ways; the Apache wouldn't be able to spot him either. He leaned up against the muddy embankment, propping his elbows on the grassy lip and holding his gun. He began to count. After thirty-four long seconds, a flicker of lightning penetrated the blackness but only for the space of a short breath. His eyes picked up no movement. He fidgeted. *How long should I wait?* The Apache very likely didn't know he had been spotted. *Even if he did, was he aware that I am armed?* He strained his eyes but could not penetrate the sooty blackness along his backtrail. He cocked the Colt and waited nervously, all senses on edge. He could hear nothing but the falling rain and the soft rushing of the rising stream behind him.

He had almost made up his mind to start into the cañon before the rising water got high enough to cover both banks of the stream, leaving him nowhere to walk. In fact, where the stream was pinched between those vertical walls, it may have already done just that. His ears picked up the click of one stone against another. He whirled just in time to catch the sound of something scuffing against gravel. He held the Colt at waist level, aiming toward the sounds, and squeezed the trigger. It went off with a blast of flame and smoke. In the muzzle flash he caught a quick glimpse of the Indian's form, still more than twenty paces up the creek bank. He knew from the angle he was holding the gun that he had fired too soon and missed. He swore and fired again, then dove to the ground. Two shots answered him. It was either his own rifle or Mac's Remington, since the Indians' carbines were all single-shots.

It was time to move. He cocked and fired once more, then scuttled away toward the mouth of the cañon. He took quick, short steps to keep his balance on the uneven and unseen gravel and sand bank. He knew he was getting closer to the cañon mouth when he began to hear a hollow echo of the rushing water. The explosion of another shot sounded behind him, but he knew he had opened the distance. The Indian hadn't seen him move but must have heard him. Maybe the Apache was being cautious and didn't want to run into another ambush. He was counting on it. He had given the Indian something to think about, and now it was time to disappear, to shake his pursuer for good.

Just as this thought crossed his mind, he stubbed his toe

hard against a rock and went pitching headlong, banging both shins. He rolled over at the edge of the water in excruciating pain. He felt as if his big toe, in the soft, wet moccasins, was broken. He limped to his feet and kept going, jamming his pistol deeply into the holster, and fumbling to get the rawhide safety loop over the hammer. It wouldn't do to lose his gun now.

He felt, rather than saw, the nearly vertical walls close about him as he entered the rocky defile. The roar of the water was much louder, echoing and drowning out all other sounds. He was forced to slow down and pick his way over and around a huge jumble of limestone boulders. Apparently part of the cañon wall had collapsed sometime past, nearly blocking the passage of the stream. The water was high here and dangerous. Over the rush of the current, he could hear rocks that were being carried with the silt, grinding along the bottom, scouring the cañon ever deeper. He didn't dare try to swim it. He had to go up and over.

A quick flash of lightning gave him an idea of what he was up against. The pile of boulders extended at least eighty to a hundred feet up the cañon wall on this side. The vertical wall dropped straight into the rushing torrent on the other side. After ten minutes of this arduous climb, his breath was rasping harshly in his throat. But he was making progress as nearly as he could tell.

A wavering flicker of lightning illuminated the cañon for a few seconds in an eerie light. Just as it faded, a gunshot boomed behind him, and a slug ricocheted off rock below his feet. When he jerked his gun and turned to fire back, all was blackness again.

Persistent bastard, he thought, saving his shot. *I'm exposed like a fly on a wall*, he gritted to himself as he took the time to slide down behind a huge boulder and reload the three cartridges he had fired.

Then, praying there would not be another flash soon, he scrambled out and continued his dark struggle over the jumbled rockfall. As he felt his way along, he wondered how many hours were left until daylight. He had lost all concept of time. He guessed it was not even midnight yet. His fear had ebbed with his fatigue. Once or twice he seriously considered stopping and waiting for his pursuer. *If that Apache is foolish enough to keep coming after me in this situation, maybe I should really discourage him!* he thought. But he had failed to discourage him earlier. Why would it be any different now? No, he would continue fighting a running battle. *Make this Apache work for it,* he thought grimly. The problem was, he didn't know how much longer his strength was going to hold out. The spider bite in his thigh was beginning to ache fearfully again with the steep climbing and constant jarring and strain. He had only nibbled on some jerky since breakfast early that morning. He had spent nine hours in the saddle and then had run for no telling how far in a driving rain, up and down hills.

He paused for a moment, gasping, and leaned his head back against a rock, eyes closed and mouth open to the slanting rain. Finally, he pulled himself up, took a deep breath and braced to start again. After all, was this any way for one of General Miles's selected one hundred white men to act? *Pompous old bastard,* he thought with a grim smile. *Wonder how he would handle this? Would he be tougher than this Apache adversary? Huh! He'd have been gunned down at the camp site.*

With that thought, he moved on, now beginning to feel all the bruises and scrapes and prickly pear spines. From the stinging and the raw spots, he felt sure he was bleeding in at least twenty places, if he could have seen them. But, worst of all, a bone-deep weariness was beginning to drag on him. It was as if someone had pulled a plug, and his strength and energy were draining out. He continued on, picking his way around and among the huge slabs of broken limestone.

Gradually he felt himself going downward again. He had finally crested the gigantic rockfall and was climbing down the other side. When he reached the bottom once more, he found himself in an even more frightening position next to the stream that was ripping and rushing along, the roar of its swollen passage drowning his senses. It was like a live serpent, whipping from side to side, as if trying to escape the constriction of the monstrous rock walls.

For a few minutes he was able to find a sand and gravel bar to walk along until he came to a point where the water was over the bar. The current here was swinging to the opposite side in a bend, and the water was almost slack. He waded along, feeling the wall, the water coming up to his knees, then higher. He felt the sand collapsing under his feet and instinctively reached for some handhold on the wall. He gripped a bush but, as his feet slipped, his weight tore the small plant out by the roots. He floundered upright again, the water now to his armpits and beginning to pull at him. He reached desperately in the dark, and his hands encountered some roots clinging to the seamed rock face. There he hung, panting, his strength fading. He called up some reserve and got his feet under him. A renewed downpour of rain pelted his upturned face. Another bolt of lightning cracked, followed by a crash of thunder, reverberating from the cañon walls.

Because of the thunder, he didn't hear the shot but flying rock chips stung his bare arms. He still didn't realize it was a bullet until the second shot came. This one, fired in the dark, was not as close and went whining off the rock above his head.

Well, this is it, Russ, old boy! he resolved with clenched teeth. In a sudden concentration of effort, he pulled himself up high enough to swing one leg out of the water and wedge his toe into a crevice. He paused, gasping, for a couple of seconds then reached one hand higher and gripped another spot on the smooth, water-worn root. He recognized the feel of a fig tree root. This tenacious plant had been here for years; it wasn't going to tear loose now. He pushed off with his foot and was able to lift his other leg clear of the water. His water-soaked moccasin slipped, and he banged his cheek bone against the hard surface, but he did not slacken his grip. He pulled again, reaching higher with his hand and then, like some awkward monkey, got both feet wedged into the serrated rock face where he clung, breathing heavily. His strength was about gone, but a flicker of lightning revealed a wedge of blackness just above him that was either a ledge or a small cave. With the strength born of desperation, he clawed his way slowly up to it. One last heave and he rolled himself into the slanting cave.

It was a good five minutes before his breathing returned to normal. The crack in the wall was just over six feet long and probably no more than two feet deep. But it was just enough to shelter him and give him a place to rest. Even in the lightning, he could not be seen here. He would just wait for the Indian to get discouraged and give up. Then he would rest and wait for the water to go down before climbing out and going for help in the morning. Now he could relax, but he would stay awake and watch, and listen. However, his strength was gone and, in spite of his resolve, he was asleep within a few minutes, lying face down on the bare rock.

When he awoke sometime later, he was disoriented for a few seconds, not remembering where he was. Then he realized, with a rush of terror, what had awakened him. Water was lapping into his cave. The stream had swelled into a gigantic river. A continuous roar filled his ears, stunning him into inaction. He was trapped. He was able to push up onto his elbows before his head contacted the roof of the crack. During the minute or two he pondered his situation, the water rose another four or five inches. He knew his only chance was to swim for it. Still he hesitated. The water rose higher. The current was running completely over him now. He felt to make sure his gun was securely fastened. Then he took a deep breath, turned his back to the stream, doubled his knees, and pushed hard against the back of the cave, catapulting his body backward into the maelstrom.

He had kicked clear of the rock wall, and he gasped at the force of the current that gripped him. Of one thing he felt very sure — the water was so deep he was safe from the rocks and boulders that were being swept along. Once in the current, his movement almost seemed to stop, as he was traveling the same speed as the water. In spite of the danger, he felt a thrill he had never known before. This was the ride of his life! *And it may be the ride of my death,* he thought as a flash of lightning revealed the steep rock walls rushing past. He turned to float on his back, his feet downstream. If he hit any rocks, at least it wouldn't be head first.

How long he was propelled along at great speed, he didn't know. But finally the roar seemed to die down slightly, and he realized that there was no echo. He had passed beyond the high walls. The current seemed to be slowing as the river spread out. He drifted along for a time, stroking to keep himself afloat as the force of the current subsided. He could still see nothing in the blackness but finally felt he was far enough out onto more level land to begin swimming slowly toward the left bank.

Eventually his feet touched a rough bottom, and he staggered erect, wading slowly up and out of the water. His arms and legs felt as if they weighed a hundred pounds each. Having no idea where he was or where he was going, he slogged along, tripping over rocks and brush, until he estimated he had gone more than half a mile. Then he dropped to his hands and knees, felt around for a soft, muddy spot, and lay down, losing consciousness almost immediately.

Chapter Twelve

He was on fire. As consciousness slowly returned to him, Norwood was aware of being hotter than he had ever been before. *Maybe this was hell.* His mouth was dry and his lips swollen. He tried to move his limbs, but he hurt everywhere. He felt like a piece of steak that had been pounded and thrown into a frying pan.

He lay face down in the sand a few more seconds, trying to gather his strength and to think. It were as if he had been drugged. His eyes were gritty as he forced the lids open a crack and squinted at his surroundings without moving his head from the sandy soil. Rough ground, rocks, the trailing limbs of a mesquite bush and, farther away, a yucca plant. With a groan, he got his heavy arms under him and somehow forced himself to a sitting position, where he paused to let a wave of dizziness pass.

"Conchita! *¡Un hombre! ¡Ven acá!*" a high-pitched feminine voice called from somewhere behind him.

He had to turn his whole body to see from where the sound came. The movement caused his head to throb. Shimmering heat waves danced in front of him as a brassy sun pounded the top of his skull and grilled the eye-piercing desert around him. He could vaguely make out the nebulous forms of two brightly-colored long dresses coming toward him. Then the world tilted crazily, and the ground smacked him in the mouth as blackness engulfed him again.

The next thing he knew a wet cloth was being applied to his face by the gentlest of hands. He was somewhere out of that blazing sun. He opened his eyes, and a face swam into focus. He licked his lips and tried to speak, but only a harsh croak came out.

"Here, *señor*, drink this."

An apparition gently cradled his head with one hand while she tipped a cup of something to his lips with the other. He swallowed a little, choked and coughed. Clear, fiery mescal burned its way down his throat. He turned his head away.

"*¡No mas! ¡No mas!*" he managed to gasp.

"I thought that would probably bring you around," the woman said in almost unaccented English. The voice sounded somehow familiar. "Now you must drink some water," she continued, pouring some into a tin cup from an earthen pitcher on a side table. How did she know the sun had sucked all the juices out of him, and he felt as dry as a piece of parchment? He accepted her offer and greedily sucked down the water, handing the empty cup back for more. She refilled it twice more, and he tilted it back, looking up at the rough-hewn beams holding up a whitewashed ceiling.

"*Gracias,*" he finally gasped, wiping his mouth with the back of his hand.

She reached around and helped him to a sitting position on the narrow wooden bed. He felt a straw tick under him as he held onto her arm to steady himself. Again he looked directly into her eyes, this time with his wits about him. The shock was immediate. It was Elena Maria Calderón!

"Where? How . . . ?" he started.

"You are one of the men who came to see my uncle with the doctor," she nodded, pulling up a chair and sitting beside his bed. "I thought that it was you . . . *Señor* Norwood . . . correct?"

"Yes. Russ Norwood."

"I would have recognized you in a moment, but something

147

has done terrible things to that handsome face since we last met."

At these words the pain in his body receded to tolerable levels. He opened his mouth to speak, but she held up her hand.

"No. First I will speak, and you will listen."

The brown face of a stout, middle-aged woman appeared at the door of the small room. Elena turned to address her.

"He is awake. Prepare the water." The head nodded and disappeared. "Now, as I was about to say, I will answer as many of your questions as I can. Then I will hear your story. Oh, do you feel well enough to sit up while we talk? You can lie back if you wish."

Sitting up with one leg over the edge of the bed, he could gaze on her lovely features. This was enough healing balm for the moment.

"You are at a fortified ranch," she continued. "It is about thirty miles from the town of Sahuaripa and about forty miles from Oposura where I live. I came here to visit two aunts, an uncle, and several of my cousins. These ranch buildings have walls around them as protection against Indians. I come here about two or three times a year to visit my relatives. I once lived here myself, but I was chosen to go to Oposura to take care of my elderly uncle, and to help the nuns care for the church."

The air in the windowless room was somewhat close, and Russ licked his lips, hoping Elena would offer him another cup of water, but he didn't interrupt her.

"Two of the women who live here, Rosa and Conchita, were going to the river for water and found you lying out there in the sun. I do not know how long you had been there."

"What time is it?" he asked.

"Late afternoon. Past five. You were not conscious for at

least two hours after we carried you in here."

He nodded. "I went to sleep there sometime in the night. It was raining and the river was in flash flood."

"The sun has burned you all day."

The stout Mexican woman reappeared at the door and said something in Spanish.

"The water is ready for you to bathe," Elena announced.

Russ slid off the bed and stood up, swaying slightly.

"Which way?"

"I will have to help you," Elena said, slipping her arm around his waist. "Lean on me."

"I can walk," he said, his desire to be close to her vying with his pride at appearing weak and helpless.

"As you wish," she said withdrawing, but eyeing him carefully in case he should fall. "Follow me."

He followed her slowly out of the room, every step painful. The cuts and bruises had stiffened his legs and back, and the cactus spines were stinging him everywhere as he moved. A large metal washtub had been dragged into the shade in a corner of the courtyard and half filled with tepid water. A square chunk of home-made soap lay beside it.

"Roberto will help you," Elena said, indicating an elderly white-haired man with a lean, seamed face. When Norwood did not start to disrobe immediately, she said, "I'll be back in a few minutes," and disappeared into a nearby doorway.

Sand and dirt fell out of his shirt and pants as he took them off. A couple of women and a man passed across the courtyard and glanced curiously in his direction while Roberto helped him bathe. Norwood caught his breath several times as the lye soap contacted the raw cuts, but he nodded to the old man when he finally stepped out of the metal tub.

"*Gracias, señor.*"

Roberto gestured for Norwood to lie down on a blanket spread on the flagstones. Wondering; Norwood complied, and Roberto spread a coarse towel over his posterior. Suddenly Elena was back along with the stout woman who had helped prepare his bath.

"What now?" Russ asked over his shoulder when he saw them approach.

"You cannot walk around with that *glochidia.*"

"That what?"

"The spines of the prickly pear cactus. You have so many in your legs, they seem to be growing out of you." Russ thought he detected a trace of a smile at the corners of her mouth.

The next hour felt to him as if he were besieged by devils who proceeded to torture him with a thousand red-hot needles as Elena, Roberto, and the older woman extracted the barbed cactus spines from his body, one or two at a time. It finally blurred into one long, searing pain. He thought ruefully of how he and Perry Babcock had laughed at Captain Lawton.

When they eventually finished, he rose from the blanket, burning, hardly aware of the fact that he was naked, and reached for his clothes. Roberto and the older woman had disappeared.

"Put these on," Elena said, handing him a pair of canvas pants and a cotton shirt. "Your clothes are being washed and sewn. They were in shreds."

"*Gracias.*"

He turned his back to dress, but he was very conscious of her presence. He felt foolish for being embarrassed in front of her. Unlike other young women of good Mexican or Spanish families, she had apparently not been reared in the strict code of modesty. More likely, she had abandoned it in the face of practicality, he thought, as he slipped the borrowed shirt over his head and found it a bit snug in the shoulders. The pants were about right.

"I see that you are larger than my cousin, Rafael," Elena

commented as he turned to face her. She cast what he thought to be an approving eye on his broad expanse of muscular chest where the shirt could not be drawn together with the rawhide laces.

"The clothes are fine. *Gracias*," he murmured. Then, with a sudden remembrance, he said, "Where's my gun?"

"It was full of dirt also. One of the men is cleaning and oiling it. You'll have it back shortly. A very beautiful weapon, *señor*. Of the latest design . . . nickel plated, ivory grips." She smiled. "Two of my younger nephews were fighting over who would get to clean it. But I gave it to their father."

"Are guns like that unusual here?"

"I myself have a pistol, but most of the guns here are *muy viejo* . . . very old muskets, most of them brought from your country after your Civil War for use by revolutionaries."

"I see." He nodded and smiled.

"It is probably better that we do not have many modern arms," she continued. "Cartridges are very expensive and difficult to obtain. Powder and lead bars for shot can be bought in bulk. And caps are easier to get." She paused and eyed him critically. "How do you feel?"

"I'm very sore but much better, thanks."

"I'm sorry we have no carbolic to disinfect those many small wounds. I'll give you a bottle of mescal if you want to use that later."

"*Gracias.*"

"The evening meal will be served in about an hour. Do you feel well enough to take a walk? The air is beginning to cool a little."

Russ thought that, if both his legs had been broken, he could not have refused this invitation.

"I would like to show you this place," she said, adjusting her pace to accommodate his painful gait. "The old ones tell

151

us that this ranch was started more than a hundred and sixty years ago. Our ancestors chose well. It is in a fertile little valley with enough wood and plenty of water. Volcanic stone was plentiful and used to construct both the original buildings and the ones that were added later. Parts of the wall are the original, I believe, on the south and east. The remainder has been enlarged and added to."

"Apaches were a threat even then?" he asked, indicating the fifteen-foot walls.

"The story that has been told to me was that my Spanish ancestors enslaved a large number of Apaches. They were the ones who were forced to build this fortress."

"If the Apaches were their slaves, then who were they trying to wall out?" he asked.

"Other bands of Apaches, the Yaqui tribes, *bandidos*. This was a very wild, isolated land in those days, *Señor* Norwood."

He started to add that it still was but thought better of it and held his tongue. Instead, he said, "Why would anyone choose to live so far from other people and from villages and towns?"

"Perhaps for the same reasons that your mountain men and ranchers do in *los Estados Unidos,*" she shrugged. "I cannot say."

"How many people live here now?"

"About fifty."

"Were you born here?"

"Yes. But when I was just a young girl, my parents sent me to live with an aunt and uncle in Mexico City. They had more money and chose to send me to a convent school in your country. Saint Teresa of Avila in Tucson."

"Ah, so that accounts for your excellent command of English."

She smiled at the compliment. "I was not considered a brilliant student, but I was eager to learn all I could. I took good advantage of the three years I spent there."

"And then you came back here?"

"Yes, by way of Mexico City. By that time, my father had died . . . killed in a raid by Apaches." She paused, the sad memory sending a fleeting shadow across her face. "He was caught working in the fields one day. Shot before he could reach the safety of these walls."

"I'm sorry."

"*Gracias,* but that was five years ago. My mother is still alive."

"Do all of your relatives live here?"

"Oh, no. I have an Aunt Consuela up north in Fronteras, but I don't see her very often. She married the prefect there . . . a man named Juan Vargas. I have no use for him. He is fat and pompous. When I visit there, he looks at me like . . . like a married man should not look at another woman." Her face clouded.

He nodded and changed the subject. "How does everyone here at the *rancho* survive?"

"Farming. They grow beans and melons and corn. There are wild berries to be gathered in season in the surrounding hills. These are made into jams. They raise a few cattle and sheep for food, wool, leather. They are kept busy making most of what they need."

As she spoke, she was leading him up a stone stairway built against the inside of one wall. He followed slowly, every step a painful reminder of his ordeal.

"Anyway, my mother decided, about two years ago, that I should go and work as a housekeeper for my great uncle, *Padre* Juan Miguel, at Oposura. It is not a large town, but she felt that my chances for meeting 'some nice young man,' as she put it, would be better there." She smiled. "Actually, I was more impressed by the quality and life of the nuns there than I was by the available young men."

She paused at the top where a walkway was built along a parapet, affording an unobstructed view on all sides of the compound. Two men in loose fitting light cotton clothes and large straw hats paced slowly along the walkway, carrying long percussion muskets. A third sentry lounged near the southeast corner of the wall, smoking a corn husk cigarette.

"We must keep a constant guard," Elena was saying. "See . . . what a beautiful view from here!"

Indeed it was. Norwood could even see the river in the distance. He could hardly believe it was the same stream, so far had the water receded in less than twenty-four hours. The sun was down behind the hills, but the sky was still a light blue. It was light enough for him to see three women carrying water jugs on their heads as they made their way slowly back from the river. A short distance from the south wall a mule, harnessed to a long pole, was plodding in a circle. A flat stone, dragging from the pole, was grinding corn on a stone pathway. A man stood to one side, shoveling corn onto the smooth stones.

He could not help feeling that he had stepped back in history at least a thousand years. The place was primitive in the extreme, even to the tiny door in the wall that was only large enough to admit one horse at a time. He might almost have been looking at some walled city in Biblical times.

"How is this ranch governed?" he asked, taking in the view.

"Oh, there is a *patrón*. You will meet him. I am not related to him, but he is a kind old man . . . Diego Sanchez." She turned to face him, leaning against the parapet. "Before we go to dinner, please tell me your story. What happened to bring you in such a condition to our doorstep?"

He briefly told the story of what had happened. As he talked, her gaze never left his face. When he finished, she drew a deep breath and exhaled.

"*Señor* Norwood, your guardian angel has been working very

154

hard. Maybe it is time to give him a rest."

"Perhaps I should, at that," he smiled. "You need a job?"

It was her turn to smile. "I don't believe I qualify."

He grinned, and even his face hurt. He automatically put a hand to his bruised cheekbone, trying to remember how that particular abrasion had occurred. Just then a clanging interrupted them from the courtyard below. He jumped and reached instinctively for the gun he didn't have.

"Time for dinner," Elena said. "Are you hungry?"

Just the thought of food made his stomach growl. "Starving," he answered truthfully. "I haven't eaten anything since early yesterday."

She eyed him critically. "You don't appear to have eaten very well at all since we last met."

"It's been a hard campaign. I guess I have lost some weight," he admitted as he followed her toward the stone steps. "But short rations have killed fewer men than gluttony."

She stopped and turned on the steps to look him in the face. "You are a most unusual man, *Señor* Norwood."

He was somewhat taken aback at this but didn't reply as the smell of fried onions drifted up from below and his stomach rumbled in response.

The meal, by comparison to his recent diet, was sumptuous — beef enchiladas seasoned with chili peppers, side dishes of corn and fresh tomatoes, and a homemade beer of some sort. But, before anyone took a bite, Diego Sanchez, the white-haired *patrón*, with a face weathered like old leather, intoned a blessing in Spanish from the head of the long table. Then, in English, he welcomed Russ Norwood to "our humble hospitality."

"*Gracias, señor,*" Russ inclined his head toward the old man to acknowledge the greeting. He was conscious of the curious stares from the half a hundred men, women, and children seated at both sides of the long wooden refectory table. He could

155

feel his face reddening under this scrutiny but hoped it wasn't too obvious behind several days' growth of stubble and the thick mustache. He kept his eyes downcast until he heard the general clatter of tableware and the hum of voices as platters and bowls were being passed. He was glad to see the food was plentiful. He hoped they were not splurging on his behalf.

"You are the most exciting event to happen here in some time," Elena whispered to him as she helped herself to some enchiladas in tomato sauce and then handed him the earthenware platter.

"You must not have many visitors," he answered quietly.

"Not too many who are welcome."

He thought again of some ancient, fortified town, walled against the barbarians without as the inhabitants sat down to eat in a banquet hall at the feet of their feudal lord. He had the oddest feeling he had emerged from that terrifying cañon into medieval Europe. He quickly shook off that feeling and settled down to do justice to the meal.

Afterward, pleasantly stuffed, he was introduced personally to the *patrón* by Elena. The old man was gracious but questioned him closely about where he had come from and the American forces in the region. Norwood, in turn, asked if the ranch had been attacked by hostiles recently. The ranch had not been bothered, Sanchez told him, but two mules and a cow had been stolen a few days previously. He was almost certain it had been Apaches, even though his people had not seen them. One of the livestock guards had become careless, he said. In parting, Sanchez told him he was welcome to stay as long as he desired.

Norwood thanked him and then was ushered outdoors into the spacious courtyard by Elena. The courtyard was completely dark. Stars shone overhead.

"Maybe it won't rain again tonight," he said, mostly to break

156

the silence. There was no awkwardness. It was amazing how comfortable he felt with her.

"Perhaps," she replied, "but this is the season for rain. We must expect it at any time."

"I'm thankful for the rain and the flash flood last night. It probably saved my life." *Was that really only last night?* Already it seemed like days ago.

"Why would that Apache want to kill you so badly?" she asked.

"I can only guess. Maybe it was his pride. I'm sure they are not used to white men escaping from them. Or perhaps he thought I went to bring help or maybe would ambush them, since I was still armed."

Silence intervened for several seconds as they walked slowly, aimlessly, in the cooling night air.

"Anyway, I'm happy that God delivered you into our safe-keeping here." She paused. "Do you believe in Divine Providence, *Señor* Norwood?"

The question took him by surprise. "I . . . yes, I suppose I do. But I made one helluva effort myself."

"I never questioned your heroic effort," she said, "but the outcome could have been much different."

He thought of the bullets that had missed him in the dark, the ledge that happened to be just where he could reach it, the gun that had not been taken from him, the high water that allowed him to be swept out of the cañon to safety. "Yes, it could have been *very* much different," he admitted and paused. "I wonder if Divine Providence took care of Stratford McGee?"

"Your friend?"

"Yes. He's probably dead by now."

"You must not question the wisdom of God. If it is His will that your friend die, then he will die."

"I just hope they killed him quickly. I hate to think what

they could have put him through before he died. And it was his quick thinking that allowed me to get away."

Apparently the anguish in his voice triggered a softer response in Elena. She placed her hand on his arm in the dark. "I'm sorry." She started to add something but stopped.

"You know," he said, changing the subject, "I'm tired. I can't believe I want to go to sleep when I was unconscious most of the day."

"You will sleep in the bed where we brought you earlier."

"*Gracias.* Is there a lamp there? I think you missed a couple of those cactus stickers."

"Yes, there's a lamp. And I'll bring you that bottle of mescal to use on those cuts."

By the time she left him alone in the small room a short time later, he was yawning and his eyes were drooping. After lighting the lamp and examining his legs and hips for the translucent spines, he doused himself with the mescal, catching his breath at the stinging of the alcohol on the dozens of raw spots. Finally, he removed his shirt and lay down on the bed. But he could not sleep. After tossing and turning for almost two hours, he got up and opened the heavy door to the courtyard. Being accustomed to sleeping outside for weeks, he felt smothered indoors. The feel of the cool night air and the view of the bright stars gave him a sense of peace as he settled down in a corner of the courtyard next to a wall, with his rolled-up shirt under his head and his wool blanket under him.

He awakened next morning to the sound of roosters crowing — a peaceful country sound that took him back to his boyhood home on the edge of San Antonio. His parents had kept a few chickens for the eggs and an occasional Sunday dinner. The morning was bright but the courtyard was still in shadow. He slipped the shirt over his head and looked down at his bare feet. Someone had taken his moccasins off while he was

158

still unconscious the previous day. But most of the other people here either went barefoot or wore sandals, so he didn't feel out of place. His feet could probably use some toughening up anyway.

"Ah, you are awake early," Elena greeted him as she appeared from somewhere, looking as fresh as when he had left her the night before.

He smiled at her as he rolled up his blanket. "You get used to that when you're on the trail with Captain Lawton. We often marched by three-thirty to avoid the heat."

She glanced at the sky. "It is going to be hot again today. But first to breakfast. How are you feeling this morning? Are you still hungry? As hungry as last night? You ate as much as two men." She laughed. "That is good. Margarita was pleased that you liked her cooking."

"If you want to know the truth, I could have eaten that much of my own cooking, but tell Margarita that her cooking was like ambrosia."

"What are you talking about?" She laughed again. "Come on."

After breakfast, she gave him a razor she had managed to borrow. "You may have use for this. There is soap and a mirror in your room . . . which you didn't use last night," she said, looking at him out of the corners of her eyes.

"It's a nice room. I was just too hot. I've been sleeping outdoors for too long. Hope you didn't mind."

"No. The stones of the courtyard are very hard, but you may use them for a bed if you wish."

He left the door open for ventilation, propped up the small mirror, then poured some water from the pitcher into the bowl on the bedside table, stripped off his shirt, and lathered his face. Someone had already stropped the razor, which was fortunate since he had no belt. As he looked into the mirror, he was startled at the white eyes of the gaunt, sun-burned stranger who peered back at him. The thick mustache was growing wildly astray; reddish-blond stubble covered the flat planes of his jaw; the left cheekbone was bruised and discolored; uncut and uncombed hair was falling across his forehead.

After he had shaved, he looked a bit more human, but he could easily see why he had drawn stares from the people at dinner the night before. He leaned over the bowl and splashed water on himself, feeling cleaner and fresher.

"Now, that's the face I remember," Elena remarked from the doorway, observing him in the mirror.

He turned to look at her.

"I have your clothes," she continued, placing the folded garments on the bed. "There were even more cactus barbs in these than there were in your skin."

He noted with relief that his moccasins were also cleaned and dried.

"*Gracias*. And please thank whoever did all this for me."

"Yes. I'll bring your pistol soon. The holster and belt are still drying in the sun." With one last look at his bare torso, she left him.

He felt even better once he changed back into his own clothes which had been not only washed but expertly sewn where needed. He didn't see Elena again until she caught up with him pacing the parapet near the guards about noon.

"You'd better get out of this sun without a hat," she said after greeting him.

"Thought maybe I could spot some of the command, but I guess nobody will be looking for us this soon."

"Come and have a bite of lunch I fixed for you."

"I didn't hear the bell."

"Some do not eat at midday. But you need to get your strength."

160

He followed her down to the dining room where several of the men and women were consuming tortillas and beans. He and Elena joined them, helping themselves to the simple food.

Afterward, the rest of the workers came in from the fields, the single gate was locked and, except for the sentries, everyone passed the next two hours resting or sleeping in the shade.

The remainder of the day Russ spent with Elena. Without realizing at first he was doing it, he told her more about himself than he had revealed to anyone except Perry Babcock. She had an easy way about her that prompted trust and confidence, and the fact that he was smitten by her looks and charm did little to discourage him. He was also struck with the thought that this girl, with her black hair and fair skin, reminded him of an Irish girl he had known in Texas — Janie Flynn — except that Janie had blue eyes instead of brown. Not only were they similar in looks, but they were both somewhat independent, he guessed mostly out of necessity. Janie had supported herself after her widowed mother's death as a maid for a wealthy cattle rancher outside of San Antonio. He had courted her briefly before he left Texas. If Janie had a fault, it was that she was too self-willed and headstrong for his tastes, although he had enjoyed her flashing smile and quick wit. He had not seen her in about fourteen years. He tried to visualize her face, maybe with a few wrinkles and a gray hair or two. She was probably married now to a storekeeper or a banker. He could hardly imagine her matched up with an itinerant cowboy or a ranch hand. How many kids?

He sighed deeply. That family could have been his. Yet back then he was looking for adventure — and trying to find himself. The last thing his father had given him was the political influence that had gotten him a commission. If his father had lived, he would have been proud of his son's years of hard service on the frontier as a leader of men. But now that was all gone, leaving him with an empty ache when he thought of a life that might have been.

"Why do you look so solemn, Señor Norwood?" Elena broke into his musing.

"Oh . . . no reason. I was just thinking of times past."

"They must be sad thoughts," she commented quietly, her dark eyes searching his face.

He shifted uneasily under her scrutiny. It was almost as if she could read his mind. He forced a smile. "The past is gone. We have only the present."

Hers was an easy smile. "Then we should enjoy it."

The next day he finally felt rested, and the food had restored his strength. His cuts and bruises were healing, and he was beginning to feel impatient to rejoin his command, wherever they might be. As pleasant as he found Elena's company, he had to find out about Stratford McGee. Time was beginning to hang heavily while Elena visited her relatives.

He napped as much as he could and even went outside into the fields and offered his help to some of the men who laughed and politely refused, indicating in broken English that he was a guest and should not work. He gave up and went back inside, again trying to rest on his bed.

It was well after sunrise the next morning when a gunshot brought him out of his room, where he had begun sleeping, into the courtyard. People were running and shouting, and two men were holding the gate open for others running in from the fields.

Norwood yanked his Colt to join in the defense of the ranch. He didn't catch much of the rapid Spanish, but one shout he did recognize.

"*¡Los Apaches!*"

Chapter Thirteen

Ignoring the soreness in his legs, Norwood sprinted up the stone steps two at a time. He ran along the catwalk to the west wall of the compound, gun in hand. There was no shooting, but a babble of excited voices still carried up from below. The only shot he heard had apparently been a warning from one of the sentries. Several of the men were entering a doorway that led into a stone tower that jutted up in the center of the compound to a height of fifteen feet above the surrounding walls. Loopholes slotted the top of the circular tower every three feet or so and, as Norwood looked, musket barrels were being thrust out of these loopholes.

He peered over the stone parapet toward the horsemen approaching from the timberline two hundred yards to the west. Several of them were Indians, but Norwood couldn't be sure about the man who rode out front. He was yelling something in English, but Norwood couldn't make out the words.

A shot came from the tower, and the leader's horse shied as dust spurted up near his hoofs. The rider waved his hat and shouted something that sounded like, "I'm white! I'm white!"

The rider walked his horse forward a few more yards, signaling the Indians to stay back. As he got closer, a sudden flash of recognition came to Norwood at the sight of the lean figure.

"Perry Babcock!" he shouted.

Another warning shot boomed from the tower.

"Hold your fire! I know that man! Those are Apache scouts with him!"

Elena had materialized at his side, and she translated his words into rapid Spanish, waving at the men in the tower above and behind her.

"That's part of my command. Lieutenant Babcock," Norwood explained.

Elena raised her voice and, with many emphatic gestures, explained to the others. The elderly *patrón*, looking up from the courtyard, signaled the door to be opened.

A few minutes later Norwood was greeting his old friend as Babcock led his horse through the low gateway.

"We were beginning to wonder what had happened to you," Perry said, the relief sounding in his voice. "Where's McGee?"

"I don't know. But I'll tell you all about it in a minute. Come on in here and get acquainted with these folks. Damn, but I'm glad to see you!"

Elena remembered the tall cavalry officer and introduced him, in Spanish, to the *patrón* and the others standing around. Norwood could not help but notice the weary, trail-worn look of Babcock. His friend was dressed only in moccasins, underdrawers, and undershirt. He was unshaven, a ragged blue handkerchief was tied around his head, and he carried the remains of a campaign hat in his hand. He was not armed.

"What about my scouts?" Perry asked, glancing at Russ and Elena.

After several exchanges, with Elena translating, the *patrón* decided, with typical caution, that even though these Apaches were with the Army, they would have to stay outside.

"We won't be here long," Perry said. "Let me go out and tell them to stand down and wait."

He was back inside in a few minutes, being offered refreshments and water to wash. The gate remained barred, and no one went back outside for a time.

After some haggling with the *patrón*, through Elena, Perry

bought a fat steer for ten dollars gold and went back out with one of the Mexicans to separate it from the herd so that it could be slaughtered by the Indians. While this was going on, Russ helped build a fire just outside the walls to roast some ears of fresh corn the *patrón* had ordered given to the visitors. Perry retrieved his pipe and tobacco from his saddlebags and hunkered down near the fire to pack a smoke.

"Okay, tell me what happened to you," he said, pressing the glowing end of a stick to his pipe bowl and puffing out a white cloud.

Russ briefly explained how he had come to be here.

"Jesus!" Perry breathed when he finished. "Mighty close." He shook his head. "I'm afraid, if we ever find McGee, there won't be much left after the coyotes and *zopilotes* finish with him."

"You don't think he got away, then?" Russ asked wistfully.

"Not a chance. They were probably so blasted mad after you escaped that they really worked him over." He spat to one side. "They take great delight in revenge." He glanced toward the scouts who, under his orders, were staying a good distance away. "Friendly scouts or not, they are still savages, and we'd do well not to forget it."

Russ nodded silently as he observed the scouts cooking the entrails and brains of the steer and cracking the bones to suck out the marrow.

"We'll pack the rest of that meat with us when we go," Perry said. "It's good to have some real beef for a change of diet."

"Has the command cut any hot trails of the hostile Apaches?"

Perry shook his head. "That's why I'm here. I was out with the scouts, and we just happened upon this ranch. You and McGee saw more of the hostiles than we did."

"Why isn't Tom Horn leading the scouts?"

"He's out with another bunch of 'em, heading north. Lawton's so desperate to pick up a trail that he's got us split into several small groups, going in all directions."

"Any chance we can look for McGee on the way back?"

"Do you remember where you were?"

Russ frowned and slowly shook his head. "Somewhere southeast of that cañon I came through."

"Pretty vague."

"I know. We had traveled a full day from camp, heading as straight as we could toward Sahuaripa, if that's any help."

"We'll swing around that way," Perry said, without enthusiasm. "Won't matter if we take an extra day. Even if we don't find McGee's body, maybe the scouts can pick up the trail of the ones who got you. How many of them did you say there were?"

"I saw five. All adult males."

"Probably out raiding for horses and arms."

"That's what I figure. But their trail's washed out, or several days cold by now."

Perry stood up and knocked the dottle out of his pipe on the heel of his hand. "That corn ought be about done by now."

"Are you certain you are well enough to travel?" Elena asked, looking earnestly at Russ an hour later as they stood just inside the gate to the courtyard.

"Thanks to you and these people, I'm in better shape than they are," he replied, nodding toward Perry Babcock and the scouts.

"But all of your wounds are not healed," she objected, gently.

He shifted his weight uneasily. "They will heal on the trail."

"You about ready to go?" Perry asked, stepping inside the gate and nodding at Elena.

"Oh, wait, I have something for you to take with you," Elena said, suddenly putting her hand on his arm.

In a flash she was gone, while the two men glanced at each other. She was back shortly with a bundle wrapped in canvas and tied with a cord.

"What's this?" Russ asked as she handed it to him. He hefted it, putting its weight at about five pounds.

"*Penole y panoche*," she replied.

"What?"

"*Penole* is small-grained corn ground fine on stone. *Panoche* is coarse brown sugar we make ourselves. Put a big spoonful of *penole* in a pint of water. Add a chunk of *panoche* about as big as my fist. Stir it up, and you have a lunch that will give you strength for even the hardest day in the mountains."

"I've heard of that," Perry said. "It was a different kind of grain, but that's essentially the same food that fed the Scottish Highlanders when they fought the English centuries ago. Gives you incredible endurance, they say."

"*Gracias, señorita*," Russ said, taking her hand.

She leaned forward and kissed him gently on the lips. "*Vaya con Dios, Señor* Norwood."

He wanted to take her in his arms, but she darted through a nearby doorway and was gone.

"It's Russ," he said absently, gazing after her.

"She'll probably catch hell from her strict aunts and chaperones for that," Perry observed, glancing at the frowns and mutterings of several older women standing nearby. "And you a *gringo* to boot," he said over his shoulder as he led the way out the gate.

Norwood, coming finally to his senses, searched for the *patrón* in the cluster of onlookers and, in a mixture of English and Spanish, expressed his thanks to him before he turned and followed Babcock outside.

"Don't have an extra horse, but you can ride double with

me for now," Perry said. "We'll just have to take it a little slower."

"I'll walk, unless you're in a big hurry," Russ said, noting that the scouts were mounted on several of the captured Indian ponies. Each man was packing a chunk of the butchered beef, tied on in whatever fashion each could manage, blood still dripping from the fresh meat. There was nothing to wrap it in.

Babcock swung his lean frame into the saddle and then hesitated. "On second thought, I think we should return to camp and get you a horse. Nothing we can do for McGee right now anyway. We'll let Lawton decide what to do from here."

By the time they reached camp, Norwood was grateful for this decision. Several miles of hiking up and down rough trails told him that his body was not yet recovered from his ordeal. But the familiar sight of the men in camp, horses and mules picketed, the smell of cooking fires, all gladdened his heart. He never realized he could miss simple things so much.

"So we have a net loss of one man, two animals, and a couple of guns," Lawton remarked when Norwood had finished retelling his story.

Norwood thought that was a rather cold way of putting it, but said nothing. Apparently Lawton caught his feeling.

"That's not to say that McGee wasn't a good man, and he will be greatly missed," he added, almost as an apology. "But, damn it, we're in a war. We have to expect casualties. These savages are ruthless!" He looked again at Norwood who still stood in front of him where he sat on a rock near his fire. "Yes, I know he was your friend, and I'm sorry," he added with uncharacteristic gentleness.

Babcock interjected himself and smoothly ended the interview, guiding his friend away. Norwood wrapped himself in an extra blanket and sat on the ground as Babcock gathered some wood and kindled a fire. As Babcock worked, he filled Norwood in on where they had marched, and what they had done while he was away.

"Your infantrymen have really pulled their weight. Hardly need an officer to give them any orders."

Russ didn't reply, but sat moodily staring into the flames as they began to crackle and blaze up. His tired brain didn't seem to want to focus on anything just now.

Perry worked silently for a few minutes, cutting some chunks of beef from a bloody shoulder he had hung from a nearby tree limb. "I know you're grieving for McGee," he said. "And you lost your mule, Plato, and your rifle. But think, man! You got away with your life and no serious injuries. I'd be ecstatic if I were in your moccasins. And besides that," he added with a smile, "you were rescued and nursed by the most beautiful girl I've seen in all of Mexico!"

Russ looked up and managed a grin. "I didn't say I wasn't grateful. I'm just dead tired. The smell of that beef is the only thing going to keep me awake long enough to eat."

A puff of wind blew dust up around them as thunder rumbled in the distance.

"Well, we had a night off from being soaked, but it looks like the reprieve is over," Perry observed. "Maybe we'll have time to eat before it hits. I've got that *penole y panoche* in my saddlebags and shoved under a rock, so it should stay dry."

Perry set the frying pan to sizzling on the fire and brought out two chunks of hardtack.

"We've started having one helluva time with blowflies," he said, sitting down on his blanket to tend the cooking. "Hard to protect the animals."

"What do they do?"

"The blowflies? Doc Sutter says they lay their eggs in any piece of moist meat and in a few hours the little screw worms

169

appear which bury themselves in the wound. Then they multiply fast and soon weaken and kill the animal. It's almost impossible to keep the horses and mules from getting raw sores and small cuts."

"What do you do for 'em?"

"Doc has some calomel that keeps them out of the wound. Hell, even our damp blankets were full of blowflies the other day. Rains so much, nothing really gets dried out."

Supper was hardly over before the nightly tempest burst over the camp, bringing on an early darkness. Fires hissed and went out in clouds of steam. Lightning crackled and stabbed and sizzled like so many striking rattlesnakes until the air was full of electricity. As they huddled against a rock bank, trying vainly to stay dry, Norwood saw something he had never seen before.

"Look!" He punched Babcock who had his hat pulled down over his face. He pointed. Where three of the infantrymen had carelessly left their rifles leaning against their packs in the open, indistinct blue balls of St. Elmo's fire glowed at the tips of the barrels. Babcock shook his head and rolled his eyes. To Russ the phenomenon only added to the eeriness of this wild country.

So glad was he to be back that Norwood didn't even mind rolling out after a sleepless night, his blanket and the ground saturated with water, and hitting the trail at six o'clock the next morning. Breakfast consisted of jerky and water since there was no wood dry enough to burn. Norwood caught himself a sturdy-looking pinto from the herd of captured Indian ponies. A wet blanket was his only saddle since there was no extra horse gear, and the animal was a lot more skittish than his faithful Plato. As it turned out, he spent most of the day walking and leading the animal anyway, since the terrain was not conducive to riding.

The column forded Nacori Creek and marched along the creek

bed for about eight miles. The sinuous creek, along with the steep walls on either side, required that the men cross and recross it constantly. Since the water, after the nightly rains, was up to their armpits and rushing along like a mill race, the march was hard on all hands, especially the infantry. Even the mounted men were not spared a pretty thorough soaking.

As it was, everyone was glad to go into camp about two o'clock after a day's march of nearly fifteen miles. Shortly after making camp, one of the men killed a cow that was apparently running wild in the area. The brand was cut out, as was the common practice, and Captain Lawton would pay the owner ten dollars gold, provided he could be found when they came to the town of Nacori.

While Babcock was building a fire to cook an early supper of beef for them, Norwood took all their gear — saddles, blankets, moccasins, and guns — and spread them on a flat rock in the blazing sun to dry.

"An exercise in futility," Perry commented as he looked up from starting the fire with a pair of spare spectacles borrowed from Doctor Sutter. "All that stuff will be soaked again tonight. You can bet on it."

"At least it'll keep the vermin out of the blankets and the mantas. I'd rather wrap up in a dry blanket than a wet one."

"You've got a point," he agreed, watching a wisp of smoke begin to curl up from the dry leaves under the concentrated beam of sun from one convex lens.

"Are we out of matches?" Russ asked, as he flipped open the loading gate and blew a few drops of water out of his Colt.

"Got plenty of matches, but they're all wet. I'll dig 'em out in a minute, and you can lay 'em in the sun with the rest of that stuff." He knelt on one knee and fed the growing fire from a small pile of sticks. "You know, I'm beginning to feel

171

I've been on this campaign forever."

"I know. I have some vague memory of another life lived in another place, another time. But I've been marching and camping and getting sun-blasted and soaked and bug-bitten for so long, it's like the only existence I've ever had."

"At least you had a little break with that Calderón girl," Perry grinned tiredly.

"I don't recommend the way I got there," said Russ dryly.

"True enough."

"If it hadn't been for McGee, I would never have gotten away from those Apaches." The pain was still sharp.

"Sorry we didn't get a chance to go back and look for him." Perry slid the frying pan onto the fire. "You know as well as I that we would never have found him alive."

"But it's the *not* knowing. If nothing else, he deserves a decent burial."

Silence fell between them for a few seconds. The strips of beef sizzled noisily in the frying pan.

"Tell you what," Perry said, "Lawton's going to have us lay in camp here for a couple of days to rest up. He's sending out the scouts. I'll ask permission to take two or three scouts and backtrack to see if we can find your camp. Maybe we can find his body, and just maybe the scouts can cut one of the hostiles' trail."

Russ thanked him with a sad smile. Then he brightened. "I've got an idea about building some bunks up off the ground. It won't keep the mosquitoes off or keep us dry, but at least we won't be lying in puddles of water."

"Great idea. Be a lot softer, and it might keep some of the sand flies off, too."

"I'll cut some of these pine boughs and get started while you're fixing supper."

"The sooner, the better."

172

Twenty minutes later Russ was dragging some pine branches to a level spot near their cooking fire, while smoke of other fires was drifting up through the shade of the larger pines. The men were drying shoes and clothing, cleaning weapons, cooking, and drying strips of meat. Russ dropped the limbs and started trimming them with a small hatchet.

"Better knock off and get some food," Perry said, sliding the frying pan off the fire onto a rock.

"Don't mind if I do. I'm starved!" a third voice interjected.

The two men looked up. Norwood caught his breath as if a fist had slammed into his stomach.

Stratford McGee stood a few yards away, looking haggard but grinning.

Chapter Fourteen

It was a joyous homecoming. Babcock and Norwood considered McGee's appearance as nothing short of miraculous. Norwood almost forgot to eat as he looked at the little man tearing into the freshly cooked beef with gusto.

"You look like you've seen a ghost," Mac remarked, licking his fingers.

"The last time I saw you those Indians looked like *they* were seeing a ghost."

"Not a ghost," he replied, chewing, "a crazy man. A babbling, howling, insane man. *Muy loco.*" He laughed at the appearance of stunned disbelief on Russ Norwood's face. "Best performance I ever gave. And I had the best incentive . . . my life! I didn't mention that, among the many jobs I've had, I even filled in a time or two with a traveling troupe of actors when one of their number was jailed and couldn't go on. Hell, it was only a simple melodrama, but it was fun. Never thought I'd have to become a thespian to save my life."

"But they just let you go?" Russ asked, skepticism in his voice.

Mac took a long sip of hot coffee before he replied. "Sure did. I reckon Apaches have seen captives go out of their minds with shock and fear. But they attribute it to being possessed by some evil spirit. And they leave a crazy person strictly alone."

"Well, your quick thinking sure saved the both of us," Russ said, finally beginning to eat.

"Hell, I was desperate. It was the first thing that came into my head. When I started, I had to play it for everything I was worth. Doubt if any real mentally disturbed person could have looked the part more than I did, even if I do say so myself. Too bad I had only Apaches for an audience." He paused to break off a piece of hardtack and soak it in some of the grease in the skillet. "'Course that storm and lightning helped a lot. Made me look even scarier, I expect."

"How did you find us?"

"After those hostiles took off with the mules and the guns, I was so grateful I didn't care where the column was. I would've gladly walked all the way to the States, if necessary. I didn't think I'd be able to find you, Russ, 'cause once you took off I figured you'd keep on going, if that Apache didn't catch you. Anyway, I walked for two days in this general direction before I finally cut the trail of the column. Took me a while to catch up, what with the trail bein' partially washed out and me not being an expert tracker." He took another bite of beef. "What happened to you?" he asked Norwood.

For the third time, Russ repeated his story.

Instead of expressing incredulity, Mac merely nodded. "Looks like the Lord wasn't ready for us, and the devil didn't want us," was his only comment.

"By God, it's good to have you back!" Russ exclaimed.

"No better than it is for me to be back," he replied, leaning against Perry's saddle, another cup of coffee in hand. "Whoa! I'm finally beginning to feel human again. Cactus pulp and a few berries won't keep your stomach from rubbing against your backbone for very long."

Shortly after they finished eating, the three of them reported to Captain Lawton.

"McGee, you and Norwood showing up in one piece is probably the best thing that's happened on this campaign so far." Captain Lawton allowed himself a rare grin. "Now, get down to the creek and get a bath. You smell worse than one of these mules."

"Yes, sir."

Another cloudburst flooded the camp that night, and the stream rose more than a foot. Norwood had become so accustomed to these nightly downpours that he could sleep through all but the heaviest part merely by covering his head with a blanket.

The sun rose and began sucking up the moisture, creating a muggy, steamy atmosphere. Lawton sent out Tom Horn with one of four small groups of scouts. Norwood and Babcock sought to escape the sultry camp by securing two rifles and tramping off to do some hunting, leaving McGee behind to rest and recuperate.

If there was anything that Norwood did not need more of, it was hiking. But he preferred this to sitting around a soggy camp. Besides, he reasoned, it would help toughen up his legs and get the soreness out of them quicker. He and Babcock had walked about four miles and were able to get two long shots at two deer, but the animals were downhill and Norwood fired high. They finally killed a wild beef and cut out the brand, taking note of where they were so they could send a couple of packers back with ropes and mules to cut up the carcass and pack it in to camp.

By the time they returned, Norwood was tired but felt good. They discovered Captain Lawton, McGee, and a packer had ridden a few miles to Nacori to meet the pack train for which Lawton had sent to Oposura. The three men returned to camp in late afternoon with word that the pack train would arrive the next morning.

It arrived on schedule along with the cavalry. Lawton then dismissed the infantry so it could return to Oposura. As a consequence, Norwood was relieved of his command responsibilities.

Doctor Benjamin Sutter was no longer the apple-cheeked young blond physician who had started out the campaign with them. The blue eyes behind the gold-rimmed spectacles were as bright as ever, but his round face now had flatter planes, and his ragged clothing now hung on a leaner frame. The campaign had been hard on all of them.

"They've sure turned into a better group of soldiers than when they first came," Russ remarked to the doctor as the infantry prepared for their seventy-five-mile march.

"Zat is so," the doctor agreed, eyeing the men. "But zere are some zat are in no condition to continue." He went on to state that Private Henry Graham had varicose veins in his legs, Marshall Hoffman weak knees, Private Reynolds an inflammation of a knee, and John Maguire had contracted malaria.

"Well, they can all recuperate in Oposura, while the cavalry takes their place for now," Russ said.

As he turned away, Norwood couldn't help wondering if the hostile Apaches, with their women and children, were also feeling the strain of constant flight.

The next morning Captain Lawton ordered the command to move several miles down Nacori Creek to a point about three miles above its confluence with the Arros River. The men marched down the bed of the stream most of the way, the water to the bellies of the horses, or deeper, most of the way. Norwood was again mounted on an Indian pony, but he now rode a spare McClellan saddle that was part of the pack train's supplies. McGee, who had also lost his mule, was riding an Indian pony with only a saddle blanket.

"Hell, it beats shanks' mare," Mac replied when Russ commented on it. But the small man refused the offer of Norwood's saddle. "I may have to get old, but I don't have to get soft," he replied with a straight face.

Norwood grinned. While comfortably shaped, the McClellan

was anything but an easy chair, wet leather and rawhide over a solid hickory tree.

In midafternoon Lawton ordered the column into camp on a grassy hill above the creek. Just as the men were dismounting, two of the Indian scouts jogged into camp and told Lawton they had spotted two horsemen about three miles ahead where Nacori Creek emptied into the Arros River.

Lawton dispatched two cavalrymen to check out this report. An hour later they reported back that they had found two clear sets of tracks and followed them down to the water's edge where they disappeared. The river was much too high and swift to attempt a crossing, so they returned to camp.

Hardly had the cavalrymen delivered their report than a heavy thunderstorm blew up and everyone went for whatever shelter they could find, which wasn't much. The storm passed in about an hour, leaving everything soaked. The sun returned, followed by thousands of small flies that got into eyes and noses and bit areas of exposed flesh. Norwood didn't know which was worse — the irritating flies or the steamy, breathless heat — but the combination was about to drive him crazy. He pulled off his high moccasins, put them on a rock in the sun, and went into the creek in his underwear.

"Might as well be wet with creek water as sweat," he yelled at Babcock. "And it's the only way I can keep the flies off." He lolled back, water up to his nose.

The next morning, Norwood and Babcock accompanied Captain Lawton, Tom Horn, and several of the scouts down Nacori Creek to the Arros River. A knot formed in the pit of Norwood's stomach at the sight of the rain-swollen river. He reined up his pony and stared. Only the tops of the willows along the bank were out of water, bobbing and nodding downstream. The river was a good one hundred and twenty yards wide, and it seemed the current was rolling downhill with the speed

178

of an express train, carrying along all sorts of flotsam — pieces of palm fronds to good-size logs.

The tracks of the two horsemen were still visible but, since the rain, it was impossible to tell whether or not the animals were shod.

"Well, we'll probably never know who those two horsemen were," Lawton said, sitting his horse and staring out at the river. "Maybe a couple of Mexicans who live around here some place. The tracks go right into the river, and that's the way we have to go, too." He called to Tom Horn to get two of his scouts to attempt to swim it.

The tall chief of scouts asked the Indians in Spanish to try the river, but all of them refused, indicating by signs that they would be pulled under. Lawton observed this shameless refusal with a disgusted look on his face.

"Hell, I'll try it," he said, dismounting and starting to remove his shirt. At that, Norwood and Horn both dismounted and stripped down to their underwear bottoms.

"Let me try it first," Lawton ordered, wading into the murky water. When the water reached his waist, he struck off in a sidestroke. After a few yards, he turned and struggled back to where he could again get his feet under him. "I'm in no condition for this," he panted, sloshing up out of the stream and wiping water from his face and mustache. "The command needs to get across this river," Lawton continued. "So we need to know if one man can make it. If so, we can probably get a line across and maybe build some rafts."

"My turn," Norwood said, stepping forward and wading in. The water was cool but not cold, and he struck out straight across the broad expanse. He heard a splash and looked back to see Horn a few yards behind. Norwood rolled onto his side and watched Horn's clumsy, heavy stroking. Norwood started again, sidestroking across the current. But he quickly felt the

179

force of the water pulling at him, carrying him downstream. He was as powerless as a piece of driftwood. By challenging this giant serpent of a river, maybe he had taken on more than he could handle. But he kept stroking steadily, trying not to think about how fast he was being carried down toward the rapids a mile or two below. As high as the river was, maybe even these rapids were now submerged.

Norwood rolled onto his other side and looked back. The figures on the shore were quickly growing smaller. Tom Horn still swam but he, too, was in the grip of the current and appeared to be struggling. Pulling strongly with his arms and kicking against the inexorable sweep of thousands of tons of water, Norwood found he was nearly in the middle of the river as now he glanced toward the far shoreline, the shoreline that seemed to be moving almost as fast as a man could run.

Why would Tom Horn have jumped in right behind him? Norwood thought the idea was to try one person at a time. Maybe Horn viewed this as a competition — a race to see who was the better man. Horn would never pass up an opportunity to enhance his image and reputation.

The next time Norwood paused to tread water and look, Horn seemed closer but was visibly tiring. "Need any help?" he yelled back.

Horn coughed and dog-paddled to an upright position. "I'm not gonna let you go down alone!" he shouted. Then he seemed to renew his efforts and swam several hard strokes, drawing closer to Norwood.

Rolling over, Norwood resumed his energy-saving sidestroke. A few moments later he was startled by a splash close by and turned to see Tom Horn nearly at his side.

"Help! Getting tired . . . !" There was panic in Horn's eyes. "Can't make it, Norwood!"

Before Norwood could reply or react, Horn grabbed for him.

It was Norwood's turn to feel panic as the scout's arms locked around his neck and shoulders. He went under with the weight of the big man on top of him. Water was being forced up his nose. To break Horn's grip, Norwood went deeper. The bigger man let go, and a foot kicked Norwood in the head as Horn flailed to the surface.

Norwood swam upward and burst out into the light, gasping. Where was Horn? Had he gone down? Before he could even turn around, he felt the death grip of the drowning man clamp around his head again and Horn's legs encircle his body. The panicked swimmer was trying to climb on top of him. as if he were some secure rock that would not sink.

Norwood used the same tactic of going deeper, but this time Horn did not let go and went down with him. Down, down they sank into the black silence, writhing in a tangle of arms and legs. Norwood knew he could save both of them, but he had to free himself to do it. That was not so easily done. He struggled to tear the arms away from his face. He was able to push the arms up and slide his head free, but the scissors lock was still around his middle, squeezing him. As they sank deeper, second by second, his lungs began to burn. He knew Horn had to be holding his breath, too. *If the scout was drowning, why wasn't he instinctively clawing for the surface? If he had already sucked in a lungful of water, his grip would be relaxing. It wasn't.*

A sudden fear stabbed his stomach. *Was Horn deliberately trying to drown him?* The thought lent him a surge of new strength. He bent double and grabbed Horn's toes, wrenching them sideways. Instantly, the legs relaxed, and the scout kicked upward.

Norwood shot to the surface, bursting free and sucking air into his tortured lungs. This time Horn was in his sight, instead of behind him. One look at the scout's eyes told Norwood that his suspicions were true. Horn was in no trouble. The bigger man lunged at him again, trying to get a choke hold to push him under. But Norwood twisted away, chopping down on the scout's wrist. Then Norwood pushed away onto his back, kicking at Horn's face. He felt the sole of his foot bend nose cartilage.

Norwood had always been good at swimming on his back, and this time he gave it everything he had, angling away so the current gave him an added push. He easily outdistanced Horn and kept swimming on his back so he could watch the scout. He gradually approached the opposite shore and finally, where the current swung toward shore on a bend, he gave a few final strokes and pushed himself into shallow water. Breathing heavily, he got to his feet and waded ashore, looking over his shoulder at Horn who was about ten yards behind him and was being swept a little farther along. The scout touched bottom and stumbled to his feet.

He had a fleeting thought of attacking him while Horn was still out of breath, but he quickly rejected the idea. *Just pretend you don't know he's trying to kill you,* he told himself. *Maybe then he won't be on his guard if it ever comes to a showdown.* Besides, as winded as he was himself right now, he doubted he could whip anybody in a fist fight. And he had no other weapons. They were both barefooted and in their underwear. As he took long breaths to calm his pounding heart, Norwood realized that if he attacked Horn, the scout would only claim his innocence — would state that he came near to going under and that Norwood refused to help him and then had picked a fight.

As he walked along the shoreline toward him, Horn came wading up, wiping water from his face and grinning sheepishly.

"Didn't mean . . . to cause you . . . any trouble out there," he panted, his deep chest heaving.

"That's okay," Norwood answered, eyeing him cautiously for

any sudden moves. He was not fooled. That had not been a look of panic or fear; it had been a look of pure hate. The fact that the scout had continued swimming easily across the wide, swift current confirmed it. Babcock had been right. The man was out to get him when he least expected it. And he was trying to make it look like an accident.

"Why don't you go on downstream a mile or two and see if you can spot the tracks of where those two horsemen came out of the water," Norwood suggested. "I'll go upstream and do the same."

"Good idea," Horn answered amiably and set off along the bank, picking his way carefully in his bare feet.

Norwood watched the back of the broad-shouldered, slim-hipped six-footer until he had gone about thirty yards. Then he turned and headed upstream.

"See you on the other side!"

Norwood looked around, and Horn was grinning and pointing back across the river. *Letting me know that he has the strength and stamina to swim back,* he thought. He didn't return the wave as he turned and resumed his tramp upstream.

Chapter Fifteen

Norwood saw no tracks in the approximately two miles he walked along the shoreline. He paused to rest and look around before slipping back into the stream and letting the current carry him as he swam back to his starting point. There was no sign of Horn who was probably screened by the brush or rocks of the next bend below.

Horn had almost caught him with his guard down. He would have to be more careful. But how could he prevent such things? As long as both of them were on this campaign, there would always be opportunities for "accidents."

Lawton was still waiting on the bank when Norwood waded wearily out of the river and walked up to him.

"Damned glad you made it. I was worried there for a while," the commander said. "Where's Horn?"

"He'll be along directly. We scouted up and down the bank for two or three miles. No sign of any tracks coming out of the water."

"Those two riders must have been swept away."

"Did Lieutenant Babcock go back to camp?"

"No. He and a couple of Indian scouts went upriver a ways to see if they could find an easier crossing point. Let's get back to camp. We'll move the column down here and try a crossing tomorrow."

Norwood found his rolled-up clothes and mounted his pony. Leaving a few scouts behind to wait for Horn, the two of them rode the three miles back to camp.

Babcock had not shown up, but he came in about two hours

later looking very tired. "We tried another spot upstream that wasn't quite as wide, but the current was really swift. Two of the scouts and I got some small logs and managed to swim across with them. It was hard going. The Indians didn't want to do it, but I showed them that, if they kept hold of the big driftwood, they wouldn't be pulled under. Anyway, we were able to find another possible crossing point."

"Wonder why Lawton doesn't wait a few days for the river to go down?" Mac asked, walking up to the pair at that moment.

"Hell, with the rainy season here it may not recede for weeks. That's a big river. It collects all the runoff from these feeder streams like Nacori Creek."

The next day, when the men returned to the Arros River, the water level had dropped a few feet, and the current was not quite as swift. The first raft the cavalry and the packers put together of palm logs they had dragged down to the river's edge was so heavy that it sank immediately. Their next try, using driftwood, was more successful, and a good-size raft was lashed together. Norwood again swam across, towing a light line that was attached to a cable made from twisting several ropes together. Two men followed, and the three of them were able to pull the rope cable over and tie it securely to a tree. From there the raft, covered with cane and reeds, was loaded with the packs, attached to the cable and, angling with the current, safely floated across. The far end of the line was then detached from the tree, carried upstream, and reattached. The raft could now return with the help of the current. In this way, the rest of the day was spent ferrying their goods across the river.

While all this activity was taking place, Norwood noticed an unfamiliar first lieutenant ride up along the shore. The next time he had a chance to look, the officer and Captain Lawton had dismounted and withdrawn to one side where they were deep in conversation.

About an hour later, Norwood was summoned to a meeting with the commander. Babcock was already standing by the grim-faced Lawton when he arrived. Lawton drew them well away from the other men before he turned to face them.

"I've just had a visit from Lieutenant James Parker of the Fourth Cavalry. He is escorting Lieutenant Charles Gatewood of the Sixth Cavalry and two Chiricahua Apaches he brought from the reservation. These Indians are of the same band as the hostiles we're chasing."

He paused, as if trying to form just the right words to proceed. "Lieutenant Gatewood has been sent down here by General Miles to make contact with the hostiles and try to negotiate a surrender." He paused again, fleeting emotions crossing his face. "I know you gentlemen are aware of the politics that are rampant in the officer corps. But this seems rather strange. Gatewood is known to be an adherent to the policies of General Crook, yet he is known and trusted by the hostiles. So General Miles has sent him as a go-between with these two Apaches who are well known to Geronimo. Even though I am more an admirer of General Miles and his methods, this action comes as a slap in the face to me, since he is telling me that our campaign has failed."

His jaw muscles worked as he gritted his teeth. Norwood realized what pain this must be causing the determined career officer, but he could offer no solace.

"I have no choice but to follow these written orders from General Miles. But, before Gatewood can open negotiations with Geronimo, we have to find him. And that's what we've been trying to do for two months or more." He started to turn away. "Once the rest of our stuff is ferried across the river, the three of us will go visit Gatewood and have a little talk."

A half hour later Norwood and Babcock broke off their work

186

with the raft, turning the remainder of the job over to the cavalrymen and packers. They accompanied Captain Lawton the three miles back to where Lieutenants Parker and Gatewood and the two Indians were camped near their own camp site of the night before.

Gatewood repeated basically the same story Lawton had told them. Gatewood, a lean man Norwood knew estimated to be in his thirties, had a rather prominent nose and a thin, light brown mustache. He did not appear to be a happy man. He stated the facts of the situation and then kept silent, a grim, pained look on his face.

"Tom Horn, Russ Norwood, and a number of the Apache scouts will be sent out immediately to see if we can pick up a fresh trail," Captain Lawton promised, perhaps showing more enthusiasm than he felt. Norwood looked at Babcock to see if he could pick up his friend's reaction to this statement. How did Lawton think that he and Tom Horn and some of the scouts were going to pick up a trail that led to Geronimo just by wishing to do so? Besides, Lawton had no idea what he was about when he promised to pair up Norwood and Tom Horn.

"Maybe if we can somehow get word to the hostiles that we want to talk instead of fight . . .," Babcock started to suggest.

"How can that be done?" Lieutenant Parker asked.

"We could pass the message to all the Mexican prefects in the region, for a start," Babcock said.

"We'll do what we can to help," Lawton promised, standing up and signaling an end to the conversation. "Gatewood, you and Parker will put yourselves under my command, since there are just the two of you," he added.

As the meeting broke up, Gatewood approached Norwood. "Do you have a doctor with your column?" he asked.

187

"Yes. Doctor Benjamin Sutter. He's down getting our new camp set up just now. I can take you to him if you wish. What's the matter?" he asked, noting the pale face of the officer.

"The doctor at Bowie tells me I have an inflamed bladder. Makes riding very painful." He made a sour face. "I didn't want to come on this trip, but Miles sent me anyway. If your doctor says I'm not medically fit to go on, I'll start home in the morning."

Norwood was taken aback at first but then realized that not only was this man sick, but he also adhered to the policies of General Crook.

"Come on. We'll go down to see Doctor Sutter," he said.

Doctor Sutter did not declare Gatewood unfit for duty because later that afternoon Gatewood came to Norwood just before supper.

"I'll be going with you and your scouts in the morning," he said. "Doctor Sutter wouldn't release me," he added in reply to Norwood's questioning look. "As long as I have to do this, I want to get it over with as soon as I can."

"Lieutenant, I don't know you very well, but I remember you when I was an officer. Frankly, I thought General Crook was the best general officer I ever served under. Since I'm now a civilian, I can tell you that I think Miles is a pompous fool. But he's apparently come around to the realization that the Army can't catch and defeat these hostiles, so he's going back to using Crook's tactics of pressuring Geronimo into surrender."

At this, Gatewood seemed to brighten up. He almost smiled. "I'm glad to hear someone who feels like I do."

"I tell you this because I want you to know we're on the same side. I'm now a civilian courier with the Army but have been functioning as an officer on this campaign. And I know

188

that we both do our duty because it's our duty, and not because we think it's always the right thing, or because it's pleasant. So, until we can get a lead on where Geronimo and his band are, I think you should stay in camp and conserve your strength. We'll do our damnedest to locate him, so you can open up negotiations and deliver Miles's message and terms of surrender."

Gatewood smiled and nodded. "Fine. Norwood, you're a good man. I'd heard some things about you earlier when you left the service, but I like to make up my own mind about a person. And you strike me as being very honest and forthright." He thrust out his hand, and Norwood gripped it firmly. "By the way, call me Charles."

"My name's Russ."

"Just between the two of us, I have no faith in this plan," Gatewood continued. "I know these Indians pretty well, and I think this time they mean to fight it out to the end. And if, by chance, we can find them and they agree to surrender, General Miles will get all the credit for it . . . and using Crook's methods, too. That's what really galls me."

"I know."

Gatewood was sitting, cross-legged, on the ground. He leaned forward, bowing his head, and pressed one hand to his lower abdomen. "I'm sick. I shouldn't be out in the field."

"Did Doc Sutter give you anything for your condition?"

Gatewood shook his head. "He has no medication but quinine and calomel. And neither of them will help me. Told me to drink a lot of clean water and to report to the post surgeon as soon as I get home."

The next morning Norwood, Horn, and twenty-five Indian scouts started out on foot. They carried no rations except some coffee and a little salt. Each man had two belts of ammunition and an extra pair of moccasins but no blankets or bedding. They rafted their clothes and a few possessions across the Arros

River and swam across themselves. One Indian who couldn't swim rode the raft. Two mounted couriers, named Edwaddy and Lang, accompanied them, swimming their animals over the river. These couriers would go with the party for a day and then swing off to cover a lot of country to the south and west.

The party marched about ten miles, gradually climbing up and away from the river valley, finally camping among some clustered bushes and thick grass high in the mountains. They built no fires but ate a supper of crackers and cactus fruit they had brought with them.

Norwood was tired but almost hesitated to go to sleep that night with no white companions but the treacherous Horn. Edwaddy and Lang had already veered off and ridden away. Norwood had attempted to have Babcock come on this scout, but Lawton insisted he needed Babcock in camp. Norwood sat up as long as he could keep his eyes open, surreptitiously watching the tall scout. But Horn, after conferring with some of the Apaches, sat by himself, whittling on a stick and ignoring Norwood. Toward dark, Norwood went off to urinate and then circled around to another spot, well away from the others to lie down under the bushes, his drawn and loaded Colt within reach. Horn could have slit his throat that night, so soundly did he sleep. Sometime in the wee hours, he came about half awake to the pelting of the nightly rain and the booming of thunder, but so used to this had he become that he dozed off again and slept until an hour before daylight.

They were up and on the march at first light. About nine o'clock they got down into a cañon where they built a fire to make a little coffee and to eat some freshly killed deer meat from a doe Horn shot. They had only one tin cup between them which they shared, neither man speaking. The Apache scouts, as usual, were grouped off to one side by themselves.

After about an hour, they kicked and scattered the fire and

started again. Another two hours' march brought them to a fortified ranch, similar to the one where Russ Norwood had been with Elena Calderón. He and Horn were very careful to approach by themselves, keeping the Indians well back, as the men and women scattered in panic from the fields. By waving and yelling in English and Spanish, the two men attempted to identify themselves as friendly. Norwood stood nervously by as Horn shouted in Spanish, and finally the *patrón* of the place came out the gate and conferred with them. This man was not the gracious host that the *patrón* had been at the earlier ranch. He had a personality to match his badly pock-marked face. He demanded, and got, the exorbitant price of $15 for a fat steer. Norwood paid him out of the American gold coins he carried for just such situations.

The Indians immediately shot the animal and began to cut it up, while Norwood and Horn built a fire. The *patrón,* his business concluded, retreated inside the walls and closed the gate, leaving them to fend for themselves. Apparently making a decision not to ask the white men for matches, a couple of the Apaches started a fire using friction and soon had a huge blaze going. Everyone sat around, roasting small chunks of beef on sticks and drinking water from their canteens.

"I think we should camp here for the night," Horn said, breaking a long silence as the two white men sat across the fire from each other.

"Fine by me. We've marched over twenty miles already today. As I understand it, the object of this scout is to cut this part of the Sierra Madre in two from west to east to see if the hostiles have swung north along the divide."

"Correct. If we don't cross some kind of trail in the next two or three days, we'll be close enough to head back to camp."

The talk was strictly business. The business over, the conversation lapsed.

That evening Norwood slept closer to the Indians than he was accustomed to doing, since lice had been a problem among them. But, if Horn tried anything in the night, maybe one of the light-sleeping scouts would be aroused. The next thing Norwood knew, the Indians were astir and preparing to march. It was still dark, and the moon was down. Norwood retrieved his Colt, holstered it, and was rinsing his mouth from his canteen when he heard Horn's low voice say, "Okay, let's move out. ¡Vámanos!"

By the time the sun rose in their eyes, they were walking along a fairly good, open trail following the ridges leading to the higher mountains ahead of them.

By late morning they had been on the march for several hours and paused to eat some more of the beef, and to roast the remaining fresh corn Norwood had also purchased. They were in good, rolling country, about a five-thousand-foot elevation, with plenty of grass and water.

After lunch, they struck off into the heart of the mountains, laboring up and down through some very rough and rocky country until they arrived at the mouth of a great cañon running down to the Arros River.

"Well, no sign of the hostiles' trail," Norwood commented as the party paused to confer about the best way of climbing down into this great chasm.

"Nope," Horn agreed succinctly. He seemed more concerned with finding a trail down into the cañon than with reading sign.

One of the scouts finally discovered what appeared to be a treacherous route down the broken rocks of the cañon wall. Led by this Indian, they all worked their way slowly downward. The footholds were narrow and the handholds few, as they went single file. From a distance they must have looked like ants clinging precariously to the rock face, Norwood thought, his breathing harsh in his throat as he followed the wiry Apache ahead of him, noting where he placed his feet to avoid the loose rock. He was careful not to put his full weight on anything for more than a second, including the tiny shrubs that projected from cracks in the wall.

Norwood glanced down once, and sweat stung his eyes. He jerked his blurred gaze away. The cañon was fully three thousand feet deep. One misstep would be fatal. There would be no second chances.

Late in the afternoon they reached the bottom, and Norwood noted that even several of the indefatigable Indians seemed pretty well done up. The twenty-two miles they had traveled since morning was equal to twice that distance in ordinary country.

Without building any fires, they ate what little cooked meat was left over from their lunch. The Indians preferred the brains, marrow, and entrails and, once everyone had finished, Norwood realized that the $15 in gold had been well spent, since nearly every bit of the steer had been consumed. He reflected idly how much this marching and hard physical exertion in these mountains seemed to excite a craving for great amounts of fresh meat. Yet no ill effects seemed to result from an all-meat diet.

After an exhausted sleep, the party pulled out of camp at daybreak and marched down the cañon for eight miles on what appeared to be an old Indian trail, crossing and recrossing the small stream in the bottom of the gorge. The steep walls on either side were covered with heavy growths of cactus and bushes, and there was absolutely no breeze to cool them as the morning wore on, hot and sultry.

After about three hours, they reached a spot where it was possible, by climbing steeply, to get out of the cañon. As they toiled upward, the column became scattered, each man seeking the best route for himself. Norwood was climbing laboriously, his chest heaving and sweat pouring off him. He paused for a few seconds to blow, glad they were not carrying anything but their canteens, sidearms, and ammunition. Even the coffee and salt were used up. It was fortunate he had persuaded Gatewood to stay in camp. He didn't think the sickly lieutenant could have made such a tramp.

Just as he started to go on, he heard a crashing of rocks. He looked up just in time to see a jagged boulder the size of a chair bounding down the slope toward him. He froze for an instant. *Which way would it bounce?* His reflexes took over, and he sprang to his right and rolled out of the way just as the projectile hurtled past. There were some shrill cries below him as two Indians scrambled frantically to safety.

The boulder finally hit a projecting part of the slope and bounded clear, falling out of sight. After a few seconds of silence, the rock struck far below with a crashing and rattling of loose shale. Norwood climbed to his feet, shaken, with cuts and bruises on his hands and knees, and looked upslope.

"Everybody okay down there?" Horn shouted.

Norwood didn't reply, and he heard some grumbling from the Indian scouts behind him. As Horn turned away, some thirty yards above him, Norwood thought he saw a slight smile on the scout's face. Another "accident" that surely was a deliberate attempt on his life. The two of them were going to have to settle this once and for all and before too much longer.

"I don't think there's any point in going farther east," Horn said when they had all reached the top. "If the hostiles are going north, there's no reason to believe they'd be any farther east than this."

"You're right," Norwood agreed, turning to survey the vast panorama of mountains and ridges rolling away to the east. "See that white speck on the Arros way down there?" He pointed.

"Yeah."

194

"I think that's one of the white tents in our camp."

"We didn't bring any tents on this expedition," Horn snorted derisively.

"That heavy white canvas that's used to cover the mule packs...Captain Lawton and some of the men drape them over the bushes to use for shelters," Norwood replied, keeping his voice neutral.

Horn turned and squinted at the distant speck. "Must be twenty-five or thirty miles away."

"That's what I'd estimate."

"We'll cut off to the right here and see if we can get down to the river as soon as possible."

"No, I think it would be better to follow the ridge as far as we can before we go down," Norwood said firmly.

Horn looked surprised at this sudden disagreement with his orders. "Then I'll take about half the Indians and go around. You can do what you want."

The two men split up, each taking about half the scouts.

It was an ill-tempered Tom Horn who arrived in camp with his Apaches about nine o'clock that night, a good three hours after Norwood and his party. It was Norwood's turn to smile.

"Ran into some box cañons!" Horn spat, striding off into the darkness.

Norwood glanced at the men within earshot who were looking at him curiously. He had further damaged Horn's reputation as a scout — certainly not a very prudent thing to have done.

Chapter Sixteen

"My guess is that, only if there are people around, will Horn try to take care of you with some sort of 'accident,' " Perry Babcock said that night. The two men lounged in front of a small, crackling fire while Stratford McGee snored softly on his blanket a few yards away.

"Then I'll see to it that we're by ourselves," Russ answered. "Give him a chance to come at me straight up, if he's so inclined."

"He's not that kind of man. Even if you're alone, he'll try to get you when you're not looking."

"I'll be ready for him, but he won't know it."

Perry shook his head. "Too dangerous. My advice is to just leave him alone."

"That's what I've tried to do, but he's almost killed me twice in the past week. I want to bring this thing to a head and end it somehow."

"It could end in one of you being killed."

"I don't want that to happen, but it's possible."

"What are you going to do?"

"Well, I'm sure Lawton will keep the command in camp tomorrow for no other reason than the condition of the scouts. Of the twenty-five Apaches Horn and I took on that five-day jaunt, seven are completely laid up, and the other eighteen are pretty well done in. The column needs fresh meat, so I'll suggest to Horn that we go hunting."

"He'll be suspicious. Wish there were some way I could watch your back. If you let your attention wander for one minute,

Horn will be on you like a mountain lion."

"My guardian angel will protect me," Russ said quietly, staring into the flames. A vision of Elena Maria Calderón drifted through his mind.

"Well, if you're determined to go, I'll lend you my rifle," Perry said, intruding on his thoughts.

"Thanks. Some lucky Indian is probably putting my Marlin to good use about now."

The next morning, to his surprise, Russ Norwood found Tom Horn pleasantly agreeable when he suggested a deer hunt. "Let me get my rifle, and I'll be right with you," the big scout said, wiping his mouth and tossing away the dregs of his coffee cup.

Norwood fortified himself with a pint of *penole y panoche*, made sure Babcock's Winchester carbine was fully loaded, and also strapped on his Colt with a full cartridge belt.

The two men hiked out of camp and headed upstream along the Arros River. About three miles out, having seen no deer, they diverted up a side cañon whose sides were not as steep. Without being obvious about it, Norwood made sure that Horn was always to one side and just ahead of him, so that he was constantly in view. While Horn seemed to be scouting for deer, Norwood was more concerned with watching his hunting companion. Without speaking, they worked their way at an angle up the left hand side of the cañon. Pine trees were fairly thick along both rims, and it was toward these that they were climbing, hoping to flush some deer from cover.

Almost simultaneously two bullets tore into the earth bank near their heads, showering them with dirt. Both men leapt for cover behind the nearest rocks as echoes of the shots slammed back and forth across the cañon. Dirt was in Norwood's mouth and eyes.

"Apaches!" Horn shouted. "Keep your head down. I can't

see 'em, but the shots came from the other side, up ahead."

Norwood was spitting out dirt and rubbing his eyes. Just as he turned to look across the cañon, he heard a shot explode close by and felt a stunning blow in the midsection that knocked him, rolling, down the slope. He couldn't get his breath; his stomach muscles felt paralyzed. He slid to a stop behind some cactus and rocks in a cloud of dust, instinctively still clutching his rifle.

"Oh, no! I'm gut shot!" he gasped, feeling quickly of his abdomen.

He looked at his hand. No blood. The numbness had given way to intense pain. Even though he was in agony, his mind was racing. Where was Horn? Norwood rolled over and looked upslope. His vision was still rather blurry from the dirt in his eyes., but he could make out the figure of the scout plunging and sliding down the steep slope toward him. It was a close shot from Horn that had struck him — not a shot from across the cañon. Ignoring the pain, Norwood levered a round into the chamber and rolled to his stomach. He was still partially hidden by the cactus and rocks as he took quick aim and fired.

"Aahhh!!" Horn yelled. He pitched over, dropping his rifle. The weapon came sliding a few feet toward Norwood as Horn writhed on the ground, grabbing at his foot or ankle. "You son of a bitch! You shot me!" he screamed.

Norwood could still not get enough breath to speak, but he kept the rifle pointed at Horn and gritted his teeth against the pain in his midsection. He didn't know how badly he was hit, but he couldn't stop now to find out. He blinked rapidly to rid his eyes of the remaining dirt. Horn had no pistol or knife. The rifle had been his only weapon, and it was out of his reach at the moment.

Horn was in a sitting position, clutching his left foot and continuing to curse. Norwood could see blood oozing from the dirty moccasin and between Horn's fingers. Horn was out of action for now, but Russ didn't trust him. He might be feigning more pain than he felt. Maybe he had a hide-out gun or knife somewhere on his person.

The intense pain was subsiding in his stomach, and he slid one hand inside his shirt as he kept his eyes fixed on Horn. There was no wetness, no wound. Surely, if a bullet had hit him from that range, it would have penetrated. His stomach muscles were very tender to the touch, as if he had been clubbed rather than shot.

No more firing came from whoever had been shooting at them. Norwood took a quick look in that direction, but saw no one. They might have fired from the cover of the pine trees on the ridge or, if they were on the dun-colored slope below the timberline, he might never pick out their copper-colored bodies against the jumble of rocks and cactus and yellowish-brown dirt. Horn was now sitting in plain sight but, if their assailants were still there, they chose not to shoot.

When Horn made no more threatening moves, Norwood slowly and painfully pulled his knees up under him and pushed himself to his feet, keeping the carbine barrel pointed, his eyes never wavering. Babcock had warned him last night that if his attention should wander for one minute, Horn would be on him. Well, the hostile fire had caused his attention to wander, and Horn had seized the opportunity.

Stepping carefully and gingerly, he moved toward Horn who was attempting to remove his moccasin to examine his wound.

"You're damned lucky you're not dead. I wasn't aiming at your foot," Norwood said, stopping a few feet away. He didn't mention that it had been a lucky snap shot that had hit even his foot. "I ought to finish you off and tell 'em the hostiles got you," he added, knowing that he would never shoot an unarmed man.

"You don't have the gumption to kill anybody!" Horn spat.

"You'll find out if you make a move toward me or that rifle."

He saw Horn's eyes go toward the rifle that was about eight feet away.

"You deny you just tried to kill me?" Norwood demanded.

"You must have more lives than a cat," Horn responded.

"That wound seems to be bleeding a lot. Hope I didn't hit an artery. If so, you can use your belt for a tourniquet, and maybe you won't bleed to death." He paused, pondering the situation. "Tell you what I'm gonna do, Horn . . . I'll send a couple of men back for you. They can pack you out on a litter. In the meantime. . . ."

He stepped over and picked up Horn's carbine by the barrel and flung it down the slope as far as he could.

"Now, since you can still move after a fashion, that will give me time to get out of range, but it'll allow you to get your weapon in case those hostiles come back after I leave. That's more than you'd do for me."

He was suddenly aware that the familiar weight of his holstered Colt was missing. His gun belt was gone, and he retraced the path of his fall looking for it, keeping one eye on the treacherous scout. Finding the gun belt near the rocks where they had been crouched, he set his carbine down and swung the belt around his waist. Then he saw what had happened. The metal buckle was bent and mangled, half torn out of the heavy canvas cartridge belt. Horn had fired just as Norwood turned to look across the cañon. Instead of hitting him square, the bullet had struck the buckle at an oblique angle, tearing it loose and causing Norwood's untensed abdominal muscles to feel as if he had been kicked by a mule.

With the gun belt slung over one shoulder and his carbine in the other hand, he started back down the cañon. As he

200

passed near Horn, he paused.

"If you want to say a hostile bullet did that to you, I won't publicly contradict you. You're through scouting for a few months . . . maybe for good. As soon as Doc Sutter works on that wound, you'll be sent back to the States. Just remember, if you ever come near me again, I'll kill you without thinking twice about it. You're a killer, Horn . . . a damn disgrace to the Army, even as a civilian. If you want my advice, you'd better be long gone by the time this column gets back to Bowie. I'd reckon the next man you try to kill probably won't be half as generous as I am."

Horn glared at him, his face ashen under the weathered skin, the receding hairline making him look older.

"By the way, if you get thirsty, there's water in the river, about a mile and a half that way," he said over his shoulder as he started down his backtrail as quickly as his sore stomach would allow.

"Damn! What else can happen?" Captain Lawton fumed when he heard that his chief of scouts was wounded.

Norwood reported that they had been out hunting deer, were fired on by some hostiles, and that Horn had been shot in the foot, both of which statements were true but unrelated.

Two soldiers and a packer were dispatched with a spare pony to rescue him, and the four of them returned without further incident about dark. In the interim Norwood had privately told Babcock the real story.

"Now it just remains to be seen what he'll say," Perry replied after he had silently listened. "You may still have to bring charges and expose him for what he is."

"Not likely he'll say anything. He can't prove that I shot him any more than I can prove that he tried to kill me several times. If it came right down to it, the only thing that I could prove with eyewitness testimony of enlisted men is that business

201

about letting the hostiles get away several months ago . . . the incident that started this whole mess." He took a deep breath and accepted the fresh cup of coffee Perry handed him. "No, let him go out as a wounded heroic chief of scouts and get a job with Cody's Wild West Show, or join the Pinkertons, or whatever he wants to do with his reputation. He won't bother me any more."

Perry looked dubious. "I still think you're being too easy on somebody who's been trying to kill you."

"What would you have me do? I could go through all kinds of public accusations, which nobody cares about now. I let the proper time for that go by several months ago when I was on active duty, when it might have counted for something at my court martial. But now all it would accomplish would be to make an enemy for life. No . . . let him go. Anybody who has no moral compunction about murder will eventually seal his own fate, one way or another."

Perry nodded. "I suspect Horn will be sent back to Bowie with Lieutenant Parker tomorrow, along with a sick trooper and a courier."

"Let's hope that's an end to it."

"By the way, those two couriers, Edwaddy and Lang, came back in today from down around Sahuaripa. The hostiles hit a Mexican pack train near Ures. It was on its way to the mines loaded with flour, canned food, and a lot of other stuff. The Apaches killed the packers and took what they wanted, including the mules. Then they struck north."

"May be the same bunch we set afoot a while back."

"Wouldn't doubt it. They've got themselves resupplied now."

"Seems like that raid on the Yaqui River was weeks ago. You have any idea what month this is?"

Perry looked slightly perplexed. "Maybe the second week of August. That's about as close as I can guess."

202

"Amazing how the trappings of civilization . . . like calendars . . . don't mean anything down here," Russ said draining his coffee cup. Thunder rumbled in the near distance. "Well, here we go again."

"The Sierra Madre does seem like another world, doesn't it?"

The next morning Russ Norwood watched from a distance as Tom Horn, in obvious pain, was helped astride a mule, his foot swathed in a thick bandage. A pair of makeshift crutches was tied to his saddle and, without a backward glance, he rode off with Lieutenant Parker and the other two horsemen.

He breathed a sigh of relief and turned away to roll up his blanket — a blanket that seemed to have more bacon fat melted into it than the bacon itself. He shook out the blowflies, making a mental note to scrub it as best he could with sand when they made camp that night. The problem was there wasn't any soap left in camp, and grease would not dissolve in cold creek water.

The column marched several miles that day to a spot on the Arros River near better water and grass. An old stone corral apparently built by Mexicans for defensive purposes when traveling in this country was discovered nearby.

Norwood had just dismounted, tied his pony to a bush, and was looking for a likely spot to drop his bedroll when he heard Stratford McGee's voice.

"Come quick! Something's happened to Captain Lawton!"

He and Babcock and several of the cavalrymen came running to find Mac crouched over the prostrate form of the commander.

"I heard him say something about feeling sick, and the next thing I know, he's throwing up. Then he kinda weaves around in his saddle and falls right out."

"Get Doctor Sutter."

The doctor was already on his way, having seen the commotion. Lawton had come to himself enough to roll over and retch violently.

"What did he have to eat?" the doctor asked, looking at the vomitus.

There was silence for a few seconds.

"I saw him eating out of one of those cans of corned beef," one of the men volunteered.

"Where is it?"

"Probably threw the can away."

"In the saddlebag," Lawton croaked weakly. "I just ate some more of it. . . ."

One of the men quickly retrieved the two-pound tin and handed it over to the doctor. Sutter looked at the remaining meat in the can and then sniffed it. Lawton vomited violently twice more and then collapsed on the ground.

"Probably ptomaine poisoning," the doctor said. "Get him down to the river."

Norwood, Babcock, and McGee, along with three others, picked up the big man by the arms and legs, face downward so he wouldn't choke, and carried him along a steep, difficult trail about three hundred feet to the edge of the river. There, Doctor Sutter directed them to make a blanket shelter over some bushes. While this was going on the doctor sent a soldier to fetch coffee. Then he had the men take off Lawton's shirt and pants and vigorously rub his arms and legs and torso. When the vomiting subsided, the doctor stimulated him with as much hot coffee as he could get him to drink.

Sutter watched him carefully for a time to see if Lawton could retain the bitter, black brew. Finally he said, "I tink he vill be all right now. He has purged most of the poison from his system."

"That was a mighty near thing," Russ said as he and Perry walked back up the hill to their camp site. McGee and one of the privates had volunteered to stay and help the doctor.

"It sure was. Food will spoil in this heat in no time."

"Yeah. He had just opened that can this morning."

"I saw a piece of fresh meat somebody hung up yesterday. It was filled with maggots from blowflies in less than two hours," Perry said. "And, speaking of medical problems, how is your stomach?"

"Sore as the devil. Good thing the rest of you had a grip on Lawton, 'cause I had to let go of him a couple of times on that trail when I stepped down and jarred myself."

"Did you have Doc Sutter look at you?"

Russ shook his head. "He'd probably just order me to rest, and I'll do plenty of that today, since Lawton is too weak to travel. I'll be all right in a couple of days. Those muscles are just bruised pretty good."

True to his resolve, Norwood rested the remainder of the day in camp, while Babcock washed his clothes and blankets, then shaved, cleaned his guns and saddle, and attended to the sore back of his mule. The Indian scouts were out in small bunches scouting for trails on their own.

"Hell, Gatewood may have been sent down here just to wind up getting mired in the same frustrations we're in," Perry remarked to Russ later that day. "If we can't find Geronimo for him, he might as well go home. There's no sense in him hanging around here. He's a sick man."

Captain Lawton gradually improved and was well enough the next day to ride his mule when the command moved out at six-thirty in the morning. They traveled slowly north and west all day toward Nacori and went into camp near some stone tanks in the rocks after covering a total of fifteen miles.

The column continued on the next morning and marched to Bacadehuachi, a town situated on a broad desert mesa, flanked on either side by ever-rising folds of higher mountains, stair-stepping away into the distance. The small town was dominated by the beautiful white-washed twin bell towers of a Spanish-style church.

From here, four pack mules and as many packers left the command to travel over the mountains directly west to Oposura to stock up on supplies. They were to rejoin the command later. Norwood watched them move away through the dusty mesquite more than half wishing he was going with them. But then, he wondered if Elena Caldersn had yet returned to Oposura.

The column remained in town only about two hours and then moved on, Russ Norwood and Stratford McGee being the last ones to ride out. Captain Lawton had instructed them to make sure all the Indian scouts were out of town. Yet, he and McGee had ridden hardly more than four miles when they noticed that the Apache scouts were straggling farther and farther behind.

"What do yuh reckon is the matter with them?" McGee remarked, twisting on his pony to survey the lagging scouts. "They're actin' about half drunk."

Norwood reined up and took a long look back. "They sure as hell do. They must've gotten their hands on some liquor while we were in town."

The scouts were passing the bottles back and forth as they came up to the waiting white men. One of the scouts said something to McGee, and Mac replied shortly.

"What'd he say?" Russ asked.

"Wants us to join 'em. They're going to shoot some Mexicans."

"What?"

"Yeah. They're lookin' for a little entertainment. I told 'em we couldn't do that just now."

"One of us had better ride ahead and warn Lawton," Russ said, suddenly alarmed at the sight of the drunken scouts who were milling around them.

"I think both of us had better ride ahead," Mac said. "This bunch is gonna be outa control very shortly."

The two men kicked their ponies into a lope and rode on until they encountered several sober scouts at the back of the column, along with a sergeant of cavalry. Norwood quickly explained the situation to the sergeant. The non-com singled out two privates and they, along with the sober scouts, returned with Norwood and McGee. The column ahead had halted at the sound of gunshots coming from the rear. The drunken scouts were yelling and firing their guns in the air and at everything in sight.

While Norwood and McGee stood back, the sober scouts tried to reason with their brother Apaches. When this failed, they waited until a man had emptied his gun and then tackled him. The soldiers used the same tactics, and then Norwood and McGee waded into the fray. Several fights were going on, and Norwood caught a fist in his tender midsection that put him on the ground. His Indian assailant suddenly collapsed on top of him, and Norwood looked up to see that one of the sober scouts had used his gun butt on the man.

It took the better part of a half hour before the row was quieted, and a rather damaged bunch of drunks was disarmed and herded on ahead, most of them bleeding and bruised. Between the hangovers and the fights, it was a very subdued detail of scouts that took the trail the next day.

Working their way northward, the command marched twelve miles that day, thirty miles the next, and twenty-two miles the following day. Aside from the unabating heat and the nightly downpours of rain, they saw and heard nothing of interest. Even the villagers in the sleepy little town of Opoto, who treated them very well, could give them no news of the Indians.

The third night after the fight a Mexican pack train, coming down from the north, pulled in and camped nearby. Two or three hours of daylight were left when the train went into camp, and Norwood noticed some of the packers paying a courtesy call on Captain Lawton.

After the Mexicans left, Lawton sent for Norwood, Babcock, and McGee. When they reported, they found Lieutenant Gatewood already there.

"If they can be believed, those Mexican packers just brought me more news of the hostiles than we've had in weeks," Lawton announced when the three men had gathered by his fire. "They tell me the Indians are up near Fronteras. They know this because Juan Vargas's home was visited by some of their women a couple of nights ago. His wife understands Apache, and they explained that they wanted to open communications with him concerning surrender, since he is the prefect."

McGee shook his head. "That doesn't sound like Geronimo . . . wanting to deal with the Mexicans."

"It does seem rather strange," Lawton agreed. "But Vargas ordered three mules loaded with food and mescal given to the women, telling them it was a gift of good will, and instructing them to take it to their people and invite the Apache leaders into town for a talk."

Babcock started to say something, but Lawton held up his hand to silence him. "You haven't heard the rest of this story. As soon as the women were sent on their way, Vargas sent out couriers to call in all the Mexican troops in his district. His idea, according to these packers, is to get the Apaches into Fronteras on the pretext of negotiating a surrender, get them about half drunk on mescal, and then murder them all with the troops."

"I can't believe that wily old devil, Geronimo, would fall for a trick like that," Norwood said.

"I don't know what to think," Lawton replied. "Maybe it

was Geronimo's way of getting free food and mescal without raiding for it. In any case, it's a lead for us. Gatewood, I want you to take your two Indians, and I'll give you several good men as escort and McGee, here, as interpreter. Head straight for Fronteras as fast as you can and get a lead on these hostiles to open up communications, according to your orders from Miles."

"Yes, sir."

"That's all for now. The rest of the command will follow along as quickly as we can," Lawton said, dismissing them.

"I knew nothing good would come of Lawton's finding out I could speak Apache," Mac grumbled to Russ and Perry as the three men walked away. "I've seen about all the hostile Indians I care to for a while."

"Better get your gear together," Russ said. "You can use my saddle."

"I think you should come along, too," Mac said.

"You know, that's not a bad idea," he mused. "After all this tramping around, I'd hate to think I might miss out on the finish."

"It could be *your* finish," Perry reminded him. "I think you've been overworking that guardian angel of yours." He grinned.

"I'll ask Lawton if you can go," Mac concluded, sounding as if he were now looking forward to the assignment. "I need to borrow a rifle anyway," he said, hurrying off.

"I'm going for a swim," Russ said when Mac was gone. "You coming?"

"Yeah. I'll join you," Perry said.

The two men had a good, cooling swim in a deep pool just below camp and then washed out some of their sweaty clothes and dried them on a rock. While they were at this, they could see and hear a cloudburst with dark veils of rain and rumbles of thunder in the mountain not far above their camp.

Just over a half hour later, as they were climbing up the bank to dress, they heard a roaring sound. Then, from around a bend in the cañon, a four-foot high wall of water came rushing at them. They scrambled to higher ground, grabbing up their damp clothing as the flash flood swept by, carrying rocks and uprooted trees and bushes along with the brown water.

An hour later they were cooking supper when Captain Lawton strode up to their fire.

"That damned Gatewood hasn't left *yet!*" he grated. "What the hell's wrong with the man? He was given an order by me, and he hasn't carried it out. I've a good mind to put him under arrest!"

"Easy, Captain," Babcock said, unfolding his lanky frame and standing up. "He's a sick man. Maybe he just wants to get a little rest and start out fresh in the morning."

"Rest, hell! That's all he's been doing since he got here. If he was sick, he shouldn't have accepted this assignment!" The wrought-up commander was practically shouting.

"Don't worry, Captain," Norwood said hurriedly. "McGee and I will get him on the trail. I'm sure he's as anxious to get this over with as we are."

"Okay, Norwood," Lawton said, somewhat less agitated. "I'll expect him out of here by midnight."

Chapter Seventeen

Gatewood finally rode out of camp at two o'clock in the morning while Captain Lawton was snoring softly on his blanket. Besides the two reservation Apaches, Kaytennay and Martine, one Apache scout, Norwood, McGee, and four cavalrymen rode with him. There was little talking among them as the ten horsemen headed north. They had a long ride ahead of them, and time was critical.

The usual nightly downpour of rain had passed, and a half moon was peeking in and out of the drifting clouds. Since none of them knew the way to Fronteras, they rode in a general northwest direction, picking their way by the intermittent moonlight. By four-thirty there was enough dawn light to see, and they increased their pace. Two hours later they intersected a well-defined wagon road and turned north along it for another hour before stopping. Eager as they were to be on their way, the horses and mules needed rest, so they spent an hour around a fire, boiling coffee and frying deer meat for breakfast.

The rest of that long, hot day was spent riding due north, following the easy road. Norwood constantly scanned the flanks of the ridges far back on either side of the road for any sign of hostiles. He noticed the others doing the same. The four troopers brought up the rear of the column, riding by twos, sometimes talking, now and then swapping chews of tobacco. Even though three of them were down to their undershirts, the black issue hats, the ragged sky-blue trousers, and the carbines slung from their saddles still identified them as U. S. cavalry.

Alternately trotting and walking their animals, they were within a few miles of Fronteras, by the time they camped an hour before dark.

"Judas! Even with a saddle my backside took a pounding," Mac remarked as he dismounted with a groan.

"Anybody's backside would be sore after the day we've put in," Russ replied, loosening his cinch. "We must've covered at least seventy miles."

No one even stood watch that night as they all slept the sleep of the exhausted.

Norwood tried not to let on, but he was still feeling the effects of the long ride the next morning, even though his stomach muscles were some better. Lieutenant Gatewood was pale and drawn, but he was ready to go after a quick breakfast of crackers and jerky.

By midmorning they were in Fronteras. The story the Mexican packers had related was true, they discovered, after they called on the prefect, Juan Vargas. His distaste at seeing them was obvious, and he answered their questions with growing impatience.

"I have brought in two hundred of my troops, a detachment at a time by night, to trap these savages. When they come into our town to talk, they will be *eliminated!*" He slammed a huge fist on the desk to emphasize his statement. "None of you will interfere with that."

"May I remind you, *Señor* Vargas, that our two countries have a treaty," Gatewood said with firm patience. "We have been pursuing Geronimo and his band for many months. I have been sent here personally by General Nelson Miles to open negotiations with these Indians for their surrender."

"We will save you the trouble," Vargas retorted, glaring at the thin, pale lieutenant.

Gatewood, who had not been in the field as long as the others, still wore a reasonable semblance of his blue uniform, identifying him as a cavalry officer in the United States Army. Vargas bore a striking contrast, being a man of about forty, short and stout, thick black hair and mustache, and a florid complexion. Freshly shaved and scented, he was obviously impressed with his position as prefect. As he became more agitated, he began puffing out his cheeks between statements.

"If most of the people in town know about your trap, what makes you think the Apaches don't know about it?" Norwood asked in a calmer voice.

"Because our only contact with those Apaches was the squaws we sent back with provisions. I was very careful to recall my soldiers at night and have kept them hidden."

Norwood shook his head. There was no reasoning with this man. "The Apaches have eyes and ears everywhere. And besides, this same trick was played on their people years ago. They have long memories. They will not be fooled again."

Vargas puffed his plump cheeks, and his short neck disappeared in rolls of flesh. "These squaws came to my house to start negotiations with *me*," he stated, perspiration beginning to show on the tieless white shirt he wore. "I sent them east into the mountains to bring their people in for a conference. Geronimo loves to make big talk. He will come. He may hate the Mexican people, but he will come. It is unfortunate that your American soldiers could not catch this devil and his band, but I will soon have them in my grasp." He formed a fat fist in Gatewood's face. "I, Juan Vargas, have done what you Americans could not do. And I will not have any interference from you now." He turned and walked back behind his desk. "You can go back to your commander and tell him what I said. *¡Buenas días!*"

The men left the office in the adobe building and started down the street to the nearest saloon. Gatewood stopped just short of the hitching rail where their animals were tied.

"I'll take Kaytennay and Martine and McGee and leave town, heading south, the way we came from," he said. "When I get a few miles down the road, we'll cut east into the mountains and see if we can pick up the trail of this hostile band. We have to make contact before Vargas does."

"I'll come with you," Norwood said.

"Suit yourself. I just don't want to take too many." He instructed the four enlisted men: "You can stay here and keep an eye on things. I can't take any soldiers where I'm going. Geronimo knows me and trusts me. But there can be only a few of us, including Kaytennay and Martine, and we must go forward under a flag of truce." He pulled his horse's reins loose from the hitching rail. "You men are free to do whatever you want today. Just keep your eyes and ears open and your wits about you. And, for God's sake, go easy on the alcohol." These were his parting words to the cavalrymen. "The rest of you, let's go."

Norwood, McGee, and the three Indians swung into their saddles and followed the lieutenant down the dusty street, heading south. They rode about six miles before Gatewood led the way a quarter mile off the road and dismounted. "We'll rest here today. At dark we'll strike east into the mountains."

Hidden in the brush, they were able to catch a few hours of fitful sleep. Just as the sun was setting behind a dark cloud bank, the small party saddled up and started east. They traveled quickly until full darkness and the first drops of the nightly rain overtook them. They camped to get what rest they could in the circumstances with no supper and were on their way again in the gray light of a wet dawn.

Later that day, by bending around and going northward, they finally managed to cut the trail of the squaws and the three

214

Author's Note

The train carrying the Apaches was halted in San Antonio on the order of President Grover Cleveland who had wanted the hostiles held at Fort Bowie until he decided what disposition to make of them. The Indians remained in custody in San Antonio for several weeks while top government officials wrangled over their fate. These Apaches were finally sent on to Florida where they were housed at Fort Marion and Fort Pickens. All the other Chiricahuas who had remained peaceably on the reservations were also transported to Florida on a separate train. An impassioned plea was received from General George Crook for the release of the friendly scouts who had given such faithful and skillful service to the Army. His plea was ignored.

In 1887 the Apaches were transferred to Mount Vernon Barracks, Alabama, where they lived until their removal to Fort Sill, Oklahoma in 1894. Geronimo died there in 1909 from pneumonia he contracted after falling, drunk, from his buggy and lying on the wet, cold ground all night. Finally, in 1913, the surviving exiles and their families were given a choice of an allotment of land or transportation to the Mescalero reservation in New Mexico.

For the most part, my fictional characters interact with historical events. However, there are a couple of possibly notable exceptions: Tom Horn may not have been present at the March, 1886 surrender conference between Geronimo and General George Crook. Horn *did* accompany the expedition that summer as interpreter and scout, but he may not have been wounded or sent home early. Al Sieber, chief of scouts, *was* shot in the pack mules. The Apache scout did most of the tracking, and the small party continued making good time the rest of the day. There was no rain that night, and the men were able to make small fires for coffee to wash down their jerky and crackers.

In the morning the Apache scout was sent back by Gatewood to inform Lawton of where the trail was leading so he could bring up his column. All that day and the next they trailed the squaws until the signs of their passage merged into the main trail of a large band. As the trail grew hotter, the party proceeded more slowly. Gatewood took an empty flour sack from his saddlebags and tied it to a stick. He rode ahead with the two Apaches through some rough and broken country, making sure the white flag was clearly visible to anyone who might be watching.

Finally, at the head of a cañon which they thought led into the Bavispe Valley, the two reservation Indians halted. They said something to each other and then, as Gatewood came up, pointed at a piece of cloth hanging on a nearby bush. It was a pair of faded canvas pants.

"What d'ya suppose that means?" Gatewood wondered aloud.

"Some kind of signal?" Norwood said.

They grouped around, silently regarding the pants. If it was some sort of sign, not one of them could make a guess as to what it meant.

Gatewood looked at the silent cañon that yawned before them. "Kaytennay, you and Martine go ahead a few hundred yards. Then Norwood and McGee. I'll bring up the rear."

The two Indians conversed briefly in their own language.

"Speak English!" Gatewood ordered. He turned in his saddle and glanced disgustedly at the rest of the party. "What're you grinning at?" he demanded of McGee.

"Your two Indians. They were just telling each other that

215

they're not greedy. They're willing to divide the glory among the whole party."

"Meaning?"

"They don't want to go into that cañon first."

Norwood grinned in spite of himself, which seemed to exasperate Gatewood even more. After a short hesitation, Gatewood said, "All right. We'll all ride in together." He again raised the stick with the white flour sack, and the five of them started forward at a walk.

The cañon was deserted.

Several miles farther on they reached the Bavispe River where the stream swept into a big bend and began flowing southward. Here the lieutenant called a halt for the night, making camp in a thick cane brake just under a hill that gave a good view of the surrounding country. Since there was still plenty of daylight, he sent Martine to the top of the hill and Kaytennay to follow the hostiles' trail for another few miles.

Reaching from horseback, Gatewood tied the flour sack to the pole of a century plant, high enough for the truce signal to be in plain view.

"You think the hostiles are watching us, Lieutenant?" McGee asked, eyeing the officer's action.

"If they are, I want to be sure they see this."

"A white flag doesn't make a man bullet proof," McGee remarked.

"Right you are. This peace commission business is getting mighty touchy. I'm just taking all the precautions I can."

At sundown Kaytennay returned with the information that the hostiles occupied a position only four miles away. They were situated in a rocky camp high in the Torres Mountains, just above a bend in the Bavispe River. Kaytennay went on to say that he had gone on into the camp and made contact with Geronimo. The war chief had told him that the approach of the small party had been under observation for some time, but he had not known who was dogging his trail. Geronimo had an easy familiarity with Kaytennay and had sent him back to say that he was somewhat offended that his old friend, Gatewood, had not come straight into his camp where peaceably inclined people were welcome.

Gatewood smiled slightly at this message, delivered in broken English. The Indian went on to say that Natchez welcomed the approach of the party as long as they behaved themselves.

Gatewood thanked Kaytennay and dismissed the Apache to get some supper and rest.

"They know we're here. Let's build a fire and get some hot coffee," Gatewood said, looking much more at ease. "Natchez is the hereditary chief. If he says we'll have safe passage, I feel a lot better. That windy old Geronimo sure can't be trusted."

In spite of these assurances, Norwood slipped his gun belt, with its loaded Colt, under the saddle he was using for a pillow when he spread his blanket in the cane brake that night. He hoped no snakes would decide to share his bed.

Before the rays of the morning sun had penetrated the camp, one of Lawton's scouts rode in. Three guns covered him until he was close enough to be recognized. He reported that all thirty scouts under the guidance of Sergeant Joe Colcannon, who had been pressed into service with the scouts after Tom Horn had left, were camped nearby.

Gatewood ordered the scouts brought up, and the combined party moved forward. When they were within a mile of the hostile camp, a lone unarmed Chiricahua met them on the trail, holding up his hand to halt the column. This Indian repeated the message that Kaytennay had delivered the night before. Then he was joined by three mounted warriors who were armed with repeating rifles. With McGee interpreting, they delivered instructions from Natchez for the large body of scouts to return to their camp of the night before. They were also to hold any troops that might come up. Natchez further suggested that the two parties meet for a conference a short distance ahead in a bend of the river where there was plenty of wood, water, grass, and shade.

After Gatewood agreed, Sergeant Colcannon led the scouts away, and the lieutenant, Kaytennay, Martine, McGee, and Norwood accompanied the three hostiles forward another mile or so to the designated meeting place on a grassy benchland in the bend of the Bavispe River.

A few at a time the hostiles came in, unsaddled, and turned out their ponies to graze. Gatewood, Norwood, and McGee emptied their saddlebags of provisions and put them on the Indians' pile of jerked horse meat and corn cakes. Gatewood added several pounds of tobacco, cigarette papers, and matches to the common commissary.

One of the last to arrive was Geronimo, apparently as conscious of his own presence as some famous stage actor. A strange chill went up Russ Norwood's back as it always did at the sight of Geronimo. It was his first look at the elusive Apache since the previous March at the surrender conference with General Crook. Norwood had the oddest feeling that all of this was being replayed with nearly the same cast — except that now the military delegation was unarmed and totally at the mercy of the hostile Apaches.

Geronimo came forward and laid his Winchester on the ground about twenty feet in front of Gatewood who was sitting on one of the Indian saddles that had been thrown over a log. Geronimo then came forward and shook hands with the lieutenant. With McGee acting as interpreter, he remarked that Gatewood was much thinner since they had last met. He asked what was wrong.

Gatewood replied that he had been sick. The Apache leader

218

grunted a non-committal reply and then sat down, cross-legged, in front of Gatewood, looking him squarely in the eye.

While this was going on, McGee passed the tobacco and cigarette papers around to the two dozen heavily armed Apaches.

Norwood was very uneasy. This was a much smaller group of peace negotiators than previously. Geronimo could not play to the camera this time. Yet, the old chief was acting just as proudly and seemingly in command of the situation as he had before.

Geronimo announced through McGee that he was here to listen to the message from General Miles. Norwood thought this was unusually abrupt for the loquacious Apache chief.

Gatewood was equally to the point as he replied: "Surrender, and you will be sent to join the rest of your people in Florida. The President will then decide what is to be done with you. Accept these terms or fight it out to the bitter end."

Norwood held his breath to see how the proud old Apache would react to this ultimatum. A long, tense silence fell on the group. If they decided to fight, they could start immediately, he realized. If they decided not to honor the flag of truce, the twenty-five hostiles could make short work of the five of them on the spot.

Then Geronimo did something totally unexpected. He rubbed one hand across his eyes and then held out both hands to Gatewood to show that they were trembling. He said something that McGee translated as, "Do you have anything to drink? We have been on a three-day drunk on the mescal that our squaws got from the Mexicans. Those Mexicans expected to play their old trick of getting us drunk and killing us, but we have fooled them and drunk their mescal."

Gatewood looked startled at this sudden change of subject. Apparently the old fox was stalling. As in the previous conference, he didn't want to give a direct, quick answer. Geronimo was again speaking. When he paused, Gatewood looked at McGee.

"We had fun with the mescal," he translated, "but our spree has passed now and we are a little shaky. You can see from the men here that we have had no fights among ourselves."

Gatewood replied that he had left Fronteras so quickly he had forgotten to supply himself with anything to drink.

Geronimo shook his head slowly, licking his dry lips. Then he returned to business. He told Gatewood they would leave the warpath only on the condition that they be allowed to return to the reservation, occupy their former farms there, and be furnished with the usual rations, clothing, implements, with a guaranteed exemption from punishment for anything they had done.

Norwood could feel sweat running down his forehead from under his hat, and his cotton shirt was sticking to his back. He knew the answer before Gatewood gave it: the Lieutenant could not promise this. Miles had told him what he could say, and he had already said it.

Then Geronimo resorted to his usual recitation of past grievances against white injustices. Norwood turned a deaf ear to this. He had heard it all before. As his eyes wandered around to the other Apaches, he was shocked to see one of them holding his Marlin carbine. The Indian was staring straight at him. He could not read the stony expression, but he boldly returned the stare. Was this the man who had pursued him into the cañon that wild night? What did the Apache think of the "crazy" McGee now acting as interpreter? He didn't recognize this Indian as one of the five who had jumped their camp. But, considering his own state of fear and panic that night, he doubted he could now identify any of them.

He turned his gaze away, removing his hat and wiping a sleeve across his brow as he glanced around at the animals, looking for Plato. But his gray mule was not among the Indians' mounts.

After his harangue, Geronimo withdrew his band for a private conference that lasted for over an hour. During this break, Norwood and McGee built a fire of driftwood, boiled some coffee, and ate some jerky and corn cakes. In spite of his nervousness, Norwood was hungry and ate his fill.

When the conference reconvened, Geronimo said that it was too much to expect them to give up all their lands to a race of intruders. They would, however, give it all up except the reservations. They would move back to the reservation, or they would fight to the death.

Norwood began sweating again.

Natchez, who had taken almost no part in the proceedings, chose this moment to say that, even if they decided to continue fighting, the small party who had come to talk to them as friends would be allowed to depart in peace, as long as they did not begin any hostilities.

Norwood drew a deep breath and relaxed slightly after this statement. But then Gatewood dropped a mortar shell among them by saying, "The rest of your people . . . about four or five hundred of them . . . who remained on the reservation have all been removed to Florida. If you go back to the reservation, you will be living among your enemies, the other Apaches bands."

This put a new light on the matter, and the hostiles again retired for a private discussion. When they returned after another hour, Geronimo declared they would continue to fight, but he apparently had some misgivings about this because he continued to talk, asking many questions about what kind of man General Miles was, what he looked like, his age, whether he talked much or little, whether he was cruel or kind. Gatewood patiently answered all his questions.

Finally, after much smoking and talking, Gatewood suggested that his party retire to their camp of the previous night about four miles downriver where the scouts were waiting. He said that Captain Lawton and his men had probably already arrived there. Then Geronimo said something very curious.

"If you were an Apache and not a white man, what would you do?"

"I would trust General Miles and take him at his word," was Gatewood's prompt reply.

When McGee finished translating this, the hostiles stood silently, looking very solemn. Finally, Geronimo announced that they would discuss it among themselves and would let Gatewood know the results of their council in the morning.

The old chief made one last try by asking Gatewood personally to ride cross-country to General Miles to ask for a modification of terms. He offered to send an escort of his warriors to ensure Gatewood's safety.

Gatewood replied that it would be useless since General Miles had already made up his mind.

The two parties shook hands and mounted their horses, riding away in opposite directions along the river.

Chapter Eighteen

"Bay-chen-daysen!" one of the Apache scouts cried, jogging in from his position as picket on the perimeter of the camp. *"Bay-chen-daysen!"*

"What does he want?" Captain Lawton asked, rising from his cooking fire.

"He's calling me," Gatewood answered, coming up as he buttoned his shirt. "That's my Apache name . . . Long Nose."

Lawton nearly broke into a grin. "And they say Indians have no sense of humor."

The rays of the morning sun were just slanting down into Lawton's camp, and Geronimo was passing the word by way of the Apache sentry that he was ready to talk.

Gatewood, McGee, and Norwood followed the sentry to a spot along the river about four hundred yards from camp where they found Geronimo and several of his warriors waiting. The hostiles dismounted, unsaddled their ponies, and laid their arms on their saddles. Geronimo alone kept a large pistol on his hip, slid slightly to the front where his hand was close to it. The Apache war chief strode to the front and spoke for several seconds.

"We have not slept for six months, and we are worn out," McGee translated. "We are ready to surrender to General Miles in person but only under the following conditions."

The conditions Geronimo wanted called for Captain Lawton and his soldiers to accompany them for protection to some point in the United States where their band of twenty-four bucks and fourteen women and children would surrender in person

223

to the new General Miles. Geronimo and his people would retain their arms until the formal surrender, and Geronimo's band and Lawton's command would have free access to each other's camps along the way.

Gatewood invited Geronimo's delegation into camp, and these terms were agreeable to Captain Lawton. The word was dispatched to the waiting hostiles, and the Indians proceeded to move their camp down closer to Lawton's.

Lawton sent two couriers, along with a corporal who knew Morse code, north to the border to send the news to General Miles by heliograph. He suggested that Skeleton Cañon, about sixty miles southeast of Fort Bowie, should be the surrender site.

"I can't believe this campaign is ending so quietly," Perry Babcock remarked to Russ Norwood when they were finally alone.

"Better than ending in some kind of slaughter or a shootout," Russ replied.

"I guess it's like Geronimo said . . . they're plumb worn out . . . and it's not just the hostiles," Perry said.

The hostiles were out of food, and looked to the Americans to supply some, but Lawton, much to his embarrassment and the Indians' amusement, had to admit that the pack train, in trying to catch up with Gatewood's party, had wandered off on the wrong trail and had not yet reached camp. The Indians slaughtered a mule and offered some of it to Lawton's command. Since no deer or wild beef could be found in the immediate vicinity, the Americans accepted.

"First time we've had to eat mule on this whole trip," Mac remarked as he spitted a piece of the raw meat on a stick to roast over the fire.

"When they have a choice, the Indians like it better than beef," Perry replied.

"That's not much of a recommendation," Mac snorted.

The pack train arrived two days later, and Lawton spent another day in camp, letting everyone get rested and fed and allowing the couriers time to get the heliograph message sent to Miles and to receive a reply.

On the morning of August 24th the column moved out slowly, marching north toward the border. They followed the Bavispe River, the brushy slopes of the gorge angling up steeply from the river.

Two days later, just as the combined columns had passed the point where the Bavispe River flowed out of the mountains and the terrain began to level out, one of the scouts returned from riding ahead to report that a large force of Mexican troops was approaching from the west. Lawton halted the command and held a hurried conference with Babcock, McGee, and Norwood. The four of them rode to a slight rise above the river from where they could plainly make out a column of infantry, dressed in white, coming over the ridge about two miles away. Lawton used a pair of field glasses to get a closer look.

"This is no chance meeting," Lawton declared. "They're marching fast and trying to head us off." He shoved the glasses back into their case and pulled his mule's head around, leading the way back to the column.

The word had been spread, and the packers were already piling the packs into breastworks, and the scouts were throwing up stone barricades in preparation for a fight. The hostile Indians were especially excited.

"Let me take Geronimo's band and make a run for it," Gatewood suggested. "You can stay behind and stall them."

"Good idea," Babcock agreed. "This could get ugly. Better to give these Indians a head start."

Lawton pondered this for a few moments. "All right. Gatewood, take Natchez and most of the band and ride like hell for the border. Geronimo and seven of his bucks will stay here for now, just in case we can't avoid a fight." He turned in his saddle and pointed. "Babcock, you and Norwood will come with me. We'll go out and meet them to parley. Give the hostiles time to put some distance between us."

Without a word, the men turned to carry out his orders. McGee stayed with Geronimo and the seven warriors who were sitting their ponies, talking excitedly among themselves and nervously fingering their weapons.

Lawton, Babcock, and Norwood rode out to intercept the Mexicans as Gatewood and Natchez galloped away with the rest of the band, three or four of the warriors dropping back to form a rear guard.

"We're probably less than ten miles from Fronteras," Norwood said as the three of them rode out toward the approaching column. "Vargas had his troops ready and waiting. I'll bet he's hopping mad."

The trio reined up near the edge of a cane brake and awaited the column that was proceeding, single file, toward them with Juan Vargas himself leading them on horseback. He wore a wide-brimmed hat and a dark jacket with fancy stitching on the lapels and collar. As soon as he spotted them, he held up one hand for the foot soldiers behind him to stop. Then he kneed his black horse forward to meet Captain Lawton. Perspiration was streaming down the stocky prefect's face, but he did not remove his hat or wipe his face. Russ thought he resembled a fat candle that was beginning to melt in the hot sun. Vargas gave them all a black look, especially Norwood.

"I am Juan Vargas, prefect of Fronteras, in case your man here has not told you," Vargas spat, indicating Norwood.

"What do you want?" Lawton asked bluntly, forcing the prefect to state his case, as if Lawton didn't already know.

"I am in charge of this district, and these Apaches, these

devils incarnate, are my responsibility. I will take them from you with the thanks of my people. We will deal with them according to our law."

It was easy to see that he was seething, barely able to maintain his civil veneer.

"Geronimo and his band have already surrendered to us," Captain Lawton said. "We are taking them across the border. They will not prey upon your people again."

"Their squaws approached us to open surrender talks. I do not believe they have surrendered to you."

"It *is* true. Are you calling me a liar?" Lawton gritted.

"I want to hear it from Geronimo himself," Vargas demanded.

There was an uneasy silence for several long seconds. Vargas's horse tossed its head and turned in a half circle. Norwood watched the Mexican's hands to make sure they did not stray from the reins as he jerked the animal's head back around to face Lawton. One signal from this arrogant leader could send a volley of bullets into them from the troops gathered behind him.

"I will bring Geronimo to you," Lawton finally conceded. He glanced around. "Up out of this cane brake. There . . . over by that grove of trees on the rise." He pointed.

"I will order my men there immediately."

"No. Bring only seven men, and Geronimo will bring seven."

It took about a quarter hour for the two parties to arrive at the designated spot. The Mexican soldiers were armed with Remington rifles. Vargas himself was wearing a fancy, ivory-handled Colt Frontier model .45 on his hip.

The Apache delegation was last to arrive. Geronimo came through the bushes into the clearing, dragging his Winchester by the muzzle with his left hand. He wore his Colt just forward of his hip, ready to his right hand.

As McGee stepped forward and made the introduction in

both languages, Norwood thought he spotted a rider approaching over a low ridge about a half mile away. But the horseman disappeared into a draw before he could get a better look.

Norwood glanced back in time to see the prefect and Geronimo shaking hands, a sight he never expected to see, even though just a formality.

"Why did you not surrender at Fronteras?" Vargas asked. Since the prefect was speaking English instead of Spanish, for benefit of the Americans, Geronimo looked to McGee for a translation. Then he replied, "Because I did not want to be murdered."

"Are you going to surrender to the Americans?" Vargas asked.

"Yes, I am . . . because I can trust them. Whatever happens, they will not murder me and my people."

"Then I will go along and see that you *do* surrender."

The old chief's face clouded when he heard the translation. "No. You are going south, and I am going north. I'll have nothing to do with you or any of your people."

In the blink of an eye Vargas snatched his long-barreled Colt from its holster and held it a foot from Geronimo's belly, hissing something in rapid Spanish. Norwood heard the clicking of hammers as seven Mexican rifles were brought to bear. Instantly the Indians jerked their rifles up and cocked them.

Geronimo's hand stopped half way to his holster as Vargas thumbed back the hammer on his big Colt. The Apache's face twisted into a grimace of hate, the whites of his eyes almost suffusing to red.

Before any of the Americans could respond, Norwood heard the thudding of hoofbeats and a horse and rider burst out of the dense chaparral some thirty yards away. The horseman yanked the sorrel to a stop almost on top of the Apaches who jumped back out of the way, still holding their rifles leveled at the Mexican soldiers.

"*¡Alto!* Stop this!" the rider shouted as the sorrel danced in a circle, kicking up clouds of fine dust.

Norwood forgot that he had his hand on the butt of his Colt as the tension was broken for the moment. He took a closer look at the rider who threw off his hat to let it hang by a cord on his back. He was stunned — paralyzed by surprise as he found himself staring at the features of Elena Maria Calderón. Her face was flushed and her eyes flashing with anger.

"Uncle Juan, you must not do this!" she cried, trying to maneuver her lathered horse between Vargas and Geronimo. But the prefect edged away, jamming the muzzle of his gun into the chief's midsection.

"Damn you, woman! What are you doing here? Get away!"

"No! You must put down your gun. All of you! Before someone is killed."

"You are the one who will be killed if you do not leave," Vargas growled, not taking his eyes from Geronimo as the stand-off continued. "This is no place for a *woman*," he said scornfully. "Go back to town with your aunt!"

Her excited horse continued to prance, so she slipped deftly out of the saddle, letting the animal go. It trotted off, then stepped on its dragging reins, and stopped. Apparently oblivious to the leveled rifles from both sides, she moved up quickly beside Vargas.

"Tell your men to drop their guns, or I will blow your guts out!" Vargas demanded in Spanish of Geronimo.

The chief made no move to comply. Only the fiendish expression on his face betrayed his thoughts.

There was no sound for the space of a long breath. Then Elena's left hand came up from a pocket of her divided riding skirt holding a small pistol which she placed against Vargas's head, just behind the ear.

"Drop your gun, Uncle Juan, or I will shoot you!"

229

"Get away from me, you meddling bitch!" Vargas hissed with terrible ferocity.

Her response was to thumb back the hammer of the .32 nickel-plated Smith & Wesson.

"This gun has a spur trigger, Uncle. Only a slight pressure from my finger will fire it. I would hate to shoot you over something so foolish as this, but I will do it in order to save many lives."

There was a resolve in her voice that Norwood had never heard before. Apparently, Vargas sensed this also, as Russ saw the expression on his perspiring face change from anger and embarrassment to one of fear. The color began draining from his face.

"All right, all right. Be careful," Vargas said. "I am putting my gun away."

He eased down the hammer and holstered the big Colt. He said something in Spanish and the seven soldiers, who were spread out behind him, lowered their rifles.

Geronimo stepped back to stand beside Norwood, Babcock, and Lawton. McGee said something to the Apache who spoke quickly to his warriors. They lowered their weapons.

Norwood let out a sigh, hardly aware he had been holding his breath.

"We will send a courier to notify you in a few days when these Indians are safely in custody at Fort Bowie," Lawton told Vargas. "For now, you must take your men and leave."

Without another word Vargas walked to his horse nearby, mounted, and savagely yanked the animal's head around, spurring him away. The white-clad infantry followed on foot as the Apaches faded back into the brush and disappeared as well.

Russ was at a loss for words as he watched Elena gather the reins of her sorrel and prepare to mount.

"May I ride to your camp?" she asked as she swung into

the saddle. "I do not believe I will be welcome at my uncle's house in Fronteras for a long time." Her expression was grave. "I have ruined my uncle," she added simply, and with sadness. "A man like Juan Vargas cannot stand for a woman to make him lose face in front of his men. He will never recover. He will lose his office and will be laughed at by all the men in the district. I just hope he does not take out his anger on my aunt."

Russ finally found his voice. "He's really your uncle?"

"Only by marriage. If you remember, I told you at the ranch that my Aunt Consuela had married the prefect of Fronteras. She is my father's youngest sister who is only ten years older than I am. I am sure my Aunt Consuela has regretted her decision many times, but her father arranged it because *Señor* Vargas is a man of wealth and influence."

Russ mounted his pony, and the two of them followed McGee, Lawton, and Babcock back toward the scouts and cavalrymen waiting near the river.

"How did you come to be here?" he asked, still bewildered by her sudden appearance. "You seem to show up at the most opportune moments."

"The day after you left the ranch, I was escorted back to the rectory at Oposura by three of my cousins. There I found *Padre* Calderón desperately ill. The two nuns and I were unable to help him, and there was no doctor. We did what we could, but he failed rapidly and died two days later."

"I'm very sorry."

"*Gracias.* I'm certain it was God's will." There was a slight break in her voice, and Russ glanced quickly across at her. She was blinking back the tears. He marveled at this woman. Of what was she made? One minute she was holding a steady gun barrel to a man's head, ready to pull the trigger, and the next she was shedding tears for the loss of an elderly relative.

231

"Anyway, after Father's funeral, I volunteered to travel to Fronteras to ask if the priest there could give us some assistance or ask the Church authorities for a replacement. Since my Aunt Consuela lives there, I went to stay and visit with her. She told me that Uncle Juan had ridden out here with his troops to take Geronimo and his band from your soldiers. My aunt tried to stop me, but I had to ride out to. . . ." Her voice was low, her eyes downcast.

To cover the confusion he felt, Russ said, "And you rode into one helluva situation. But thank God you showed up when you did. You distracted him just enough to save many from being killed."

"Do you remember when I asked if you believed in Divine Providence?"

He nodded.

"I believe this was another example of it."

"Perhaps. But where did you get the gun?"

She looked her surprise at him. "I always carry it when I travel. This is a dangerous country, señor."

"Tell me something. Would you have actually shot him?"

She averted her eyes, and they rode in silence for several seconds.

"Do not ask me such a thing, señor," she finally murmured.

Chapter Nineteen

Captain Lawton was not happy to have a woman traveling with the column but, considering that Elena had just tipped the scales at a critical moment, he could hardly refuse.

"I'll keep an eye on her, Captain," Babcock said. "She's like my little sister. I doubt she'll need much looking after though. She's got a lot of sand in her craw. Besides, she can't go back to Fronteras now."

Lawton, in a hurry to catch up with Gatewood and the rest of the hostiles, acquiesced.

Norwood, McGee, and two scouts were sent forward. On the way one and then another Apache jumped up from hiding beside the trail as the riders passed and jogged after them to take up rear guard positions farther along. The first time this happened, Norwood felt a prickle of fear up his back as the brown body materialized out of the landscape.

"Mighty glad they weren't waiting to bushwhack us," Mac said, echoing Russ's thoughts. "I never saw that buck."

After about three hours of hard riding they managed to catch up with Gatewood who had halted with the hostile band. Norwood filled him in on the strange outcome of the confrontation with the Mexicans. McGee translated the story for Natchez, who grunted his approval.

The band went a short distance farther until they were able to find just enough water in some stone tanks to give the animals a drink and to make coffee. When the rest of the command had not arrived by dark, they built no cooking fires and scattered out to sleep in the wet grass. It was best to take no chances of being caught off guard by any pursuing Mexican forces.

At ten o'clock the next morning, Norwood and McGee rode back in search of Lawton. They located the command in camp about five miles south of the San Bernardino ranch. Captain Lawton had gone to a hilltop near the ranch just on the Arizona side of the border to send a heliographic message. When Norwood and McGee found him, his orderlies were folding up the tripod and putting the mirrors away in their cases. One look at Lawton's face told Norwood something had gone wrong.

"Miles is now stalling about where and when he wants to meet with Geronimo," he stated disgustedly as he stalked off down toward the abandoned ranch buildings below. Norwood and McGee followed him. "I can't get him to give me a definite answer about where he wants to meet them — or *if* he wants to meet them. After all this work and trouble, you'd think he'd be anxious to get this over with." He was talking over his shoulder as they descended the steep, rocky hill. "I don't understand that man. It's almost as if he were afraid of Geronimo."

"Maybe he just wants to milk this surrender for all it's worth, sir," Norwood offered. "The country is watching. He's bound to grab for all the glory and credit he can get for bringing in Geronimo."

Lawton reached the bottom of the hill and turned to face Norwood as if he were going to reprimand him for making such a statement about his commanding general, but he let it pass and said nothing.

Lawton rejoined his command and, with Norwood and McGee leading the way, rode east to Gatewood and the hostiles. The combined column then moved a couple of miles northward and camped in Guadeloupe Cañon, on the Arizona/Mexico border.

"The hostiles are getting nervous as they get closer to the line," Perry Babcock remarked as he and Russ and Mac sat by their cooking fire that night. Elena Calderón had automatically joined their mess and sat quietly sipping a cup of coffee. Her face, in the fire light, looked a little more weathered, and her hair was in disarray. Russ couldn't keep his eyes off her.

"What do you think, Russ?"

"What?" He had been totally oblivious to the question from Babcock. He could feel his cheeks burning as he looked at Perry.

"I said, do you think Geronimo will try to bolt again if he gets to thinkin' he's gonna be hanged by the civil authorities in Arizona?"

Russ shrugged. "I hope not. I think he trusts Gatewood . . . and the rest of us . . . to protect him and his people until we get to Fort Bowie."

"If we can keep the lid on the boiling pot until they're safely on the train to Florida, then we can take a deep breath," Perry said. "Not before. Lawton is up ahead at their camp trying to reassure them now."

"This is the durndest 'capture' I've ever seen," McGee observed. "The Indians are marching ahead of us, fully armed, and can leave any time they want to."

"Well, it won't be long now," Russ said. "Tomorrow we get to Skeleton Cañon. I think Miles will finally agree to meet there."

The next day the command started north again, crossing into the United States at some indefinite point along the way. They marched about fourteen miles, arriving at Skeleton Cañon in late afternoon where they went into camp near an old, abandoned ranch. Only a few adobe walls were still standing, filled with burned timbers.

All the following day couriers were coming and going with all sorts of official messages. At three in the afternoon General Miles and his staff arrived. Since there was no fresh meat in camp, Lawton sent Norwood out to hunt, along with Natchez, as a gesture of solidarity.

The two men found several wild cattle in the brush about two miles from camp. Two beeves were shot and later were cut up and packed in by some of the soldiers and packers. Everyone feasted on fresh beef that night, although there was very little to eat with it.

The following day, September 4th, was slightly overcast and sultry. With very little formality General Miles, who had been having long conversations with Geronimo since his arrival, accepted the surrender of the hostile Apache leaders and their people.

The next morning Miles left camp with Geronimo, Natchez, two of the general's staff, an Indian named Perico, and one squaw. They planned to push hard to see if they could cover the remaining seventy miles to Fort Bowie. The rest of the command and the Indians were to follow at a more leisurely pace.

Marching and camping, it took the column three days by way of the foothills of the Chiricahua Mountains then Cave Creek and Gilaville finally to reach the adobe buildings of Fort Bowie itself. The surrendering hostiles went along peacefully and halted unexpectedly only once when a young Indian woman delivered a baby. Spurning any assistance from Doctor Sutter, she was helped by two squaws. An hour later she was back on the trail, carrying the infant and looking rather pale but apparently all right.

Elena Calderón had been unusually quiet, Norwood thought, during these final three days. She seemed very tired, but Russ put it down to her being in unfamiliar surroundings. He had offered her his blanket to use, but she had returned it with a grimace, pointing out that it smelled of rancid bacon grease and smoke. She had said her own saddle blanket was cleaner, but that she preferred to sleep without a covering.

At last the hostiles gave up their arms at Bowie and were put under guard in one of the empty adobe barracks buildings. One of the cavalrymen recognized the Marlin carbine among the confiscated weapons and returned it to Norwood.

That night, a weary quartet of Russell Norwood, Elena Calderón, Stratford McGee, and Perry Babcock sat down to supper in the sutler's store on the post. Bathed and shaved and somewhat cleaner, they still wore the grimy, smoky clothes of the trail.

"These may be out of a can, but they sure are a welcome change from fresh meat," Russ remarked as he forked an oyster into his mouth and chased it with a cracker.

"I would like to propose a toast," Perry said, raising his beer mug. "To the successful completion of the longest, hardest campaign of my life. May we never have another one like it."

"And thanks to God that you are all still alive and well," Elena added, clinking her glass against the others. They drank, and Russ looked over the top of his mug at the dark eyes of the girl across from him. She seemed even lovelier in the soft light of the low-burning coal-oil lamp, her black hair pulled back and fastened at the nape of her neck.

"Where will you go from here?" Russ asked her. "Back to Oposura? My job as courier is over. I'd be glad to escort you."

"Actually," she said, cutting a slice of bread for herself, "I may not go back to Mexico. At least not right away. I have no family left in Oposura, and I won't be welcome in Fronteras. I'll still visit my mother and other relatives at the fortified ranch, but for now I want to go to Tucson. I went to school there, and I have good memories of it. One or two of my friends are still there. Perhaps I can find a job and live there. Who knows, I may even become an American citizen."

"What about you, Mac?" Perry asked.

"I reckon I'll be let go as a packer or a scout or interpreter, or whatever the hell I was," he replied. "Not much need for my services any more. This campaign has let me know that I'm too old and tired to go to prospectin' again. I don't know. Just keeping my options open. Something will turn up."

"Well, I'll have the job of helping escort Geronimo and the rest of that band to Bowie Station tomorrow and see that they're put aboard the train for Florida," Perry said.

"Miles isn't wasting any time, is he?" Russ remarked.

Perry shook his head. "No, he's not. Once Miles makes up his mind to do something, he gets right to it."

"I'll be back before dark," Russ said at eleven the next morning as he and Elena stepped out onto the wooden porch of the officers' quarters.

"Must you ride with them?" she asked, a trace of impatience in her voice. "The soldiers will take them to the train."

"I know. But I've been on this campaign from the beginning, and I want to be there at the end."

He looked across the sunny parade ground at the soldiers who were taking the hostiles from the makeshift guardhouse and loading them into wagons.

"Bowie Station is only a few miles north of here. We should have the Apaches on the Southern Pacific cars and on their way by two o'clock." He looked at her. "How about an early supper when I get back?"

"That would be good," she smiled.

"I'd better get my pony and get saddled," he said, stalling as if reluctant to leave her standing there.

"Would you like to ride my mare?"

"Better save her if you plan to start for Tucson tomorrow." He looked away from her at the Indian women and children settling themselves in the open wagons. "I might have some business in Tucson myself."

"*Bueno.* Then we can ride together."

Her whole being was suffused by her smile. Without thinking, he took her in his arms and kissed her soundly, passionately, oblivious to the stares of two nearby officers. She was flushed and breathless when he finally released her and strode quickly out onto the parade ground.

Instead of turning toward the corral immediately, Norwood paused to watch Geronimo and Natchez climb into a wagon with several other warriors. General Nelson Miles, an officer, and an aide sat their horses a few yards away, supervising the operation. Then the guards continued to herd the Apache scouts toward the wagons, pushing them with their carbine barrels. Norwood was startled and looked toward Miles to see if he were aware of the mistake. The commander sat, stoically observing.

When Kaytennay and Martine were treated the same way, Norwood looked around for Babcock. Not seeing his friend, he boldly approached the general.

"General Miles, those are the friendly scouts they're loading into the wagons. They're not part of the hostile band."

Miles looked down at him. "Who're you?"

"Russell Norwood. I was a courier on this campaign, sir. These scouts did some great service for us, tracking the hostiles. Without them, we would have gotten nowhere."

Miles regarded him coldly, as if disdaining even to reply. Finally he said, "They're all Chiricahuas. They're all being shipped out of here to Fort Pickens, Florida."

"But, sir, these scouts should be rewarded not treated as prisoners of war like the others."

"Do you presume to tell *me* what to do, Mister . . . uh, Norville, or whatever your name is?" Miles snapped. "Draw your pay and get off this post. You're through!"

Russ could feel himself losing control. "You arrogant bastard!" he shouted, starting toward the mounted officer.

At that moment Perry Babcock appeared out of nowhere and Russ felt Perry's long arms wrap him up, forcing him away. "Easy, easy. Don't say any more," Babcock whispered urgently in his ear.

Just then the order was given to mount, and Russ vaguely, as through a fog, heard the whips pop over the mules' backs as the wagons began to lumber away, the cavalry escort flanking them.

"Are you coming, Mister Babcock?" It was General Miles's icy voice as the commander rode up near them.

"Yes, sir. I'll be right there," Babcock replied, releasing Norwood with a last warning look.

The general turned his white horse away. Norwood watched in disbelief as the blue-coated back receded after the rumbling wagons.

"You can't let him do this!" Russ said in desperation. "He's betraying his own men!"

"I know. I know. It makes me sick."

"Did you know he was going to arrest the scouts and banish them too?"

"Not until this morning."

"We can't let him do it!" he insisted.

"There's not one damned thing we can do," Perry told him. "This is politics at the highest level . . . a power struggle, a clash of wills, a chess game between the commanding generals of the Army and the President of the United States. This is way out of our power to control."

"Damn!"

Norwood backed away, gritting his teeth and swallowing the frustration that was beginning to choke him.

"Listen to me, Russ. Miles is trying to make himself a hero

240

with the white population. Most whites don't make any distinction between a scout and a hostile. To the settlers an Apache is an Apache, and they should all be hanged or banished from the territory."

"I can't believe such bald-faced dishonesty from a man in his position."

"Then you don't know much about politics," Perry said, bitterly. "And rumor says that Miles has presidential ambitions."

"God help the country!"

"Babcock!"

Perry paused as he was about to mount. Russ recognized William Thompson, Assistant Adjutant, walking toward them. He had a strange smile on his face and, when he got close enough, Norwood smelled whiskey on his breath.

"I've got something here that would stop this movement of Indians," he said, patting his uniform pocket. "But I'm not going to let the old man see it until the train's gone. Then I'll tell him about it."

He winked, conspiratorially. It was obvious he was feeling his liquor.

"What is it?" Babcock asked impatiently.

"A telegram from Washington ordering Miles not to move any of those Indians out of Arizona until President Cleveland decides what to do with 'em." He paused for the reaction from Babcock. When none was forthcoming, he continued. "I'll tell the old man the wire got here too late. If I give it to him now, there'd be no end of confusion. You know . . . the uproar in the papers, the Arizona politicians yellin' to hang the hostiles, and all the ruckus that would cause with them tryin' to get custody of the Apaches from the Army." He waved a hand drunkenly. "You better get goin' if you're gonna catch up with the wagons."

Norwood looked toward the dust cloud that was drifting up

from the brushy draw where the column of wagons and cavalry was disappearing.

"Don't get too smug about that message, Thompson," Babcock said, swinging into the saddle. "I'd bet my commission that Miles already knows all about those orders."

He spurred his horse and cantered away as Norwood stared after him. Elena materialized at his elbow. The hoofbeats faded beyond a building.

"Buy you a drink?" Thompson offered.

"No, thanks," Norwood replied, pulling himself together. He glanced up at the faded flag that was flapping lazily overhead. "This young lady and I have some business to discuss."

Thompson grinned knowingly.

Russ guided Elena away, adding in a lower voice, "Let's throw some sand into the works. An unsigned telegram to the right place might just sidetrack that train before it gets across Texas."

She gripped his arm in agreement.

foot, but this happened in 1887 at the San Carlos reservation during the escape of the Apache Kid, a notorious renegade.

The feud between Tom Horn with Russ Norwood, while completely my own invention, is nevertheless consistent with the known character and personality of Horn who subsequently worked as an operative for the Pinkerton Detective Agency. In the 1890s he was hired as a stock detective by several Wyoming cattlemen to stop the rustling of their herds. His zealous shooting of real and suspected outlaws eventually led to his arrest for the murder of a fourteen year-old boy. After a controversial trial, he was convicted in 1901 and hanged in Cheyenne in November, 1903.

Let me conclude with a salute to the late Doctor Leonard Wood whose diary of this expedition furnished many of the incidents and day-to-day details included in this narrative. Many thanks also to Stephanie Varnado, Connie Bailey, and Greta Sheets for their assistance in helping to type the manuscript.

Tim Champlin, born John Michael Champlin in Fargo, North Dakota, graduated from Middle Tennessee State University and earned a Master's degree from Peabody College in Nashville, Tennessee. Beginning his career as an author of the Western story with *Summer of the Sioux* in 1982, the American West represents for him "a huge, ever-changing block of space and time in which an individual had more freedom than the average person has today . . . For those brave, and sometimes desperate souls who ventured West looking for a better life, it must have been an exciting time to be alive." Champlin has achieved a notable stature in being able to capture that time in complex, often exciting, and historically accurate fictional narratives. He is the author of two series of Western novels, that concerned Matt Tierney who comes of age in *Summer of the Sioux* and who begins his professional career as a reporter for the Chicago *Times-Herald* covering an expeditionary force venturing into the Big Horn country and the Yellowstone, and Jay McGraw, a callow youth who is plunged into outlawry at the beginning of *Colt Lightning*. There are six books in the Matt Tierney series and with *Deadly Season* a fifth featuring Jay McGraw. In all of Champlin's stories there are always unconventional plot ingredients, striking historical details, vivid characterizations of the multitude of ethnic and cultural diversity found on the frontier, and narratives rich and original and surprising. His exuberant tapestries include lumber schooners sailing the West Coast, early-day wet-plate photography, daredevils who thrill crowds with gas balloons and the first parachutes, Tong Wars in San Francisco's Chinatown, Basque sheepherders, and the Penitentes of the Southwest, and are always highly entertaining. *Swift Thunder* is his latest title.

WR